UNIT 9

By Robert S. Conboy

This book is a work of fiction. Any references to historical events, real people, or real places are used fictitiously. Other names, characters, places, and events are products of the author's imagination, and any resemblance to actual events or places or persons, living or dead, is entirely coincidental.

DEDICATION

For my wife Ruth who inspired and supported me; Sara Robinson, who guided me, taught me, and endured my journey with her amazing positivity and beautiful smile- who both bring sunshine and grace to wherever they travel; and for the men and women everywhere who toil in the prisons of the world.

ACKNOWLEGEMENTS

I would like to acknowledge the work of Sarah Domet. Her book <u>90 Days to Your Novel</u> helped me get past page fifty, where I had been stuck for ten years. It is a wonderful guide for all beginning authors. I must also acknowledge the help I received from Sara Joyce Robinson. Her willingness to continue to be my reader and tutor was invaluable. Her knowledge and method of teaching pushed me to a new level, while never letting me become discouraged. I would also like to thank my wife Ruth, who supported me throughout this project by spending countless hours editing, and providing me emotional support.

UNIT 9

PART I

1

Bruce Dernson sat in a holding cell fidgeting with his shirt. The hard metal bench cut into the bottom of his legs so he repositioned himself, moving away from the inmate that was talking to himself. Bruce was in the former Men's Prison in Chino, California. Now it was the Evaluation Center for the National Department of Rehabilitation and Modification. He was not sure why he was summoned to Dr. Isaac's office. He did not have an appointment. He just saw his psychologist yesterday.

He closed his eyes and thought about his wife and daughter. Elise turned eleven last week and he missed her birthday. He felt awful about it. She was the light of his life. Disappointing her had devastated him. Why did he ever let his friend Charlie talk him into that stupid credit card fraud scheme? He had been doing alright working at the tire center. He had never done anything illegal before. He was just trying to make a better life for his family. It was the banks that would suffer. They were not stealing from other people. That's what Charlie said to convince him.

The custody officer at the desk called out his name and Bruce snapped back to reality. "Dernson, go back to the doctor's office, he's waiting for you."

Bruce stood up and walked down the hallway to his doctor's office. He knocked on the open door. "Come in Mr. Dernson," Dr. Isaac said.

As Bruce took a seat, a nurse and a custody officer entered the room.

"Stay seated sir," the custody officer said.

Bruce's eyes grew wide and he flinched, trying to run. The custody officer grabbed him by the shoulders and pushed him down into the chair. The nurse stepped forward and stuck a needle into his neck. Within moments, Bruce was unconscious.

* * * * * * * *

Six hours later, Bruce Dernson woke up. He was in an operating room. Medical staffs were scurrying around him. The lights were so bright they hurt his eyes. He squinted a little. He panicked when he saw a large robotic drill move toward his face. He wanted to fight against the restraints, but he couldn't move. He didn't feel any pain, but he was awake and aware of what was happening to him. The metallic smell of bloody flesh and bone filled the air as the drill bore into his forehead. The putrid smell nauseated Bruce. He wanted to scream, but he couldn't make a sound. He wet his pants. The drill withdrew and made a second hole in the top of his head. As the drill withdrew from the second hole the drill bit retracted, and a 22 gauge 6 inch needle appeared. It moved to the site of the second hole. The techs in the operating theatre turned to view the procedure on video monitors. They showed 3D scans of his brain.

"Initiate phase two," a doctor said.

The robotic arm pushed the needle into Bruce's brain and the video monitors lit up. Hundreds of Nanites flooded into his skull. It felt like a thousand ants crawling across his brain. They looked like microscopic bed bugs, but were far more deadly. They encircled his amygdala and attached to his brain. They joined with one another to form a cohesive unit. The needle withdrew and approached the hole in his forehead.

One of the nurses had a worried look on her face. "Doctor, his pulse rate is rising and his breathing is shallow."

"Give him another 5cc of Secretal," the doctor said.

A tech injected Secretal into the IV line, and then stepped back. After a moment she turned to the doctor. "Vitals are stabilizing."

"Continue with phase two," the doctor said.

The needle entered him again, and more Nanites rushed out. The video screens lit up with the second onslaught. This time they encircled his frontal lobe. The needle withdrew and the doctor in charge looked at the monitor readings, "Attach the implant and initiate the connection."

Another robotic arm moved toward Bruce's forehead. It inserted a micro-transmitter/light into the hole. It glowed emerald green when the connection was initiated. Instantaneously Bruce's anxiety was relieved. He had no emotional sense at all, but he could see what was going on around him. He recognized the medical staff that had been working on him. He knew who he was and who his family was, but he felt numb. Other than that, physically, he was fine.

"Vitals are still stable doctor."

The doctor removed his gloves and looked at the monitors. Then he directed the techs, "Apply the healing gel to the drill points, and move him to recovery"

In the recovery room Bruce Dernson's forehead glowed as he stared at a television. He would never again experience love, anger, or any other emotion. He also had no understanding of what just happened to him, but then, he would have no understanding of anything in the future. He would simply follow directives and orders. His reasoning ability was compromised. He was completely docile. He was a Mod.

2

Above the theatre in the observation room, Edward Miller, the superintendent of the Modification Center, sat comfortably in a plush leather chair. He watched the procedure as it was performed on Bruce Dernson. When it was completed, he headed back to his office.

Miller was a slender man, with dark hair and pleasant features. He was raised in foster care in San Bernardino, California. San Berdu, as it was called, was a low income/high crime area. He learned to fend for himself at an early age. Miller was often described by his colleagues as a cold-hearted, aggressive individual, who would do almost anything to get ahead. He was a self-made man who managed to get a college degree, and worm his way up the bureaucratic ladder. Now he was in charge of the Modification Center.

Miller was adorned in the latest Smart Jacket from Ardent Clothing. It had phone and home controls built into the sleeve, and a microphone in the shoulder. A 3-D projection emanated from the pocket producing a video feed of his caller, or a video of the website he was viewing.

When he got back to the office he received a call. The vid phone connected, and the face of Gavin Jordan, CEO of Ardent Corporation appeared in a 3D Hologram. Ardent was a major clothing manufacturer. They had a contract with the government to receive Modified inmates. The Mods worked at Ardent's manufacturing plants.

"What do you have for me Eddie?" Jordan asked.

"I will deliver another fifteen Mods by next week. And I told you not to call me Eddie," Miller said, "Or to call me here at the office."

"That's good Eddie," Jordan sneered at Miller. "Let's just hope you don't disappoint me this time." The connection ended abruptly.

Miller stared out his office window, but he didn't see anything. He didn't notice the bright sunny Southern California day, or the hummingbird sucking nectar out of the gardenias in front of his office. His palms were sweaty. He knew there was no way he was going to be able to provide fifteen Mods by next week

3

The engine hummed as Michael Taylor engaged his supercharged hover car. He turned off the auto-pilot. He could make much better time if he drove it himself. He was late and he didn't want to disappoint Liz by missing her graduation party. She just graduated from County High School, and her folks were throwing her a major bash. Michael finished high school six months earlier. He completed his credits at the continuation school, and got out as soon as he could. He was booted out of regular high school for fighting. He was not a violent person, but sometimes he needed to stand up to the pompous rich kids. They didn't like the fact that he dated Liz. She was one of them, and they didn't think he deserved her.

Problem was, their families used influence to get them out of trouble. Michael got the short straw, which in this case was continuation school. He didn't care since he got to avoid all the Rah Rah dramas of high school, and still get his diploma. Now he was going to community college. He didn't need to worry about them anymore. They would all move on to their fancy four-year colleges.

Michael loved Liz. They had been an item for about a year now. They met through a friend of hers. His mind drifted back to the first time they were alone together. Her parents were away for the weekend. They had her parent's home to themselves. She was still a virgin. He remembered how nervous she was, how she trembled as they laid together.

Michael and Liz were good together and dating her helped him see the world a little differently. Before Liz, Michael had a bad attitude and a nasty temper. He was even working on controlling his temper.

Michael cruised up to the front of Liz's home and secured his hover car by the valet station. He gave his key fob to Jimmie the valet before making his way into the party. Jimmie was dressed in black slacks, a white shirt, and red blazer.

"Nice jacket," Michael laughed as he slapped the valet a high five.

3

Michael knew Jimmie from continuation school. They were never close but had some friends in common. He was a good guy that got kicked out of mainstream school for attendance problems. He had to work to provide for his family when his father became sick with cancer. His father had two separate types of cancer with two tumors at the same time. The doctors said it was a very rare condition. The continuation school worked out well for Jimmie. It gave him a more flexible schedule.

"How's it going Taylor?" Jimmie asked.

"Not too bad, just going in for Liz's big graduation bash. What about you?"

"Cool, just workin and playin whenever possible."

"Cool," Michael said. "Take good care of my baby," he said as he pointed toward his hover car, "and no joy rides."

The valet smiled and shook his head. "Why would I want to drive this piece of crap when I have my choice of these beauties?" he said. He waved his arm toward a row of the latest and most expensive hover cars.

"Good point, maybe you could switch my key for that Z-Rocket when I leave," Michael said.

"In your dreams, homie."

Michael chuckled to himself as he made his way up the main walkway. As he saw the crowd he began to feel a little anxious. He liked Liz's parents, but he was a little out of his element with their friends. He was wearing his best suit in an attempt to look the part, navy blue with a cream colored shirt. No tie, but his best leather shoes polished to a high sheen. It was old school though. He couldn't afford the latest on-board Data-Wear, but he still cut a handsome figure with his dark hair, blue eyes, and chiseled six foot two inch frame.

He made his way through the house to the backyard. The party was in full swing now. There was well over a hundred people. The yard was alive with white lights, torches, and colorful flower decorations. Food tables were set up to the right of the pool, buffet style, and garnished with graduation centerpieces. He wandered through the crowd looking for Liz, and then he heard his name.

"Hello Michael."

He turned to see Liz's parents, Oliver and Anastasia Hansen. They were dressed like they were going to the President's ball. Her father was an important man in the banking business. Michael heard he made a lot of money after the last recession buying up farm properties, and that he could be a cold and ruthless businessman. He was not as tall as Michael, but was fit and tan. Her mother had never worked a day in her life. She was a trust fund kid who married Liz's father straight out of college. She occupied her time working for charities and organizing fundraisers for the arts. She was a beautiful woman, and the obvious source of Liz's good looks.

"Nice to see you son," Mr. Hansen said as he extended his hand to Michael. He looked Michael in the eye and grimaced.

Michael shook his hand with a firm grip and smiled. "Thank you, sir."

"And you look so nice," her mother said.

"Thank you for inviting me," Michael said.

"Well, you know you're always welcome here," her mother said.

Michael had always been very respectful to Liz's parents, and they saw how well he treated their daughter. They could also tell how much Liz cared for Michael.

"Yes, you are, you know," her father said, as he looked away from Michael into the crowd.

"Have you seen Liz?" Michael asked, attempting to extricate himself as quickly as possible.

"She's over there with her friends," her mother said, as she pointed towards the Cabaña behind the pool.

"Okay, I'm off," Michael said. He smiled and walked away.

Michael spotted Liz right away as he approached the Cabaña. She looked beautiful. Her shoulder length auburn hair shone under the lights. A sleeveless green silk party dress hugged her petite frame, accentuating her fabulous figure. She laughed and threw her head back enjoying the moment, flashing her beautiful smile, and sparkling blue-green eyes.

"Congratulations party girl," Michael said from behind her.

She turned and squealed when she saw him, throwing her arms around his neck and squeezing him as tightly as she could.

"You came," she said.

"Of course," he said.

She felt like chocolate silk in his arms. Warm and smooth. He held her tight, and wished it could be just the two of them. He handed her a single long-stem red rose that he brought her as a gift.

"Here, this is for you,"

"How lovely," she said.

A photographer came by at that moment and took some pictures of the happy couple.

"Would you like a copy of any of these?" the photographer asked.

"Sure, let me have one of Liz," Michael said.

The photographer reviewed the images on a data pad and then pushed a button. A hard copy of an image of Liz materialized on the screen. He handed it to Michael who smiled and showed it to Liz. Then he put it in his wallet for safe keeping.

"Now I will always have you with me," Michael said.

They both laughed, and then Michael and Liz enjoyed the party. They danced, ate, laughed, and cuddled. When they sat at a table Michael put his arm around Liz's shoulder. He stroked her arm. She turned to look at him and smiled, and Michael leaned forward to kiss her. Liz was the center of attention and she loved it. She glowed with the affection from family and friends.

"Are you having fun?" He asked.

"Yes, this has been a great night," she said.

"Well, you deserve it," he said.

Michael got up to get some drinks. As he headed toward the bar he noticed the activity at the shoot-tube. The shoot-tube was a molecular deconstruction and reconstitution tube which offered quick and easy movement around the city.

The tube was setting visitors on an arrival dock in the back yard. One had to be very connected to have a shoot-tube station right on their property, even if it was a temporary one installed for the party. The shoot-tube was individualized public transportation. Michael preferred his hover car because it gave him more control over his movements.

Michael saw Liz's best friend Stacy exiting the shoot tube. He walked over to her and helped her off of the dock.

"Oh hi Michael, where's our girl?" Stacy asked. She gave Michael a big smile and hug as she climbed off of the dock

Stacy's parents were also wealthy. They had her genetically programmed in utero. If you had money you were allowed to choose two genetic alterations for your children. If you had alterations you were called a Normal. Any more than two alterations caused psychiatric instability. It hit when an individual reached adolescence. That had been determined the hard way. In fact, that is how the Modification technology was initially developed. The first generations of Genbots, as they had been affectionately named, were genetically altered children. They became so unruly and dangerous they had to be controlled with the Nano technology used in the Modification process. Simple incarceration did not work for them. Now you could only choose two alterations, unless you dealt with an unscrupulous doctor on the black market.

Occasionally you would run across someone who seemed a little too edgy, or sure of themselves. Chances are, they had more than two alterations. Those individuals were destined to a life taking Horanian. Horanian was a medication that was developed to help Genbots deal with the psychiatric conflicts associated with too many genetic alterations. It had been developed after the Modification process. As a result a generation of adolescents was lost. Most of them had been Modified. Later on a few lucky ones were saved by Horanian. The latest generations of successfully altered individuals were all under twenty five years of age.

Stacy's parents chose two interesting genetic traits for their daughter. They chose supermodel visual appearance, and prodigy musical talent. So Stacy played cello like a master, and looked great while she did so. She knew she was a beauty but still had a kind and loving way about her. She was also unusual because not many parents chose supermodel beauty. There were enough beauty enhancements available through surgery or cosmetics, so most parents didn't waste one of their choices on something they felt was easily attained. But Stacy's beauty was truly a cut above everyone else's.

Liz's parents chose extreme empathy and educational ability. They felt that with her mother's looks, she would come out fine in that department. Her mother was also a kind soul, but she had concerns about the father, so she was the one who suggested the empathy characteristic. Michael always wondered if he would be with Liz if she had not had the empathy alteration. Michael's parents didn't have money for any alterations. He was referred to as a Darwin, because he had to rely solely on natural selection for his genetic makeup.

"Liz is over here at the table," Michael said, as he led Stacy through the crowd. "She will be very happy to see you."

Most of the men in the area turned to watch Stacy as they walked. "Do you ever get tired of that?" Michael asked, as he laughed at the phenomena.

"Not really," Stacy said. "As long as they don't become touchy or aggressive I enjoy the attention."

Liz stood and came to greet Stacy when she saw her walking toward her.

"Sorry I'm late," Stacy said, as she gave Liz a hug.

"Don't worry about it," Liz said, as she hugged her back. "What's important is that you're here now."

Stacy sat down, and the girls immediately began to discuss the events of the evening. Michael went to retrieve the drinks he forgot when he saw Stacy arrive. As he approached the beverage bar, Michael encountered Brock Nitchzke. Brock stood with a drink in his hand, leering at Michael as he approached. He was with two of his buddies. Brock was Liz's boyfriend when she met Michael.

He had been enhanced for athletics and academics, and was the captain of the football team. He was invited along with all the other members of the graduating class. Brock was not pleased when Liz dumped him for Michael. Michael and Brock had fought each other because of it, with Michael coming out on top. It was a bitter pill to swallow for Brock's ego. He still wanted revenge.

Michael attempted to avoid Brock and his boys by going to the opposite end of the beverage bar, but Brock was intent on confronting him. He moved toward Michael and put his arm out blocking Michael's way. Michael stopped and looked Brock in the eye. He could feel his temper rising. He looked to his side to see what the other two other were doing. If he twisted Brock up, he didn't want to get suckered from behind, but they were just standing there with dumb looks on their faces. Michael reached out and grabbed Brock's arm.

"Well isn't this cozy, hello boys," Mr. Hansen walked right between Brock and Michael. "Enjoying the party Brock? Michael?"

Brock stopped in his tracks and flushed red. "Yes sir."

"That's good Brock," Mr. Hansen put his hand on Brock's shoulder. "Because I want to make sure everyone enjoys the party. Understand?"

Brock got the message that no fighting or disruptions would be tolerated, and he knew better than to mess with Mr. Hansen. Brock turned away and stormed off into the crowd.

"Can I get you a drink sir?" Michael asked, as he smiled.

"Yes Michael, I'll have a rum swirl, thank you." The two of them stood there waiting for the drinks in silence. Michael knew that her father was upset when Liz left Brock for him. Brock had a great future ahead of him. What did Michael have? But he knew her father was not going to let anything interfere with the party.

The drinks arrived, and Michael handed Mr. Hansen his rum swirl. "Here you go sir," he said. He picked up the drinks for himself and Liz. "I need to deliver these now."

"Yes of course," Mr. Hansen took a long drink as he watched Michael walk away.

Michael returned to his table and set the drinks down.

"Let's dance," he said to Liz.

"Okay, sounds like fun," she said, as she got up. The two of them went to the middle of the dance floor and embraced as they moved back and forth to a slow song. The party roared around them but Liz only saw Michael. She leaned forward and kissed him. He hugged her and then glanced at his watch. "Let's hope it's just the beginning of a fabulous summer," she said. "That's the time we have before I have to leave for school in the fall. Are you going to miss me when I go?" She asked.

"Of course I am," he said.

"Will you come to visit me in San Luis Obispo?"

"You couldn't keep me away," he said. "You know how I feel about you Liz. Being with you has given me a new outlook on life."

"Well someday we will spend that life together," she said. "I have big plans for you Michael Taylor. So you better not disappoint me."

"I'm afraid that right now I might. It's time for me to leave," Michael said.

Liz frowned at him and made a pouty face.

"Don't worry," he said. "If you want me to keep you in the lifestyle to which you've become accustomed, I can't lose my high paying job on the night shift at the grocery store."

They both laughed and hugged each other. The song ended, and they walked hand in hand back to the table. He said his goodbyes to the other people, and then he said his final goodbye to Liz.

"See you soon," she said, kissing him on the cheek one last time.

"You can bet on it," he said. He stroked her hair and looked in her eyes, basking in her beauty.

Finally Michael made his way out to his car.

"I see you made it out alive," Jimmie said.

"Barely a scratch on me,"

"Have you seen the Chicken Man around lately?" Jimmie asked.

The Chicken Man was one of their classmates at the continuation school.

"No, haven't you heard?" Michael asked. "He got arrested for selling stolen cars. During the arrest he resisted and injured a cop. He was sent to the Evaluation Center and got into some fights, so they failed him. He ended up getting Modified."

"Holy Shit, not the Chicken Man," the Valet said.

"Yeah, it's messed up. Now he's off sewing clothes or picking strawberries somewhere. Hardly even knows who he is," Michael said.

As the Valet gave Michael his key fob, he had a look of horror on his face.

"Take care of you, man," he said. Then Jimmie handed Michael a packet of legal Cannabis cigs. "Here's a little graduation present for you."

"Wow, Hong Kong Gold. Thanks Jimmie." Michael was impressed. This was a very expensive gift.

"You're welcome. I got a carton from my uncle for graduation, and I've been spreading the wealth. They are real kick ass, so enjoy." Jimmie smiled broadly and looked very pleased with himself.

Michael shook his hand and gave him a hug. "You too," Michael said.

Then Michael got into his hover car and went off to work. He couldn't help thinking of the Chicken Man. What a waste. This Modification Law was nuts. Everyone was a little freaked out since it passed five years ago.

4

The metal crates pinched Michael's fingers as he stacked them in the main cooler.

"Damn it," he said. It had been over four hours since he left the party at Liz's home.

He yanked his hand back and looked at the blood blister already forming. He was tired and now his hand hurt. He finished his work in the cooler and quickly drank an energy drink to stay awake. Then he went to the restroom to wash his injured hand. Michael worked at a grocery store part-time while going to school. The store was part of a large regional chain. He worked the night shift stocking deliveries as they came in. Tonight they had received a shipment of dairy goods. He had come directly from Liz's party and had changed clothes in the men's room. He had been working at the store since he turned sixteen and was legally able to work.

It was hard at times, physically demanding, but he often enjoyed that part of it. It was like getting paid to work out. When he came out of the restroom he ran smack into Laura Jenkins. She was one of his co-workers.

"Sorry Michael," Laura said. "I didn't see you there."

Laura wrapped her arms around Michael's waist. She looked up at him smiling as she pushed her size 42 bust into his chest. Michael laughed as he reached down to pull her arms away. Laura was a Darwin like him, but you would never guess it by looking at her. She was gorgeous with an amazing figure.

"Really Laura, I'm way too tired to play your games today. Please let me go."

"Oh Michael, how can you treat me like this, after all we've been through together?"

"I'm sorry Laura, but I'm with Liz now. I've told you already that I won't play around on her."

Michael kissed her on the cheek and pushed past her. Laura put on her best pouty face and batted her eyelashes. Michael smiled as he felt himself almost give in to her charm. They'd had a brief and highly physical relationship during Michael's junior year.

Michael ended it when he met Liz. Laura had been a good time, but she could not compete with Liz's personality as far as Michael was concerned.

"Now I have to go back to work," Michael said.

As Michael returned to the main floor he could still sense the feeling of Laura's voluptuous body on his skin. He licked his lips and the flowery taste of her perfume lingered. He was jolted back to reality when he saw his boss Charlie walking toward him.

"Can you finish that canned corn display at the end of isle five now, Michael?" Charlie asked as he slapped him on the back.

"Sure enough boss," Michael said.

Charlie was a hard guy not to like. Despite the fact that he dressed like a square with his crew cut, Snap-On tie, orthopedic shoes, and pocket full of pens. He was a good egg, and had been at the store for eighteen years. He had given Michael the job. He was fair and easy to work for. Michael thought that Charlie would probably be doing this work for the rest of his life. Charlie was unenhanced like everyone over thirty.

Michael sometimes wondered what he would be doing when he was Charlie's age. He didn't have any real plans for a future profession. He was just trying to make it through the day most of the time. He worked, went to school taking general education classes, and had fun.

Michael headed to the end of aisle five to begin work on the canned corn display. He cut open boxes of canned corn then placed the cans into the display module. He found himself half nodding off as he did the monotonous work, until he noticed a woman and a little boy walking past him. He noticed them because not many customers actually shopped at this early hour, even though the store was open twenty four hours a day.

Michael watched them mosey through the store as he methodically stacked cans of corn. They looked tired and dirty, like many of the homeless he had seen. The mother was around thirty something years old with stringy blonde hair. She wore old style denim pants, dirty athletic shoes, and an old military coat that was several sizes too large for her. The boy looked to be about eight years of age. He was holding a ragged looking teddy bear in one hand and hung onto his mother's sleeve with the other hand. The woman was moving a little too fast for the boy. He was forced to half run and half walk to keep up.

The mother was obviously a Darwin but Michael could not tell about the boy. It was difficult to tell about children unless they were doing a specific task such as playing an instrument, or painting. That is when the genetic enhancements really showed.

The woman gave Michael a furtive glance as she turned the corner to walk down aisle eight, the refrigerated aisle. Curious about this duo Michael stopped moving cans of corn and walked toward aisle eight. When he turned the corner he saw the woman stuffing a package of lunchmeat into her coat. She didn't notice him as she walked toward the door with the boy in tow.

Michael shook his head in disbelief. He was concerned because he knew the store's surveillance system would catch her. The store had a policy of prosecuting shoplifters. She would most likely lose her son to child services.

Moving quickly Michael cut through the floral section to head her off. He could see the security drone flying overhead making its way toward the woman and her son. Michael reached them first. He grabbed the woman firmly by the arm and turned her to face him.

"Hi Shirley," Michael said as if he knew her. "Are you here to get those twenty dollars I owe you?"

Startled and confused the woman attempted to pull her arm away from Michael's grip. "What?" she said.

Michael reached into his pocket and pulled out a twenty dollar bill. "Here," he said. "Now you can pay for your lunch meat. You wouldn't want the security drone to stun you." Michael glanced into the air toward the drone. The woman's eyes followed Michael's. Suddenly she went limp.

"Look Mom, it's a drone," the little boy said.

The woman blinked her eyes and then reached out and grabbed the money. "What do you want for this mister?"

"Nothing lady, It's just that I wouldn't want your son to have his mother turned into a turnip over a piece of turkey. You need to be a lot more careful. What's your boy's name?" Michael asked as he released his grip and stepped back.

"Clark," she said.

"Hi Clark, I'm Michael." Michael smiled at the boy, and he smiled back.

Then the woman turned and headed to the checkout terminal to pay for the lunch meat without saying another word.

Michael watched her go, "You're welcome Shirley," he said under his breath. Michael headed back to the corn as Laura walked up behind him. "You're such a White Knight Michael Taylor." She giggled as she pinched his side and then ran ahead of him.

"Just keep that to yourself" Michael yelled after her.

When he got back to the corn display the store's director, George Ditka was standing there inspecting the display. Michael was startled by his presence and stopped in his tracks. Ditka looked at him with a scornful smirk and shook his head. Michael thought that he always looked like he was ready to tear someone's head off. Everyone thought he was a Genbabe who was taking Horanian because of too many genetic alterations.

"You know Taylor, you may think you did that woman a favor, but I don't think so. I believe you only put off the inevitable for a brief time," Ditka said.

Michael did not respond. He only shrugged as he watched Ditka's face contort. Ditka was the only Genbabe that Michael knew. He found it fascinating to watch him.

Ditka took a can of corn and handed it to Michael. Then without another word, he turned and walked away. Michael placed the corn back onto the stack as he watched Ditka walk away. His gait was unlike that of other men, most likely because of his enhancements. He loped as he moved, somewhat like an animal on the plains of Africa. Michael had seen wild animals move that way in a movie at school.

Michael finished the corn display. Then he checked the time. It was the end of his shift. He headed into the back room where there were lockers, tables, and chairs available for the employees. A television was hanging on the wall. Charlie was eating a sandwich and watching a replay of last night's basketball game.

"How's the game?" Michael asked.

"It's okay," Charlie said. "It's just not the same these days with all the Normals. All those physical enhancements." Charlie threw his sandwich down on the table in disgust. He watched Michael retrieve his party clothes from a locker.

"Good job tonight, Mike," Charlie said.

"Thanks boss," Michael said. He grabbed his bag of personal effects and headed toward the door. "See you next time," He walked out to his hover car and slid into the front seat.

Michael was exhausted. He had been awake for almost twenty four hours between school, Liz's party, and work. The sun was up, and he was glad he didn't have school today. As he pulled out of the docking area he turned on the auto pilot. He opened a window to let the warm southern California air blow through the vehicle as he headed home. The music function played some new alternative techno rap music.

He tapped his fingers on the steering column as he flew. It wasn't bad music but it wasn't his favorite. He liked old twentieth century Rock and Roll. It was impossible to get that on any of the music streams anymore. The music was all techno and completely controlled by the corporations. It was all produced electronically and embedded with subliminal advertising messages. Everyone knew it, but they would listen anyway. There weren't any alternatives when you were streaming. Right now it was helping to keep him awake. That and the twenty ounce power drink he downed in the milk cooler.

5

Michael slowed down as he turned into the docking area of his mother's house. He saw that his brother Ryan's hover car was there. He got a knot in the pit of his stomach. Ryan stayed there less and less these days, and that was fine with Michael. Ryan was ten years older than Michael. He was lucky enough to have missed the mess of the early genetic experiments.

Ryan had made Michael's life miserable from day one. They had no father around because their dad died of A.L.S. when Michael was three. His mother became a single mom who worked all the time. Ryan was left to run rough shod over Michael since he was a toddler. Ryan always seemed to take his older brother role to the next level. He often physically abused Michael.

Michael opened the front door and entered the house. His mother was in the kitchen making Ryan something to eat. Ryan was lounging on the sofa, a worn piece of furniture that had been around Michael's entire life. They lived in a small three bedroom home in an older neighborhood of North Orange County, California. It had small rooms, and the original stainless steel appliances that broke down regularly. Michael tried to keep the house painted and the yard groomed for his mother, while Ryan never helped.

"Hi honey, are you hungry?" His mother asked. She smiled at him as she handed Ryan a plate of food.

"No thanks Mom," Michael said. "I'm just tired."

He went over and kissed her, she smiled at him. The years had not been kind to his mother. She had let her hair go completely grey and cut it short. She was thirty pounds overweight. She struggled with diabetes the last three years. She worked too much and had too little. Michael glanced at Ryan and nodded his head. He watched Ryan shovel a tuna sandwich into his mouth.

"Sup bro," Ryan said. Michael said nothing as he turned away and headed toward his bedroom. Michael closed the door and flopped down on his bed. He kicked off his shoes and took a deep breath. His room was small, but tidy and clean, somewhat Spartan. He slept on a twin bed. He had a dresser and a night stand that did

5

not match. He had one poster on the wall. It was of a twentieth century rock band called Led Zeppelin. He also had a framed picture of Liz which he kept on the nightstand. His school books were piled up on the dresser.

He grabbed his bag and dug out the pack of cannabis cigs Jimmie had given him. Michael rarely got high by himself, and he never bought his own drugs. He was going to enjoy this. After the day he had, he needed a buzz. He lit a cig joint and took a hit holding the smoke in his lungs. He felt his throat burn and his lungs convulsed. He coughed out the smoke and felt the rush in his head. He took another hit and held it. Again he blew out the smoke, creating a large blue cloud that engulfed him. He looked out his bedroom window. He could see the sun over the top of the neighbors' houses and palm trees. He closed his eyes and felt a sense of mellowness throughout his entire body. Michael picked up his data pad and turned it on to see what was streaming. The social media channel was showing some posts by kids in China doing a group dance. Michael found it quite entertaining. The announcers were also laughing at it.

That's when Ryan came bursting through his bedroom door. "I thought I smelled some hooch," he said.

Ryan leapt on Michael, putting him into a half-nelson while sitting on his other arm. Ryan had fifty pounds on Michael, and he was as strong as a bull from working construction. Michael could smell the tuna fish on his breath.

"Get off me," Michael yelled.

He struggled but was unable to move his arms or torso. He kicked his legs but that had no effect on Ryan. Ryan laughed as he tightened the half nelson.

"Relax bro. Don't you want to share?" Ryan asked. With his free hand he grabbed the pack of cigs off the bed. "My my," he said. Ryan put his nose to the pack and smelled it. "Fresh," he said. "Thank you very much."

Michael felt ten years old again with his arm twisted back and his neck bent forward. Ryan had been twisting him up and taking his things his entire life. He stopped struggling, and thought. It would have been different if Dad was around. He would have stopped Ryan.

Then Ryan punched Michael in the stomach. Michael doubled up from the impact. "Don't think about coming after me now Bro," he said.

Then, in a flash Ryan was off him and out the door. Michael jumped up and looked for the lit cig joint. He found it smoldering in his blanket, he grabbed it and put it out.

"Asshole!" Michael screamed.

"Michael, watch your language," his mother said as she walked past his room.

"Really Mom?" he said. Frustrated, he stormed out of the house. "I need to go get some fresh air," he yelled to his mother.

Michael ran up the street and turned right. He ran toward his favorite refuge, the baseball dugout at the local park. Michael ran the entire three blocks to the park. It was empty except for a maintenance robot. It was painting the outside of the restrooms. Michael made his way onto the baseball field.

He climbed down into the dugout. He could feel the cool darkness of it already beginning to calm him. It smelled musty from the dirt on the floor. He had been coming here since his childhood. It was a safe haven from Ryan. He lay back on the bench and leaned against the wall.

He was angry at himself for letting Ryan get to him. He took some deep breaths and looked out over the field. The infield was all dirt. It was kept fairly smooth for a city field. Most had been left to deteriorate due to the same budget problems that brought on the Modification law. The outfield grass was overgrown, and needed to be cut. When it got long it was dangerous. The field was uneven. Players tripped on the bumps or twisted their ankles in the holes.

Michael was thirteen years old when he almost broke his ankle running for a fly ball on this field. He could still feel the pain in his right leg. At the time it swelled up so badly he could not wear shoes for two weeks. He laughed to himself when he thought about trying to walk with crutches, and falling on his butt.

The sound of his phone alert startled him. He still had an older model hand held vid phone. It was one of the first models with the holographic display. He looked at the Caller ID and recognized the name, Jason Koppe. Jason was another former student of the continuation school. He and Michael had been close friends once. Jason was also a Darwin. Michael hesitated before answering. He had been trying to distance himself from Jason because he heard he was doing some illegal work.

Michael gave in and pressed answer. Jason appeared in a hologram. "Hey buddy," Jason said. "What are you up to?"

"Just chillin," Michael said.

"Is that the dugout you're in?" Jason asked.

"Afraid so," Michael said.

"I would guess that brother Ryan was around today, eh?" Jason asked.

"So what's up?" Michael was tired and not in the mood for idle chit chat.

"Not much, it's a beautiful day and I got some cash. How about if I buy you breakfast?"

Michael hesitated again. There was usually some type of hidden agenda with Jason.

"I can swing by the park and pick you up in five minutes," Jason said.

Michael was hungry. He hadn't eaten since the party and hadn't slept. Breakfast sounded like a good idea.

"Okay," he said. "See you in five."

"Cool," Jason said. "See you then."

6

Michael saw a hover car approaching as he walked toward the edge of the park. It was the latest luxury model. Jason pulled up and Michael climbed into the front passenger seat of a new, 17 Series Hover Car.

"What's up bro?" Jason asked as he clasped Michael's hand.

"I'm good," Michael said. "What's up with this ride?"

"You like?" Jason asked. "I'm a successful businessman now. I deserve a good ride."

"What kind of business?" Michael asked. "Never mind," he quickly answered himself. "I really don't want to know. Let's get some food." Michael sat back and tried to relax.

"Sure thing, except that's something I wanted to talk to you about, but let's wait on that. Let's go get some chow, but we need to make a quick stop first. Wilson is going to have breakfast with us."

"Wilson," Michael said, suddenly feeling wide awake. "No kidding. When did you start hanging out with the elite?"

Wilson was part of the upper class. He always had the latest sporty hover cars and money to burn, but he tried to act like a regular guy. He was also a Normal who had intellectual enhancements that increased his IQ.

"Let's just say we like similar things," Jason said. "Check out this sound system."

Jason lit a cig joint and handed it to Michael as he cranked up the stereo. He had a built in custom stereo so he wasn't streaming. It was playing the new song by the Hidden Knuckles. They both liked the Knuckles. They smiled and moved to the music as they cruised. Fifteen minutes later they arrived at Wilson's apartment. Jason pulled up and docked in front of the building.

"Let's go," Jason said.

The boys got out and Jason walked to the rear storage bin where he retrieved a backpack.

"What's that?" Michael asked.

"Just some stuff I borrowed from Wilson, I need to return it to him."

They made their way up the walkway and rang the doorbell. Wilson answered the door wearing sweat pants and a Lakers' jersey. The Lakers were the perennial power in the professional basketball league for as long as anyone could remember. Wilson never actually watched sports, but he liked to be a part of the crowd so he wore their colors. He shook their hands and invited them in. It was a modern apartment outfitted with the latest tech and trendy furniture. They sat on the sofa and Jason laid the backpack on the coffee table.

"Would you gentleman care for a beverage?" Wilson asked.

"No thanks," Jason said. "Let's just get this over with."

Jason leaned forward and unzipped the bag. He pulled out a large bag of Zylapheron pills. It was the latest pharmaceutical drug on the street. It was three times more potent than Heroin but less addictive. It made you euphoric and more alert. It was very popular with the well-to-do.

Michael's eyes widened as he sat up.

Wilson walked over and picked up the bag. Then he asked Jason to extend his arm and Jason did so, Wilson then held a data wand over his arm. Michael heard a "beep."

"Check it," Wilson said.

Jason bent his arm in front of his face and worked the interface on his sleeve. A moment later he looked up at Wilson. "The deposit is in, it looks good," he said.

"I guess that's all then," said a voice in the hallway. The boys turned to see who was there. As they did the front door burst open. Three police officers ran into the apartment.

Jason looked at Wilson. "You bastard," he said.

"Sorry Dude," Wilson said. "But they had me by the short hairs. It was either me or you."

Michael could not believe what had just transpired in the last ninety seconds. He stood up and raised his hands in the air. One officer put a pulse collar around his neck and handcuffed him. Another pointed a pulse gun at him.

PART II

7

After Michael's arrest, he was sent to the Adjudication Center for trial. He was housed in a dormitory with other men who had been arrested for a variety of crimes. The men stayed there until their audience with the Judge. There were no jury trials anymore since the Modification Law was enacted. The process was fast and there were no appeals.

The cost of incarcerating hundreds of thousands of individuals had become too expensive. The government had to do something. The Patriot Act in the early twenty-first century opened the door for more government control. During the last recession the cost of prisons became prohibitive. They repealed the Eight Amendment which prevented cruel and unusual punishment. Then they enacted the Modification Law.

The Modification Law combined the state and federal justice systems into one entity. The government did not need both systems now. Since then, the penal codes had been combined, and streamlined. They were adapted to allow them to send everyone through the Modification gauntlet. No longer were career criminals going in and out of prison. No more warehouses full of felons. Only twenty percent of those convicted of crimes qualified to go to Rehabilitation. The rest were Modified to serve society.

* * * * * * * *

Michael had been at the center for two weeks. He was allowed to make one phone call to let his mother know what happened. She cried when he told her. He asked her to let Liz know what happened to him. There was no visiting at the center except with attorneys. Families were notified of hearing dates via e-mail. Michael was assigned a public defender. So far he had seen her one time for five minutes.

Michael lie on his bunk with his eyes closed trying to calm himself. Today was his hearing. He was on the middle bed of a triple decked bunk. No one was on either of the other two beds. The dorm could house a hundred prisoners but it was only half full. With the Modification law prisoners were processed out of the Adjudication Center very quickly. Michael still wore the clothes he had been arrested in minus his belt and shoe laces. They took them for safety reasons.

He took a couple of deep breaths, opened his eyes and sat up. He could see a prisoner being transported at the front of the dorm. He was strapped onto a gurney and appeared to be unconscious. The guards took him through the main door and out into the hallway. The door shut, and Michael could no longer follow his progress. He didn't need to though. He knew what was happening to the prisoner. He had seen this scene acted out many times over the last two weeks. It was common knowledge among those who had been there for a while. A ride on the gurney ended at the Modification Center.

Michael heard his name called. He was directed to the interview area to meet with his public defender. He made his way through a maze of bunk beds and entered the room where his attorney sat waiting for him.

Michael sat down across from his public defender, Ms. Phillips. She was in her early twenties but had already managed to pass the bar exam because of her intellectual enhancements.

Without looking at him Ms. Phillips launched into his case. "Okay, so you have been charged with dealing a controlled substance. You have a clean slate in the past except for your school record, and your crime associate indicated you had no part in the operation. Nevertheless you are faced with a real sticky situation. Do you have any questions about the possible outcomes?" Ms. Phillips asked as she looked at her data pad.

Michael did not respond. She looked over at Michael. He was staring out the window. He had not been outside since his arrival. In fact, this was the first time he had seen natural light since his initial meeting with Ms. Phillips.

"Michael, hello," she said, as she slapped the table trying to get his attention.

"What?" Michael asked. He was startled and turned to look at her.

"I said do you have any questions about the possible outcomes?"

"Well, let me see," Michael said, as he leaned forward. "They can choose to send me directly to Modification and turn me into a turnip. Or, they can send me to be evaluated. If I go to be evaluated and am found unfit, then they send me to be turned into a turnip. How am I doing so far Ms. Phillips?" He threw his arms up in the air, and sat back feeling frustrated and helpless.

"Look Michael," she said. "I understand how difficult this is, I didn't make the law. But we all have to live by it, all of us. I had an uncle Modified myself. So I feel your pain. But that's the way it is now." She set her data pad down on the table and sat back crossing her arms.

"Thanks for the history lesson," Michael said. He stood up and pushed his chair hard into the table. "Just tell me what my chances are of not being Modified."

"Actually Michael, I think your chances are pretty good. I know you don't have much trust at this point, but try to have some faith. I think you are going to come through this alright." She stood up and laid her hand on Michael's shoulder.

Just then a guard appeared at the door to the office. "Taylor you're up," he said.

Michael looked at the guard. He had a data chip on each temple. The guards were all enhanced beyond the typical genetic changes. The additional enhancements improved their strength and agility. It also provided them with live interface communication with each other. Overall it allowed for efficient control of the lockup.

"Well I guess it's time to find out what your chances are," Ms. Phillips said.

Michael looked at her and she smiled. Then she walked out the door. Michael followed as the guard brought up the rear. Ms. Phillips turned to the left, but the guard directed Michael to the right. He entered a small Plexiglas chamber with a single chair in it. The guard secured him to the chair with straps at his ankles and his wrists.

The guard left the chamber after he secured Michael and shut the door behind him. Michael found the restraints were strong. He could not move his legs or his arms. He looked out through the Plexiglas and realized that he was in the courtroom. His chamber was along the eastern wall, along with two additional chambers located to his right. They both had prisoners restrained in the same way. In front of the prisoners were two tables for attorneys, and they faced the judge's bench. There was a gallery at the back of the courtroom for the families. That area was separated from the main courtroom by Plexiglas. Michael scanned the faces of the people in the visitors' area. He did not see his mother or brother.

Michael could hear people talking through a speaker above his head. One of the attorneys was pleading his client's case. The judge suddenly cut him off.

"I've heard enough thank you, Mr. Walters," the judge said. "Please have a seat while I render my decision." He pounded his gavel as he spoke.

The judge turned toward the prisoners and spoke to the man in the chamber next to Michael. He was a large Asian man. "Mr. Chung I find you guilty. You are sentenced to immediate Modification."

Mr. Chung immediately began to scream and raged against his restraints as the door to his chamber opened behind him. A nurse with a syringe and a guard entered. Mr. Chung managed to break his right hand free. He swung at the nurse who was attempting to inject him in the neck. He caught her flush on the right temple knocking her out. She went down in a heap.

Meanwhile Mr. Chung's father rushed the Plexiglas wall and was pounding on it with a chair leg that he had broken off. His father was screaming something that Michael did not understand, but he had a good idea what it meant. Guards quickly rushed in and secured Mr. Chung's father, then they dragged him out of the family area.

A second nurse appeared in Mr. Chung's chamber and retrieved the syringe from the floor as the guard held down Mr.

Chung's arm. She injected him in the neck, and he immediately went unconscious. They quickly removed him from the chair. They placed him on a gurney waiting for him in the hallway.

Michael watched all this from three feet away. He had never seen anything like this before. He began to sweat and breathe heavily.

"Next case please," Michael heard the judge talk through the speaker and watched as a new set of attorneys made their ways to the tables. A clerk read the case number and charges for Mr. Castillo. Again Michael scanned the family area looking for someone, anyone there to support him. He saw Liz sitting by herself in the back. Their eyes met and she smiled at him and waved. Michael tried to muster a smile. He weakly smiled back at her. She blew him a kiss, and that made him laugh.

It took twenty minutes to hear Mr. Castillo's case. Michael watched again as the man was sedated and carried off on a gurney. What was it that Ms. Phillips said, have a little faith?

Now they were talking about Michael in the courtroom. Ms. Phillips was standing up while she explained the situation. Michael watched the judge as he scanned the computer monitor embedded in his desk. It didn't seem as though he was listening to her.

Ms. Phillips finished her presentation and took a seat. Now the prosecution attorney stood to speak. Michael sat up in his chair and listened intently. The prosecution attorney was a middle aged man dressed in the latest data wear. It looked to Michael like he was too old to have been enhanced.

The prosecutor spoke, "Your Honor, the government agrees with the defense in this matter. We support a disposition of placement at the Evaluation Center in Chino."

Michael felt his heart leap. He may be saved. The prosecutor took a seat, and the judge looked at Michael. "Mr. Taylor, the court rules that you will be sent to the Evaluation Center in Chino to be evaluated for Rehabilitation."

The door to his chamber opened and a guard entered. He released Michael from the chair and led him to a holding area.

"Have a seat Taylor. You will be transferred at the end of the day." His body felt numb as he stumbled over to a bench. The guard left and Michael was alone in the holding cell. He looked at his hands, they were shaking.

"Get a grip," Michael said to himself. He took some deep breaths to calm himself. Then he settled in to wait.

By the end of the day fifteen more prisoners entered the holding cell with Michael. They held one hundred and five trials that day.

8

Michael was in a transport bus on his way to the Prison Evaluation Center in Chino, California. The morning sun was up now. If he was found capable of change and being a productive member of society, he would be sent to the Rehabilitation Center. If not he would be Modified. He was grateful for that at least. He had been given a chance.

Michael's knees were jammed into the metal seat in front of him. He was handcuffed and shackled around his waist. Another chain connected his hands to the restraints around his waist and his feet. The sun was shining through the window and the glare was blinding him. He could not lift his hand to block it. He closed his eyes and tried to breathe through his mouth. He tried not to smell the stench of the man next to him, or the stench of the bus. It had transported thousands of inmates like him over the years. Michael could not believe these old buses even ran anymore.

Jason was also sent to the Evaluation Center. His case was processed more quickly than Michael's. He was pushed through the system because it was clear that he was guilty, but he made a deal. He gave up the name of his supplier to avoid immediate Modification. Michael wondered if he would see Jason in Chino. Would he would still be there? He may have failed already. That would suck! Jason had some problems, but he didn't deserve to be turned into a turnip. Did anyone?

Michael and Jason had not seen each other since their arrest. Since Jason was a snitch he was housed in protective custody at the Adjudication Center. Michael was very angry at Jason. He was equally angry at himself for his own stupidity. He knew Jason was trouble but he went with him that morning, all because he was feeling sorry for himself.

As they pulled into the grounds of the prison, Michael could see fences topped with razor wire surrounding large old buildings. He saw a corn field to the right of the main building. Men were walking through the field tending to it. They moved slowly and methodically.

"They're Mods," the man next to him said.

"Like Zombies," Michael whispered.

Michael had never actually seen a Mod before. The Mods had mostly been confined to working in factories. A large gate opened and the bus pulled into the sally port leaving the Mods behind them. The gate closed behind the bus. The bus was now between two gates in an enclosed area. Michael could see a guard in a tower working the gates. The front gate opened and the bus pulled into the prison yard.

Chino was an older prison left over from the former State System. The prison was ancient by today's standards, but the government still used it as an Evaluation Center. It had been refurbished but was still in disrepair. Most new funding was devoted to the Rehabilitation Centers where the treatment was done. The Modification Centers cost very little because they consisted of only an operating room, and simple housing. There were three Evaluation Centers in California, one in the north, Chino in the south, and one for women in central California.

Michael struggled to get off the bus with the chains attached to his body. Eventually all the inmates exited and were standing in the hot, dusty parking lot. When the chains were removed the inmates shuffled single file into the reception area to be processed. For the next four hours Michael was stripped, searched, interviewed, given a physical, a brief psychological evaluation, had his picture and fingerprints taken, and was given a data tag on his left hand that contained all the information that was just garnered.

After his intake he walked toward his living unit with four other new arrivals. They all carried a bed roll, a towel, a "Fish Kit" filled with a toothbrush, toothpaste, a small plastic hairbrush, dental floss on a stick, and deodorant.

They were escorted down the main hallway by a custody officer. He was a well-built black man wearing the standard blue uniform and cap. A pulse wand was attached to his belt. He had obviously been genetically enhanced for athletic skills. Michael noticed data chips on his temples similar to the guards at county jail.

The guard moved very efficiently, no wasted movements. All of the guards at the county jail moved in the same manner. The guard was not rude, but he dealt with them in a professional and direct manner.

The group stopped outside a doorway and the guard spoke to Control through his interlink system. "Four 10-15's for Unit 9, at the door," he said.

Michael could not hear the response, but he looked up and saw the words "Unit 9" stenciled on the wall above the door. The automatic door release clicked and the door creaked open.

The guard looked at them and spoke. "Inside gentleman, single file, stand on the yellow line on the right."

All the inmates including Michael made their way into Unit 9 and lined up. The Unit was very spacious inside. Three tiers, or floors of cells, rose up to the ceiling. A three story wall stood twenty feet opposite the tiers creating a large open space. A combination of sunlight through the windows, and florescent lights, created an odd mix of light. A fence separated the entry area from the tiers and a metal staircase. Michael looked down the tiers and could barely see the other end of the building. The custody officers had a small office area with a desk and three chairs in the front entry area. Michael could see a door with a window behind the officers' desk. It led into the Dayroom according to the name stenciled over the door. A shower area was behind Michael.

A custody officer yelled out cell assignments telling them where to go. Michael was assigned to cell 215. That meant it was on the second tier. He walked through the gate and climbed the stairs. Then he made his way down the tier toward his cell. He passed the other cells on the tier as he made his way to 215. Inmates were standing at the front of their cells as he walked by. They were curious to see the new arrivals. They let out cat calls as Michael walked by.

The front of the cells had bars that were covered with metal mesh to keep inmates from throwing things like feces and urine at the guards. That feature was a holdover from the old days when

Chino was a state prison. Now most inmates at least tried to be civil toward the custody officers.

Michael finally reached 215 and stopped in front of the cell. He heard an officer say, "Rack 215." The door to the cell moved to the left and Michael stepped forward. The cell was dark despite the fact that the light in the ceiling was on.

On his left was a bunk bed. At the end of each bed was a built in video screen with a data reader. In front of him on his right was a metal sink attached to the wall and back in the corner was a metal toilet. Next to the sink was an open metal locker for each inmate. The cell was seven feet wide by ten feet long, and about eight feet high. The space he was standing in was the only open floor space.

"Welcome to paradise," his cellie said. "I'm Billie." Billie was lying on the bottom bunk reading a book. Billie stood up. He was white, a Darwin, with tattoos on his neck and arms. He was muscular with his face and head shaved. He had bright blue eyes and a mischievous smile.

"Thanks, I'm Michael."

"The top bunk is yours." Billie said.

"Guess so," Michael said.

He threw his bed roll and other belongings on the upper bunk and climbed up. He lay back on the bunk and supported his head with the pillow. He could feel the metal frame of the bed through the two inch mattress. Above him he could see where prior inmates had scratched their names and other choice words of wisdom into the ceiling. "Eat Me," and "Fuck the Government." The cell was painted a putrid dark tan color and smelled stale. He sent Liz a quick e-mail to let her know his address and that he was thinking about her. Then he closed his eyes and tried to conjure up the memory of Liz at her party. He didn't know how his relationship with her would hold up with him in prison. A tear rolled down his cheek, and he closed his eyes in an attempt to rest.

9

Rick Carson lay embracing his wife Natalie. He could feel her soft, warm skin, as he stroked the small of her back. His hand moved around to rub her stomach, and then he caressed her breast. She flinched and he could feel her tighten up. She did not want him to touch where her other breast used to be. She had it removed six months ago due to cancer. She chose not to have reconstructive surgery yet. Rick kissed her neck and laid back. Then he leaned over to look at the clock. It was time to get up, but he had a good sleep and felt rested. He rolled over, and pushed a button to open the window shade. The bright morning sun came streaming in. His wife groaned and pulled the covers over her head. He could hear his daughter moving around in the hallway.

"Time to get moving," he said to his wife.

"Do we have to?" Natalie asked.

"No, but we should," he said.

Just then their dog Mattie jumped up onto the bed and burrowed under the covers so she could lick Natalie's face. Mattie was a black and white Papillion less than two years old with bundles of energy.

"Okay, you don't need to gang up on me, I'll get up," Natalie said.

Rick and Natalie both laughed as she threw back the covers and stood up. Rick watched her as she walked to the bathroom. He caught up to her at the sink and wrapped his arms around her waist. She turned toward him and kissed him.

"Perhaps we were a bit hasty," Rick said. "A few more minutes won't make a difference."

"Too late darling," Natalie said. "You'll have to wait until tonight." She turned and broke free from his grasp, then stepped into the shower. She smiled at him as she laughed. "I love you." Then she turned away as she gave instructions to the shower's data center, "Full stream, and water at 88 degrees." The shower erupted with water from the five sprinkler heads which were positioned to cover her entire body.

Disappointed, Rick turned his attention to shaving himself. After showering and dressing, he sat in his study trying to catch up on some work. Mattie lie at his feet as he listened to smooth jazz music, and edited work reports. Rick was a psychologist who worked at the Chino Prison Evaluation Center. He was dedicated to his work and had published two books on Forensic Evaluations. He converted a portion of the garage into his home office. It was small with a desk, one file cabinet, an overhead fan, and his favorite leather chair. It was also outfitted with the latest computers, and he had access to the most comprehensive library database available.

Rick looked at the report reflected in a 3D display in front of him and shook his head. The name at the top read, James Shinley. James had been convicted of car theft and was sent to the Evaluation Center because it was his first offense. He was given a chance to go to Rehabilitation. After getting to the Evaluation Center, however, James had been involved in several incidents. Most recently James had assaulted a staff member. Rick had no choice but to send James to be Modified. Rick closed the report and sighed deeply. He believed people should be punished for their crimes, but he hated being responsible for anyone being turned into a mindless drone.

"Breakfast is ready Rick." Natalie called from the kitchen.

He rose to go to breakfast. Before he left his office he quickly downloaded the latest issue of Runners' Weekly onto his data pad. He would look at that later. Tall and lean, Rick dressed in business casual. He had what he called 'prison clothes', which were basically inexpensive clothes he could throw into the washer. He never knew what he was going to get on himself in prison, so it didn't pay to dress for success. He enjoyed the casual nature of that. Rick was never one to stand on ceremony. As he entered the kitchen his mouth began to water from the aromas of fried eggs and turkey sausage.

Unlike Rick's office, the rest of the home was decorated in contemporary furniture and appliances. It also had Natalie's trademark artistic touch.

"Smells great," Rick said.

"Good morning Dad," Rick's daughter Ashley said. She was seated in the breakfast nook.

Ashley was their only child. She was bright, intelligent, and very engaging. Rick and Natalie could only afford one enhancement, and they chose intelligence. Ashley was in her final year of high school.

"Good morning, Sweetie," Rick said.

He kissed Ashley on her cheek and went to get a cup of coffee. A fresh watercolor landscape was leaning on the counter.

"What's this, you're latest Hon?" Rick asked smiling at Natalie.

"Yes, do you like it?" she replied, as she plated some eggs.

"It's beautiful Mom," Ashley said with a mouth full of toast.

"Yes it's really nice, very colorful," Rick said as he turned toward Ashley. "Please don't talk with food in your mouth."

Ashley covered her mouth with her hand and made an apologetic smile.

Bridges, the Carson's eight year old tabby cat jumped up on the counter and sniffed at the painting. "Get off Bridges," Rick scooped up the cat and set him down on the floor.

Rick poured himself a cup of coffee as Natalie moved across the room. He looked at her thinking of the sweet smell of her hair and the softness of her skin that he enjoyed that morning.

As they ate their breakfast, Rick noticed that Ashley had a data pad tucked under her plate. She kept her left hand on it and seemed excited but restrained. Rick was proud of Ashley for her academic accomplishments. She was the top student in her class. He often thought that a parent could not ask for a better kid.

Natalie also noticed the pad. "What's that you have there? "She asked.

Ashley looked up to see both of her parents staring at her.

"I have something to tell you," Ashley said.

She pulled the pad out from under the plate and set it on the kitchen counter. After she pushed a button, a hologram of a woman in a Stanford jacket appeared. She was talking to Ashley and congratulating her.

"I've been accepted to Stanford."

"Congratulations!" Both Rick and Natalie blurted out as they rushed to Ashley to give her a hug.

Ashley's face beamed. "I'm so excited. I got the notice yesterday, but I wanted to wait until we were all together to break the news."

"Wow," Rick said. He sat back in his chair and looked at his daughter. "What about the other schools you applied to?" Rick asked. "Have you heard from them? Are there any other contenders for the great Ashley Carson?"

"Yes," Ashley said, "But Stanford was my number one choice because of their environmental studies program. So that's the end of it I want to go there."

Rick and Natalie looked at each other, smiling proud parents. Then Rick got lost in thought about the upcoming expenses he would incur over the next four years. Natalie and Ashley began to talk about what was going to happen next, but he didn't hear them. Rick wondered if he would need to write another book to supplement his income.

10

Rick made his way to the shoot-tube station near his home. His mind was preoccupied with thoughts of Ashley going to Stanford. He was happy for her, but they would need to make sacrifices to pay for her education. Rick thought the shoot-tube looked like an unfinished sewer junction. It had large bright metal tubes on top of a metal platform. As Rick made his way onto the platform, his shoes made sounds like hollow aluminum drums. Everything was automated at the station so there were no attendants. Rick took his place at the end of a short line of people. While he waited for his turn, Rick observed the bright glow of the shoot tube. It went through a rainbow of colors from yellow through light blue. He found the visual effect rather pleasing. He recalled an interesting article about the impact of colors on human emotions. One of the administrators at his last assignment attempted to test the effect by painting holding cells blue. Blue was supposed to have a calming effect. No one actually knew if the color of the room had any effect on the inmate's moods. Inmates were already enraged or suicidal when they were placed into the rooms.

When his turn came, he scanned the data chip on his wrist band to pay and set the destination. Rick took a seat on the facilitator which moved into and out of the main tube. He closed his eyes. A panel slid down and sealed the opening as the tube closed, Rick was instantly dematerialized, and then reconstituted. The facilitator at the end point moved him out of the tube. He stood on the platform and paused for a moment to let his dizziness pass. After he regained his senses he made his way down the aluminum stairs. He always felt like he had just taken a carnival ride when he used the shoot tube. Rick smiled to himself as he thought of vomiting from carnival rides as a young boy. At least he didn't vomit now.

Rick began the one block walk to the prison. A strong Santa Ana wind blew dust into his face. He brushed his salt and brown pepper hair out of his eyes, and leaned into the wind. It was a warm day, and the sun shone brightly. It was still early so the sun was bright, but not at its peak heat yet. The glare hurt his eyes and made him squint even more than the blowing dust. His legs ached a little. He was still feeling the effects of the Los Angeles Marathon he ran last week. It was his fifth year running. He had steadily improved his race times. He was in the top ten percent for his age group.

Rick reached the main gate and showed his ID to the guard. He walked through the entrance to the prison grounds. He noticed a large black crow eyeing him from the top of the razor wire on the perimeter fence. Another strong gust of wind blew as he approached the building. The crow left its perch on the razor wire and flew directly over Rick's head. Rick flinched as it swooped low in front of him and snatched something from the sidewalk. Then it arched back into the sky. He continued along the fence line on the outside of the housing unit. He could hear inmates yelling out of the windows to each other. It was an odd and disturbing experience if you were not used to it. It was how inmates talked to one another when they were three or four cells away.

The building looked imposing from the outside. It was very large and surrounded by fences topped with razor wire. The administration offices were in the front of the building with the housing units in the back and on the sides. Rick walked past the living units and made his way to the front of the administrative area.

As Rick entered the main building he was greeted by the familiar scent of bodies that showered too infrequently, and were packed together too closely. Over the years he had become almost immune to the smell. But on days like this, with the wind stirring up the sediment the smell was impossible to ignore. It smelled like a feedlot for cattle. It made his nostrils pucker as though he smelled rancid milk.

As Rick entered the secured area, he gave his bag to the custody officer working the entrance. He recognized Ms. Rodriquez, as she was at this post most mornings

"Good morning Doc," she said.

Rick handed her his lunch cooler and his briefcase. "Good morning," he said.

She scanned his bags and placed them on the other side of the machine.

"Doc, all ready for you," she said.

Rick walked into the full body scanner and put up his arms. Ms. Rodriquez viewed his image on a video monitor.

"Looks good Doc," she said. "You can proceed."

"Thanks, you have a good day," Rick said.

All staff had to be scanned to ensure they were not bringing in any contraband: video equipment, phones, guns, tobacco, etc. Over the years many staff had been caught bringing in contraband to sell to the inmates. They risked their jobs to make a few extra dollars. It could also create a serious safety and security risk. One time an attorney snuck in a gun and gave it to an inmate. Then the inmate made an escape attempt. He took three office staff hostage, and shot one before it all ended.

Rick proceeded to equipment checkout. He had his personal data-chip scanned, and the guard gave him a personal alarm and a protective vest which he put over his head. He pushed a button and the vest constricted to encase his torso. Violence was a way of life in the prison. Many of the inmates would be sent on to be Modified. They didn't always take it lying down. They didn't always get along with each other either. Rick left the security entrance and walked down the large main hallway of the building.

On his left was the initial reception area. Large cages called holding tanks lined the walls. They were often filled with inmates who just arrived. They were waiting for their housing assignments. When the tanks were full, the inmates were very noisy. Today they were empty except for three inmates sleeping on the benches. Most of Rick's colleagues avoided going this route to the Unit. They would go through the Medical Department. They wanted to avoid the noise or inmates asking for restroom breaks.

Rick reached the end of the hallway. He was in front of the door leading into Unit 9. Instead of entering the housing unit, he turned right and went into the evaluation unit. As he entered the office area he was greeted by the custody officer who worked the area, Lucy James. "Morning Doc."

"Good morning Miss J.," Rick replied.

Rick moved down the hallway toward his office, and unlocked the door by scanning his data-chip. He situated his bags, and sat in his chair. His office was comfortable but not luxurious. The offices were built by Prison Industries which was responsible for most prison construction. It was designed like a cell with a six inch wide window that ran three feet high. The view outside was two parallel fences, and the outside of the Medical building. Not exactly stunning, but at least he had some natural light. He tried to decorate the office with pictures of exotic locations like Hawaii. He had several chairs, a desk, computer, and two bookcases with old paper books. He still enjoyed looking at old paper books, and collected them as a hobby. He also had some therapy aids built into the walls.

He logged into his computer and pulled up his new assignment roster. He looked at the roster. It had three new names on it. The name on the top of the list was Michael Taylor.

11

It was Michael's first morning on the Unit. He lie on his bunk with his eyes closed thinking about Liz. He could visualize her smile and the feel of her skin. He missed her a lot and hoped to hear from her soon.

He had already been to breakfast this morning. Some of the food he found edible, and some he did not. The oatmeal had been horrible. He sat up onto the edge of his bunk with his feet dangling over the side. Billie was standing by the lockers.

"So what's this we're going to do?" Michael asked.

"It's called the dayroom program," Billie said. "It's one of the only times we get to just chill out, play some dominos, you know," Billie said. "The rest of the time we're in groups, talking to our primary Docs, taking tests, or doing structured programs, like chow and showers."

"How long have you been here?" Michael asked.

"About two months," Billie said.

"What are you in for?"

"Assault," Billie said. "I had too much to drink and went off on my neighbor because his dog kept going after me. A stupid ass dog and a stupid ass owner. What about you?"

"I was charged with dealing a controlled substance," Michael said. "I trusted an old friend and it cost me."

"That sucks," Billie said. "What do you think your chances are?'

"Of what?"

"Of going to Rehabilitation."

"I don't know. I've never been in this situation before," Michael said.

"Well let me tell you, be real careful. Some strange things have been going on around here lately."

Billie had an easy manner about him that Michael liked, but he felt cautious about taking advice from another inmate. "What do you mean?"

"Nothing really, it just seems that some cool people have been scooped up and sent to Mod. People I was close to who were not gangsters, or bad players. People, who just messed up, made one bad decision. Sometimes they are messed with, and get into trouble because of it. It doesn't always make sense. Then, the next thing you know, they're gone."

Michael could see a look of concern and disappointment on Billie's face.

"Are you worried about yourself?" Michael asked.

"Of course! And you should be worried about yourself too. That's what I'm trying to say, Bro. I have Dr. Isaac, and his guys seem to get the worst of it. You'll find out who your Doc is pretty soon."

Billie turned and grabbed the bars at the front of the cell squeezing them so hard the blood left them, turning his hands pale white.

"I had a good Bud in here that got scooped up last week. He was in a fight and the next thing you know, he's gone. It was totally fucked up. The fight wasn't even his fault. His doctor was Isaac."

"Sorry to hear about that," Michael said.

"Thanks," Billie said. "But there's nothing we can do about it now. So let's just go to the dayroom and try to chill."

Billie released the bars and turned back toward Michael as he leaned against the lockers. He forced a smile, and Michael thought he looked like an abandoned puppy. It made Michael aware of his own vulnerability. Just then the door to their cell opened releasing them for the dayroom program.

Billie smiled, "Let's go have some fun," he said. Then he walked out of the cell and turned left towards the stairs.

Michael jumped off his bunk. Just then a large cockroach ran out from under the bed. It stopped in front of Michael, turned, and ran out of the cell. Michael cringed as he moved out onto the tier walkway. He sensed someone behind him and turned around. Several inmates were directly behind him.

"Let's keep moving dude," one of the inmates said.

Michael turned back and walked down the stairs. The dayroom was on the bottom floor on the other side of the Unit. The inmates filed into the dayroom and spread out to sit at tables. The room was fairly large with a high ceiling. It was lit with bright florescent lights. There were eight metal tables in the room. Each table was attached to the floor. Metal stools were attached to the tables with a frame that made them look like silver spiders. Four people could sit at each table. Twenty-five inmates were allowed to participate in the dayroom program at one time.

Michael could see pulse rifles mounted to the ceiling and cameras mounted in the corners of the room. Gas jets jutted out of the baseboards, and were located about every ten feet. On the left, about fifteen feet up, the wall was made of safety glass. Behind the glass was a room with a control console. A custody officer sat at the console and observed the dayroom ready to respond to any disturbances.

All the inmates were dressed in orange jumpsuits with black slip-on tennis shoes. Michael followed Billie to a table and took a stool. The metal stool felt cold and hard on Michael's backside. The stool was small, and Michael struggled to maintain his balance on it. There were two other men sitting at the table.

"Boys, this is my new cellie, Michael," Billie said. "He's in for selling a controlled substance."

"I'm Kevin," the inmate sitting next to Billie said. Kevin had red hair, pale sallow skin, with freckles, and an acne problem. He was very slender, obviously a Normal.

"Hi Kevin," Michael said.

"I am Victor," the other inmate said.

Victor was sitting next to Michael on his right. He looked at Michael with steely grey eyes. He appeared older than the rest of the guys, and he had a slight accent. He also had a large scar on his face that ran from his right ear across his face to the edge of his mouth. He had short stubby blonde hair which looked like it was never combed.

"Where's your accent from?" Michael asked.

"Russia," Victor said. "I have been in United States for three years now."

Michael could not help but stare at Victor's scar.

"You like my face, huh?" Victor asked.

"Sorry," Michael said. "I didn't mean to stare."

"It's okay," Victor said. "I am used to it."

"How did that happen?" Michael asked.

"It's called Joker," Victor said. "I got while in prison in Ukraine. It's because I am Russian. They cut your face with razor. Someone walk up to me and just cut me, starting here." Victor pointed to the edge of his mouth. "They cut back to here." He touched his ear. It make you think twice about going into Ukraine again, stealing their business."

"You escaped?" Michael asked.

"No, I did time," Victor said. "Why you ask that?"

"How did you escape Modification?" Michael asked.

"They don't have that bullshit in Ukraine, didn't have genetic Modification when I born either." Victor said. Michael couldn't help but to keep one eye on Victor. He looked weathered, and tough.

Billie slammed some dominos down onto the table, crack, crack, crack. Dominos was a favorite prison game for decades. The administration still made it available because it was easy to provide and inexpensive. "Come on boys, let's cut out the sewing circle shit and throw some tiles." They all laughed, and started grabbing dominos.

12

Liz looked around the coffee shop and spotted Stacy sitting in the back. She smiled and waved and then went to a kiosk to order. Loud techno music played in the background of the brightly lit shop. After placing her order she went to Stacy and gave her a hug and a kiss.

"Hello Lady," Stacy said. "You're looking good as usual."

"Thanks," Liz said as she took a seat. "The truth is I'm a little freaked out by everything that's going on." A hole opened up in the middle of the table and a pedestal appeared through the hole with Liz's drink on it. She took the drink, and had a sip. "My gosh, I need this."

"Have you heard anything yet?"

"Yes. I went to Michael's hearing last week. He made it to the Evaluation Center. He has to pass a ninety day program to go on to the Rehabilitation Center. This is so nerve wracking."

"Well at least he is still safe." Stacy took a sip of her own drink and sat back as she watched Liz.

A man walked by the table and stopped to stare at Stacy.

"Can we help you?" Stacy asked.

"Yes, I mean no, I mean, sorry," the man stammered and then walked away as he hurried out the front door.

The girls laughed and then Liz sat forward. "Michael also sent me an e-mail. He wants to know what I am going to do. You know, am I going to dump him, or what."

"What are you going to do?"

"As long as he is not modified I am going to stand by him. He needs me. I can't imagine what he feels like. It wasn't even his fault. It was that boy Jason's fault."

Stacy smiled as she grabbed Liz's hand and squeezed it. "Good for you. I really like Michael, and I think if he gets through this you guys will be great together. I know he really cares for you. He's the only guy who I know personally, that has never made a pass at me."

Liz wiped a tear from her eye and reached into her handbag for a tissue. She sat back as she wiped her eyes and took a deep breath. "I know he wants to be with me, and I want to be with him. I leave for school this weekend. I am hoping that will take my mind off of his situation."

"I'm sure it will. Are your parents moving you up there?"

"No, my father is busy as usual so he hired someone to help me."

Stacy smiled and shrugged her shoulders as if to say "sorry" as she took another sip of her drink. "Well let's be sure to keep in touch. Okay?"

"Of course we will," Liz said. "Just because you are going to be in New York studying music doesn't mean we won't stay best friends."

Stacy finished her drink and stood up to leave. "I love you friend and I hope everything turns out well for you. I have to run now."

Liz stood up and the girls hugged and kissed. Stacy grabbed her handbag and waved from the door as she left.

Liz sat down again and looked around at the other people in the coffee shop. They were all going about their business, oblivious to the life and death struggle that Michael and people like him were involved in. She opened her data pad and wrote Michael an e-mail.

"Dear Michael, I got your e-mail, and I am thrilled that you have been cleared for the Evaluation Program. It was very nerve wracking watching you in court. I was so relieved you were not modified. I want to let you know that I am your biggest supporter. I will help you in any way that I can. I still care about you. I will leave for school this weekend. My father hired someone to help me with the move, so I will say goodbye to my parents before I leave. Stacy sends her regards, and hopes you make it through to Rehabilitation. Please take care of yourself. Love, Liz, XO."

Liz pushed send and then sat back to finish her drink. She watched two people snuggling in the far corner as they laughed and kissed each other.

13

The next morning Billie sung as Michael lie on his bunk cringing.

"Do you really like that stuff?" Michael asked. "Country music?"

"I love it," Billie said. "It makes me feel connected to other peoples' stories, you know. Some of them remind me of my life."

"I know, but do they have to do it in such an annoying way?"

"Mama, don't let your sons grow up to be cowboys," Billie crooned.

"Oh my God," Michael groaned as he put his pillow over his ears.

"Taylor-215, get dressed and prepare for a doctor's ducat, five minutes," a voice came over the loudspeaker.

Michael blinked as he listened to the announcement. Butterflies filled his stomach as he sat up to get dressed.

"Well, I guess you will find out who your Doctor is today," Billie said.

Michael jumped off the top bunk and slipped on his tennis shoes. They were about two sizes too big and difficult to keep on his feet if he walked too fast. He zipped up his orange jumpsuit and stood in front of the gate waiting to be released.

"Good luck," Billie said.

Michael glanced back at Billie who was reclined on his bunk with a concerned look on his face. "Thanks,"

The door to the cell suddenly came to life as it jiggled and clanked open moving to the right. Michael made his way downstairs, leaving the unit to walk across the large hallway to the Clinic.

The Staff at the Clinic checked him in by scanning the data chip attached to his wrist. He had a seat in a holding cell with three other inmates. It was stuffy in the holding cell. Michael did not recognize the other inmates. They sat on a bench that went around the perimeter of the holding cell. It was an enclosed room with two large windows made of safety glass. Inmates could watch the staff moving about the Clinic, and staff could watch the inmates.

Eventually a female custody officer opened the holding cell. "Taylor, take it down to room eleven," she pointed down a long hallway. Michael exited and made his way down to room eleven. When he arrived the door was open so he stood in the doorway and waited.

Rick Carson stood up from his desk and waved toward a chair. "Come in, you must be Mr. Taylor, Michael. I'm Dr. Carson, have a seat"

Michael looked at Rick and entered the office. He took a seat in front of Rick's desk. Rick sat down and looked across the desk at Michael. "Do you understand what you are here for Michael?" Rick asked. "Do you understand the purpose of the evaluation process?"

"Sure," Michael said. "It's your job to decide if I'll be turned into a turnip or not."

"We're here to determine if you are likely to commit more crimes against the community, to break laws," Rick said.

"What if I didn't break the law to begin with?" Michael developed a lump in his throat. He began to tear up as his frustration rose.

"It's not my place to retry your case. I simply make a recommendation. My job is to evaluate your ability to benefit from personality treatment, so you can be a constructive and positive member of society. If I believe that you can, then you will be sent to Rehabilitation, if not you will be sent to Modification."

"So you get to pass judgment on me!" Michael could feel his temper rising as his voice became louder.

"In a way," Rick said. "But it's not only me. You will be administered a battery of tests, attend group therapy where a social worker will evaluate you, and meet with me individually. All that information is accumulated, and then I have the final decision for the recommendation to the government."

Michael gripped the armrests on his chair and his breathing became labored as he listened to Rick. "How could these people do this? How could he have ended up here?" he thought.

Rick could see that Michael was getting angry. He leaned forward in his chair and talked to Michael in a soothing voice.

"Michael, I understand you feel angry about this whole process. That's okay, I know it is your life on the line. I need you to trust me in this process. I am not out to get you. I only want to help you get through this. I have reviewed your court documents. I realize that you may have been dragged into this unwittingly. Is that true?"

Michael looked up at Rick. "Finally," he thought, "someone who might get it". Rick looked like a nice enough guy, and he wasn't that Dr. Isaac that Billie had warned him about.

"Yeah, that's right," Michael managed to blurt out. "I am not a drug dealer. I took a ride with a friend who offered to buy me breakfast, and the next thing I know I'm in prison."

"Okay then," Rick said. "It will be up to us to work together to do this. So we will meet on a regular basis to talk about you, and your life. That will help me understand you better so that I can help you, okay?"

"Okay." Michel spoke hesitantly as he glared at Rick through tearful eyes.

"No guarantees of course, but we will give it our best." Rick said. Then he outlined for Michael the schedule of tests, group therapy, and interview sessions. Michael left Rick's office with a slight sense of hope for the first time in weeks.

14

The next morning in the Chow Hall, Michael took his tray and sat next to Billie and Victor. The menu for today was scrambled eggs, bacon, toast and half a grapefruit. Michael looked at his tray and poked the eggs with his fork.

"Are these supposed to be eggs?" Michael asked.

"Powdered," Victor said as he shoved a piece of toast into his mouth. "If you don't want, I take them."

Michael looked down at the runny yellow slime on his tray and pushed it over to Victor. But not before he snatched the bacon and toasts off the tray.

"After you've been here longer, you will appreciate any hot food you get," Billie said.

"So, what do you have for today?" Billie asked as he waved a piece of bacon at Michael.

"Some kind of a brain scan," Michael replied as he bit off the end of a strip of bacon.

"Piece of cake," Victor said. "They want know if your brain works properly. If MRI shows no activity in limbic system, you go Modification. They say no activity in limbic system means you likely reoffend, or even worse, you are psychopath."

"What are you now, Dr. Frankenstein?" Billie asked.

"No Cowboy, I watch documentary on evaluation process before I arrested," Victor said as he ate Michael's eggs.

"So what does all that mean?" Michael asked. "How do I activate my system?" He crossed his arms and laid them on the table feeling frustrated.

"You can't. It either is or isn't. If isn't, you fucked pretty boy. You go straight to Mod," Victor said. "Some people say you wiggle your toes may help."

Michael looked at Victor who was shoveling eggs into his mouth. He was very confused. He had no idea how to prepare for this test.

A buzzer sounded signaling the end of the ten minute chow period. Everyone stood up and headed for the exit. Michael offered his hand with the data card to the Correctional Officer at the door. The officer scanned his card and directed him to the station at the end of the big hallway. Michael made his way down the hallway with all the other inmates who were going to their appointments. Custody officers were stationed every twenty yards. There was a group of three officers at the central control station in full combat gear. They were ready to respond to any disturbances.

Michael arrived at the MRI station and walked in. He offered his data hand to the Custody officer at the desk to scan. He was put into a holding cell by himself. After a short wait a nurse came for him and led him into the MRI room. Michael noticed the nurse was a very pretty Asian woman with long black hair. She smiled at Michael and had him lie on the MRI machine. She positioned him so his head entered the scanning element of the machine. As he lay there, Michael moved his toes around to test their mobility.

"Now just lie very still," she said. "This will not hurt. It is a simple brain scan. In particular we are assessing activity in your anterior cingulate cortex. But please don't move during the test. When you are moved into the scanning chamber there will be a video screen in front of you. You will see words flashed up on the screen. The words will be the names of colors. What we would like you to do is think of the word that you see. For example, if the word says, red. Then you think, red. Do you understand?"

"I guess so."

"Good," she said as she patted him on the arm. "Now it is very important that you do not move during the test. Try to stay as still as possible. Any movement will cause an inaccurate reading. Then we will have to redo the test. Just so you know, wiggling your toes will not help you pass the test. If anything, the movement will stimulate a different part of your brain. That will cause confusing readings, so no movement, okay?"

"Okay," Michael said. He felt very foolish for believing Victor.

Michael was moved into the scanning chamber, and the machine began to perform the scan. Above him was a video screen. A word flashed on the screen. The word read "green," but the color of the letters was red. He thought, "Red." The next word flashed onto the screen. It was blue, but the colors of the letters were yellow. Michael thought, "Yellow, Damn." He got angry with himself for missing the first two questions.

The machine hummed, and the dorsal area of his anterior cingulate cortex lit up on the MRI scan indicating activity. That meant that Michael was most likely not a psychopath. Psychopaths were like sociopaths on steroids. They were manipulative and amoral. They lacked the ability to love or establish meaningful personal relationships. The Evaluation Center went to great lengths to weed out psychopaths, because their behavior could not be changed. The test continued for the next ten minutes.

The nurse finally finished the scan and helped Michael up off of the machine. Michael smiled at the nurse with his "go to" endearing smile. "So what do you think? How does it look?"

"Oh, I don't have any idea. It has to be read by a radiologist and a neurosurgeon. That will take at least two weeks. So just continue to go about your business as usual," she said as she returned Michael's smile.

Then she escorted Michael to the door, and he headed back to the unit. After returning to his cell he lie on his bunk, and wrote Liz an e-mail.

"Dear Liz, I'm so happy you wrote to me. I know you are busy getting ready for college, but I wanted to answer you right away. It means so much to know you are still going to stick by me. I really need something to look forward to. This is my first week here but they keep us really busy. I have a cellie named Billie. He is okay so far. The food is terrible, and the place where I live is old and run down, but I will try to keep my spirits up. I think of you and all the good times we've had. I will write when I can and I hope you will do the same. Love, Michael."

After he sent the e-mail Michael laid back and opened his dinner sack. The sandwich looked half eaten, so he dumped the bag out onto his bunk. A mouse tumbled out of the bag with the food. Michael leapt off of his bunk, and shook off his blanket. The mouse fell off onto the floor, and then ran out under the cell bars. Michael swore to himself as he gathered up his remaining food, and threw it into the trash.

15

The next morning at chow Michael bore the brunt of Victor's toe wiggling prank. The guys had a good laugh at his expense. After chow he headed to the group room for his first group therapy session.

He was a little nervous about what group would be like. He was waiting in the group room when social worker Susan Atkins burst through the door. She had a bag of data cards and a pocket reader in her hand. She moved with confidence and purpose. Her red hair was pulled back into a bun. She greeted the seven inmates seated in a circle with a big smile on her face. "Good morning everyone," she laughed. "How are you all today?"

"Good morning Miss Atkins," most of the inmates replied. This was Michael's first group and his first encounter with the inimitable Ms. Atkins. He observed her with a curious eye. She looked at the Correctional Officer standing by the wall and nodded to him. He turned and left the room leaving her alone with the inmates. He would wait outside the door. The group therapy sessions were confidential. Only the clinical staff remained in the room.

She sat in the circle and introduced herself as the social worker in charge of the group. Then she had the inmates go around the room and introduce themselves, state their crime and how long they had been in the group. In addition to Michael there were two other new guys, Roberts and Jimmie. Michael already knew his cellie Billie who was sitting next to him, and Victor and Kevin whom he played dominos with during dayroom. Also in the group was Zack Cole, a Darwin whom Billie said acted like a junior staff member. Zack had a habit of confronting other inmates about their issues.

"For those of you who are new," Ms. Atkins said. "This is group therapy and part of your evaluation. This is what is called a process group. In here we discuss feelings, emotions, behaviors, actions, and alternatives to our destructive criminal acts. It is not an educational group. I am here to observe your ability to interface with others, while engaging in an honest and open discussion of your personality. I will write a report on your participation and make a recommendation for Modification or Rehabilitation, just like your primary clinicians, or doctors. Any questions?"

Ms. Atkins looked at seven pairs of eyes staring at her, but nobody said a word.

"Alright then, let's hear from one of you newer gentleman." She picked a data card out of her bag and inserted it into the pocket reader. "Michael Taylor. Tell us about yourself Michael."

Michael sat up in his chair as his back stiffened. He had never been in a situation like this before. "What do you want to know?"

"Why don't you start by telling us about your family," she said as she smiled at him.

Michael felt uneasy, but he started to tell the group about his family. "My mother raised me and my brother Ryan. She did it alone because my father died when I was three years old. He had a disease called A.L.S. I really don't remember him, but my mother told me a little about how horrible his death was. I guess I'm glad I was too young to know what was happening. Mom is a good woman, she tries hard. But she never really knew what to do with two boys. She has been sick with diabetes the last three years. This thing with me really sent her into a tailspin. She has been very upset. My brother Ryan is twenty eight years old. He is ten years older. We have never been close."

With that Michael folded his arms, stopped talking and looked at his feet. Everyone in the group looked at him, but nobody said a word.

Ms. Atkins looked around at the other members of the group one by one. Finally she spoke up. "Does anyone have a reaction to Taylor's comments?"

"Yeah, I've got a comment," Zack Cole said. "Thanks for sharing and all, but that was a little skinny on the real low-down. Especially regarding your Bro, he's ten years older than you, that's it?"

Michael looked up at Zack. He had never spoken to him before. He looked to be around Michael's age, maybe a few years older. He was about Michael's height, lean and muscular. Most of the inmate's had tattoos. They identified where they were from, names of deceased friends or 'homies', names of girlfriends, or information on their gang affiliation. Zack did not display any gang signs in his tattoos, but his neighborhood information was displayed prominently. He was had the letters SD and EC tattooed on his arms, El Cajon, a city in San Diego County known for its violence. Michael never had any extra money for decorating his body, so he didn't have any tattoos.

Michael looked into Zack's eyes which looked empty. He could see a slight smirk on Zack's face. He knew Zack was trying to call him out.

"Is there something else you want to tell us about your brother, Michael?" Ms. Atkins asked.

"Like what?" Michael did not feel like telling them anymore about Ryan.

"Like how many times a week he kicked your ass?" Zack asked as he started to laugh.

All the other inmates also began to laugh at Zack's comment.

Michael gripped the side of his chair so hard the plastic edge cut into his fingers. He felt his temper flare. It was similar to how he felt the day of the fight that got him sent to continuation school. Todd Chalmers had made a joke at his expense in chemistry class. Michael had taken a glass beaker, and broken it over Todd's head.

"Maybe I should just kick your ass to show you how he did it!" Michael said.

Everyone stopped laughing immediately. Ms. Atkins deftly moved her hand to the personal alarm secured to her waist. She pushed the alarm to alert the custody officer in the hallway.

"Come on then, new boy, jump!" Zack said laughing again.

Just then Billie laid his hand on Michael's arm to calm him. "Easy Buddy," he said. "We all know you can take care of yourself. That's how it goes in here. Just take a breath and chill."

Michael turned and looked at Billie. He had a look of grave concern on his face. "Chill out, Michael," Billie said.

At that moment the door to the group room opened and a custody officer appeared.   Ms. Atkins looked at the officer and said, "I think Mr. Taylor has had enough for today officer. Can you escort him back to the Unit?"

Michael looked at her, and she smiled at him. "It's alright Taylor. Just go back to your house, and we'll pick this up next time, okay?"

Michael calmed down and stood up to go with the officer. As he was leaving, he saw that Zack Cole still had a smirk on his face. Michael and the officer walked down the main hallway toward Unit 9. The officer did not talk. Michael walked a few feet ahead of him.

Michael began to think that he had messed up. Was he going to be sent to Modification already? Why couldn't he control his temper? He began to realize this was a very different situation than he had ever been in before. He started to have doubts that he could get through it. As they reached the unit the officer called in their arrival through his embedded communication chip. Michael waited for the unit door to open. The officer looked Michael in the eye. That was very unusual for them to do that. Not one officer had ever looked him in the eye at County.

He smiled at Michael as he talked. "Don't sweat it Taylor," the officer said. "It's your first week here. It's good that you didn't do anything dramatic. Just watch that temper of yours."

Michael was stunned but grateful for some human concern from a custody staff member. It was the first sense of humanity he had felt from a line staff.

"Thanks," Michael said. "I appreciate the heads up."

The door to the unit opened and the officer pointed toward the door.

"In on the yellow line," he said.

Michael turned and walked back into the unit.

When Billie came back from group, Michael was lying on his bunk eating an apple from his lunch sack.

"That was quite a show man," Billie said to Michael as he sat on his bunk and took off his shoes. "I thought for sure you were gonna blow."

"I know, thanks for talking me down," Michael said.

"It's that asshole Zack Cole," Billie said. "I warned you about him. He's a slippery bastard who seems to know how to incite other people. But you know, he never goes off himself. It's kind of curious."

"Yeah, he reminds me of some of the rich assholes I used to go to high school with," Michael said.

"Well you were lucky today. If you had gone off you would be in Ad-Seg right now, or worse."

"What's Ad-Seg?"

"The Hole, that's where you go if you get into trouble. It's the lockup unit," Billie said. "You don't want to go there. It's a fucked up way to do time."

Both of the boys then laid back on their bunks to rest. Michael fell asleep and dreamt of Liz and her birthday party. He was a long way from the party now.

16

The weekly case conference was attended by all the clinical staff and supervisors. Rick found a seat next to Dr. Dean Cooper. He was Rick's best friend and main ally. Dean was old school. He went to Harvard; the number one rated educational institution in the country. He insisted on wearing a Harvard coat over his stab-proof vest to let everyone know how accomplished he was. Rick was fond of Dean though, and found him intelligent, funny, and gregarious.

Dr. Isaac sat down on the other side of Rick. Ms. Atkins was seated on the other side of Dr. Isaac. Dean always referred to Dr. Isaac as the "Vile Little Man." He had a petite build, and long, black, slicked back hair. He always seemed to have a sardonic smile, and never looked you in the eyes when engaged in conversation.

Rick's boss Dr. Brayden was sitting at the end of the table. Dr. Brayden was not a physically imposing man, but he was a driven individual, and very direct.

"Okay people," Dr. Brayden said. "Let's get started. First let's review the weekly statistics. We received thirty-five new inmates this week. We transferred ten inmates to Modification, and thirteen to Rehabilitation. That leaves our total census at three hundred and seven inmates. Our ratio for referral to Rehabilitation for the last month is fifty-six percent. Down from seventy-two percent."

Rick stole a glance at Dean when he heard that they had been referring a larger percentage of inmates to Modification. Dean raised his eyebrows at Rick and nodded toward Dr. Isaac to indicate that he was responsible for the increase.

"We want to be mindful of our responsibility to society here folks," Dr. Brayden continued. "We do not want to be sending a criminal element back on the streets. I think it is prudent to err on the conservative side. If in doubt send them to Modification. Their future victims will thank you. Okay, so let's go over some cases, shall we. Dr. Isaac would you like to begin?"

Dr. Isaac went through his cases and then began to review Michael's cellie. "The next case is Billie Johnson," Dr. Isaac said. A holographic picture of Billie appeared and his test data and demographics appeared on the doctor's monitors.

"Johnson has passed the initial screens, but in individual sessions he does not seem to have a level of psychological sophistication that would allow him to benefit from Rehabilitation. He is poorly educated and has a sketchy vocational background. Both of those factors would impact his ability to find suitable work in the community, and be a contributing member of society. I am currently leaning towards Modification for Mr. Johnson."

"He does seem to do well socially however," Ms. Atkins spoke up. "He recently helped defuse a volatile situation in one of my groups."

"That may be," Dr. Isaac said as he cut Ms. Atkins off in mid-sentence. "I will of course consider that in my final analysis, but as I said at this point I am leaning toward Modification."

"Thank you Dr. Isaac," Dr. Brayden cut in. "Let's move on now. Dr. Carson, let's review your inmates."

Ms. Atkins sat back in her chair and folded her arms over her chest as she let out a deep breath. She looked frustrated from having her input minimized

Rick started the review of his new inmates. Michael's face appeared in the holographic display and his case information appeared in the monitors on the table.

"My last case is Michael Taylor. He's had an average start so far. He just started the testing phase as you can see. He had one session with me, and that was a little rocky. I believe he has started to attend groups. Is that correct?" Rick asked as he looked at Ms. Atkins.

"Yes," she said. "He has attended one group so far, and I had to have him escorted back to his cell. He almost started a fight. He has quite a temper."

"Well, let's keep an eye on him Doctor," Dr. Brayden said looking at Rick. "If he becomes a behavioral problem, we don't want to waste a lot of time on him."

"I will keep an eye on him as I do all my inmates. He does not have a prior record, and his involvement in his commitment offense is questionable according to the court report." Rick said. "I am certainly not going to rush to judgment. He is allowed three months before we render an opinion. I will give him his due time and due process."

Dr. Brayden was scowling at Rick as he listened. "Of course Doctor, but as I said earlier, we need to be mindful of our responsibility to society. Let's move on then. Dr. Cooper please review your caseload."

"Let me see, alright." Dean typed into the keyboard in front of him to start the hologram and informational display on his first inmate.

Rick sat forward in his chair with his arms on the desk. He was looking at the display but not seeing it. He wondered, "What is Dr. Brayden up to? Why is he pushing Modification so strongly?"

The meeting finally finished about eleven-thirty. As they were leaving the conference room Rick noticed that Dr. Isaac lagged behind. He was in a deep conversation with Dr. Brayden. Rick caught up to Dean and held him by the arm.

Rick whispered to him, "Let's try to get together and have a chat sometime this week."

Dean looked at Rick and nodded. "Sounds like a real good idea Doctor. I would like to run some cases by you. I will check my calendar and let you know. We should go to Luigi's."
Luigi's was Dean's favorite restaurant.

"Sounds good Dean, let's talk later."

Rick and Dean walked down the hallway to their offices as an alarm went off. Two custody officers came bursting through the main door into the office area. Then they went through the side door to the medical department. Before the door shut behind them, a rush of O.C. Spray blew into their office area. O.C. was oleo capsicum, an agonist spray used to subdue unruly inmates. It stung Rick's eyes, and Dean began to cough uncontrollably for a minute. They both moved quickly down the hallway away from the open door.

"Just another day in Heaven," Dean said.

"Exactly, talk to you later."

17

The next day was Rick and Dean's bi-weekly carbohydrate festival. The scent of garlic filled the air, and the antique ambiance of Luigi's was always a welcome sight for Rick. It was an oasis in a world of high-tech, low calorie, organic, gluten free restaurants that populated the area near the prison. The restaurant specialized in traditional Italian food like pasta dishes, pizza, and calzones with home-made sauces, and some of the best garlic bread in the universe.

The hostess sat Rick and Dean in a booth. The table was covered with a white table cloth, and a candle stuck in old Chianti bottle sat in the middle. They ordered a bambino-sized pizza as an appetizer, and penne pasta with Italian sausage and marinara sauce. Bottles of wine adorned the walls, but they ordered lemonade to drink.

"Are you sure you want to do this?" Dean asked as he laughed.

"I know, what a carb fest, huh. But it's only once in a while that we come here. I will run it off this weekend."

"That's fine for you but what about me. I will pay the price with a week of salads for lunch."

The waiter brought their garlic bread and pizza as an accordion played over the sound system.

"So what do you make of Brayden's comments yesterday at case conference," Dean asked as he tore into a piece of pepperoni pizza.

Rick set his bread down and looked at Dean. "Seriously, that guy bothers me. He seems to be pressuring us to send people to Modification. He doesn't want to come out and say that directly. He hides behind platitudes. I'm not sure what his motivation is to push this issue."

"I agree. How many of the ten referrals from last week were yours?"

"One," Rick replied. "How many were yours?"

"Two, which means seven of them were Dr. Isaac's. That's preposterous!"

"Wow, I had no idea he was referring so many. I was a little put off by his insistence about Billie Johnson. He cut Susan Atkins off when she spoke up in support of him. I also saw Dr. Isaac and Dr. Brayden in a serious talk at the end of the meeting."

"This whole Modification process bothers me period. With the economy suffering from its ninth year of recession, any money spent on criminals is resented by the populace. The last five years since they implemented the law have been really hard. I'm not sure how long I will be able to be a part of this circus," Dean said.

"I know what you mean. I often have my doubts as well. When the law was implemented, I was working in a treatment program for mentally ill individuals. They had all been incarcerated for a murder of one type or another. They were all Modified during the transition. It was very disturbing to me. That was five years ago. Now I try to be as fair as possible."

"I don't like being pressured," Dean said. "We have a right to come to independent conclusions regarding these folks." He looked at Rick.

"I agree, but what are our options if we really start to get pressured to refer people to Modification?" Rick was feeling frustrated the more he talked about it. He picked up a piece of pizza.

"We could speak to the Attorney General's office, or I suppose we could talk to the folks at the Civil Law Office," Dean said. He was speaking in a hushed tone.

"I guess those are both options, but in the meantime we will have to wait and see how this plays out. I am not going to refer anyone to Modification who has a chance." "Neither will I, I refuse to be herded by that incompetent boob," Dean said. They both laughed at the thought.

The kitchen door opened as the waiter brought out their meals. Rick saw a Mod in the back washing dishes. He could see the man stooped over the sink. Mods were all dressed the same, so they could be easily recognized. They wore navy blue shirts, blue slacks, and simple blue athletic shoes, with name tags sewn onto the front of their shirts, right above the left pocket. They had their heads shaved for the convenience of the person in charge of them, and the emerald green light on their forehead glowed.

"I didn't know Luigi used Mods," Rick said to the waiter.

"He just got his first one," the waiter replied. "It's very helpful to have him here."

"Do you recognize him?" Dean asked Rick.

"No, do you?"

"No."

"Suddenly I'm not so hungry anymore. I think I will get my food to go."

"Good idea," Dean said. "Let's get out of here."

18

Michael and Billie were lying on their bunks munching on their dinners of bologna sandwiches, potato chips, carrots, and a carton of milk. They got one hot meal a day, breakfast. They got a sack lunch and dinner. It cut down on labor in the kitchens to only serve one hot meal a day in the chow halls. They picked up their lunches at breakfast, and their dinners were delivered to their cells at the end of the day.

"Do you think we will come out of this alright?" Michael asked.

"Of course, Dude," Billie said. "We will make it, no problem."

"I know, I just feel like I'm going to explode every day. I am so angry about this whole situation. It's really messed up."

"You just need to learn how to relax. Do some progressive relaxation or something," Billie said.

"Progressive what?"

"You know, breathing, meditation. Man you need to talk to your Doc to get straight. You need to learn how to chill out."

"Did Dr. Isaac teach you how to do that?"

"Not actually. I learned by myself when I was on the street. I tried to learn how to check my temper so I went to a counselor. But as you can see by the simple fact that I'm here, it didn't help. But that doesn't mean it won't help you," Billie said.

"What has Dr. Isaac taught you to help you control your anger?"

"Not much really. He treats me like I'm stupid or something. I sometimes feel like he wants to fail me so he can send me to Mod."

"That's a drag. Have you asked him about it? Asked him to help you more?"

"He blows me off. He said his 'primary function is to determine if I am suitable for treatment, not to provide treatment.' He is one stuffed shirt."

Michael shifted on his bunk and lay on his side. He could hear Billie breathing heavily.

"Does he tell you if he thinks you are a candidate for rehab?"

"Not really, he plays it really close to the vest. He has a rep for being a real dick though. He's known for dropping it on guys when they least expect it. The other docs all give their guys the full three months to try and prove themselves. Provided they don't test out on the sex pervert scale or something. Isaac sends guys anytime. Randomly."

"You mean you never know when it could happen to you?" Michael asked.

"Exactly."

Michael could sense Billie becoming more agitated as he spoke. Gesturing with his arms and getting louder.

"The man has a method. I heard from some guys who were in the Doc's office area when it happened. He calls you into his office for an interview, and then he tells you you're going to Mod. As he is telling you, custody storms in with a nurse. She sticks a needle in your neck, shooting you full of a drug that knocks you out flat. That way you can't go all crazy on him. I hear the next thing you know, you wake up in the chair in the Mod Center, with a drill in your face."

"Holy shit! That is really messed up. But you said the other docs don't play it that way?" Michael asked.

"Not from what I hear. They all let you run for three months and then sit down with you like you're a person. Those guys are shackled up and transported while they are awake, unless of course they go crazy or something like that."

Michael watched a cockroach crawl across the wall above the sink. "I don't want to be Modified."

"Me either."

"It's so confusing here. It's like you have to solve a puzzle but there is nothing written on the pieces. They're all blank," Michael said.

"I know, just try to stay out of trouble the best you can."

"How's that been going for you so far?" Michael asked.

"So far so good, but like I said that doesn't mean much when it comes to dealing with Dr. Isaac."

"Just keep hoping I guess," Michael said.

Michael heard his e-mail alert ring. He sat up and looked at his latest e-mail from Liz on his data pad.

"Dear Michael, I hope you are doing well. I'm finally settled in at college. I live in a small dorm room by myself. I like being on my own though. It is the first time I have ever lived away from home. My classes are alright. Some are interesting, but when you start out you take a lot of general classes about everything. I like my music appreciation class the best. It is interesting to hear about all the old forms of music. I miss you very much and can't wait to see you again. I will be able to visit you when I go home during one of our breaks. I will give you more details about that later. Please take care of yourself, I am counting on you. Love, Liz."

Michael finished reading and wondered what they would be doing right now if he hadn't been arrested. He would love to see her, but at the same time he didn't want her to see him like this, as an inmate.

19

Michael was in the middle of his second week in Chino. He sat down with his tray and attempted to balance himself on a metal seat in the Chow Hall.

"Why is it I can never seem to get comfortable on these seats?" Michael said looking up at Billie and Victor. "And what exactly is this?" Michael pointed to a piece of green colored meat on his tray.

"Bologna," Victor said. "You always complain about food, pretty boy. Why don't just eat or not, always complaining."

"This is so nasty it's wrong. How can they serve this shit?" Michael pushed his tray away in frustration. The other inmates at the table all looked up at him but did not stop eating.

"Maybe you go to Mod, and then you don't care what kind of shit they serve you," Victor said.

"Easy boys, let's just chill out, nobody's going to Mod today," Billie said. "Here let me take that off your hands." He reached over and snatched the green meat off Michael's tray.

Michael watched Billie shove the food into his mouth and felt his stomach turn. He was always amazed and somewhat disgusted by Billie's capacity to eat anything. He was like a dog that ran along the street gobbling up any piece of flotsam and jetsam he came across. It was a miracle that he never seemed to get sick. Michael shifted on his seat again and looked into his lunch bag. He pulled out a plastic wrapped piece of the same green colored meat.

"You have got to be fucking kidding me. They gave us the same green meat for lunch."

He threw the meat on the table, and Billie reached out and snatched it up. The buzzer sounded indicating the end of breakfast, and everyone stood up to leave. Michael crunched his lunch bag in his hands. He was fuming and disgusted. He had to go to medical to complete some blood work. When he got into the main hallway he turned right, and headed down the hallway toward the medical department. The hallway was full of inmates heading to their first activity of the day. The custody staffs were stationed up and down the hallway. The hallway seemed more crowded than usual. Michael could feel other inmates all around pushing him from behind. He found this particularly annoying, as he didn't like being manhandled. He extended his arms and elbows in an attempt to gain some personal space.

He finally reached the Medical department. He entered and had his data chip scanned by the custody officer at the desk. The officer told him to have a seat in a large holding tank that was full of inmates. Michael entered the holding tank and found a seat on a bench. It was the last available seat.

More inmates arrived for medical appointments. Now people were standing in the rows between the benches. Michael closed his eyes and tried to imagine himself in his hover car with the music playing and the wind on his face. He felt like a cow at the feedlot like he had seen on television. The cows were all jammed into a pen together with no room to even fall down.

"Get up fool, and let me sit down."

Michael opened his eyes. A large individual was standing in front of him. He was talking to the inmate sitting next to Michael. The inmate who was talking was huge. Not particularly muscular just large. His hands were enormous and his arms were the size of Michael's legs. He had short stubby hair and a tattoo of a snake on his arm. His breath came in wheezes and it smelled like green meat.

Michael looked at the inmate next to him. He did not recognize the guy. He was smallish with glasses and no tattoos.

"I said get up, fool," the large man repeated.

"Get up where?" the man next to Michael asked. "There's nowhere to get up to."

"Just do what I said," the large man said as he slapped the inmate next to Michael.

Now Michael sat up straight. "What the hell," he said. "Why don't you relax Big Fella? There's no room in here, and you're making things worse than they already are."

"Who you callin Big Fella?" the large inmate asked as he turned his attention to Michael. "Mind your own fuckin business," he said as he reached out and hit Michael in the shoulder.

Michael's temper flared immediately. "Look Pal," Michael said. "Nobody wants any trouble. Why don't you just back off and quit fucking with people?"

"Fuck you," the large inmate said as he hit Michael again.

Michael moved with lightning speed. He jumped up onto the bench and started punching the large man on his face and head. Then he punched him in the throat and the man began to gasp for air. In desperation the man rushed into him and pinned Michael against the metal wall of the tank. Neither one heard the alarm blaring in the Medical department. The other inmates were all rushed out of the tank and into the main hallway by custody officers.

The custody staff sprayed the two men fighting with O.C. Michael's eyes burned like they were on fire, but he could not stop fighting because the large man would not stop.

Then a custody officer hit the large man with a pulse baton. The surge of electricity went through the large man and into Michael. Both men stopped fighting as their bodies seized. They fell to the floor where they were restrained with handcuffs and a shock collar.

After a few moments Michael's head began to clear. He realized that he had wet his pants, and that he was in handcuffs. He looked around and saw that he was surrounded by custody officers. His eyes and face burned intensely.

"Stand up Taylor," a custody officer said. Michael attempted to stand but his legs were weak and rubbery. That was a side effect of the pulse baton. A custody officer helped Michael to his feet. He was escorted to a shower area in the Medical department where he stood under the shower. There he rinsed his eyes and pants out. After his eyes cleared he was escorted down to the Administrative Segregation unit. Ad-Seg, or the Hole, as it was called.

Michael was assigned a new cell in Ad-Seg and given dry clothes. He was interviewed by the Sergeant in charge and given a fact sheet about the program on the Ad-Seg unit.

"You will be here for a week, and you will be single cell status, no cellie," the Sergeant told him. "You will be in your cell twenty-three hours a day. You will get one hour of program which may consist of showering, a walk in the exercise area or a medical appointment. Your cell on Unit 9 will be held for you until you are released from Ad-Seg. Anytime you come out of your cell, you will be handcuffed and pulse collared, so we need you to cooperate with staff on this process. Just so you know, three trips to Ad-Seg constitute a reason to send you directly to Modification. My records indicate that this is your first time here. Do you understand everything I said?"

Michael looked up at the Sergeant and shook his head up and down. His eyes were still burning and his legs were weak as he was escorted to his Ad-Seg cell.

After he entered the cell and the door was shut, the custody officer removed his pulse collar and handcuffs. Michael changed into dry clothes and stood at the cell door. He looked out at the rest of the Ad-Seg unit. He had hoped he would never see the inside of it. He was being housed on the third tier so he had a pretty good view of the whole unit.

Unlike Unit 9 where the cells just faced a wall, this unit was built in a rectangle with cells on three sides facing inward. The control center was on the bottom floor.

Michael saw the big man he had the fight with being escorted to a cell on the first tier. There were three custody officers with him and he looked like a Brahma Bull being herded into a pen. Michael recalled the time he went to a bullfight with some friends. They had snuck down to Mexico without their parent's knowledge to drink alcohol, and have some fun. The slaying of the bull and the danger for the Matador was both disgusting and exhilarating. Michael had drunk too much Tequila on the trip and had gotten sick. Afterwards he felt similar to what he was feeling at this moment, nauseous, with a killer headache.

Custody officers were on each tier passing out sacks of food that would be the inmates' dinner. There were a lot more staff on the Ad-Seg unit. Michael noticed that they wore more protective gear than the officers in the other parts of the facility. They had on headgear with a plastic face shield, and form fitting stab proof vests.

A custody officer appeared in front of Michael and offered him a sack of food, and a carton of milk. Michael took the food and went back to sit on his bunk. He was hungry even though it was early. He had not eaten much breakfast, and he had thrown away his lunch.

He opened the bag and emptied the contents out onto his bunk. He picked up the items one by one and looked at them. A piece of cheese wrapped in plastic, a bag of chips, an apple, two slices of bread, a packet of mustard, a packet of relish, and a piece of green meat.

20

It was Michael's second day in Ad-Seg. The isolation was beginning to take a toll. The endless hours of being alone played on his mind. It was breakfast time now. They were served their hot meal in the cell in Ad-Seg. He tossed a package of crackers onto his locker for later, and then looked into his bowl of cold oatmeal. He dug his spoon into it. The entire glob of oatmeal attached itself, lifting up out of the bowl. It was a disgusting ball of sticky, gelatinous, nasty slop. "Just like my life," he thought. He put the bowl down and fell back onto his bunk. He grabbed his pillow and put it over his face while he screamed. He had to be in Ad-Seg for another five days. He heard that back in the day, before the Modification Law, inmates would spend up to a year in Ad-Seg. He could not imagine how they could take it.

The cell itself was similar to his other cell. It was dark and dingy, but it had a single bed and only one locker. It had the same smell as Unit 9. The setting was depressing.

Michael kept himself occupied by exercising and reading on the cell's video reader. It was a data pad attached to the end of his bunk similar to his other cell. There was a library of books one could access while in Ad-Seg, but nothing else. No e-mail access. It was not easy to exercise in the cell. He tried to do pushups but there was not enough space on the floor to stretch out. That is if he could tolerate lying on the floor. He had to exercise by doing pushups against the wall. He had cleaned the cell his first day there with an extra towel and soap a custody officer had given him. The frequent cockroach sightings were not encouraging. Occasionally a rat would make an appearance but thankfully they seemed to be interested in something other than him.

He was not in the mood to read right now. He was worried. He felt he had let himself down by losing his temper. He allowed himself to get into a fight, and it could cost him severely. He was starting to think that maybe he should open up to Dr. Carson. He might need some help to change his behavior if he was going to survive this ordeal, and make it to Rehabilitation.

It's just that it was hard for him to trust anyone. He had been fending for himself his whole life. Sure his mother gave him some advice from time to time, but, generally he made his own decisions.

'Tap, Tap, Tap.' Michael heard a tapping sound at the wall vent. He rose from his bed and put his ear to the vent.

"Taylor, are you there?" He heard a voice in the vent coming from the next cell.

"Yeah, I'm here," Michael said.

"This is Flako," the inmate in the adjoining cell said. "How you doin man?"

"I'm cool," Michael said. He smiled to himself. He had met Flako during a dayroom program. He was a friendly Hispanic man who was in for stealing Hover cars for an organized theft ring.

"I got rolled up for stealing a secretary's wallet," said Flako. "These motherfuckers are threatening to send me to Mod."

"Sorry to hear that, Flako," Michael said as he flattened himself on the wall to be able to hear better.

"Yeah, this is the second time in a month they put me in Ad-Seg."

"Be careful," Michael said. "You don't want to be turned into a turnip."

Flako laughed. "A turnip, you're a funny guy, Taylor." Then he asked, "Do you have any food?"

"Sure I have a package of crackers."

"Maybe we can exchange, I'll send you something tomorrow." Flako said.

"Sure thing," Michael said. "Get on your door and fish it from me."

"Thanks Taylor, I owe you."

Michael got his crackers and fished them to Flako. Fishing was a technique used by inmates to exchange things between cells. They would attach an item to a long string that they made by shredding their sheets. Then they would fling it out onto the tier by sliding it under their door. The other inmate would snag it by attaching a hook, which was usually made out of a paper clip. Then they would pull it into their cell.

"Okay, I'll check you later," Flako said, after retrieving the crackers.

"Later," Michael said.

Michael returned to his bed feeling a little better. He wondered how his mother was. He had not heard much from her. He understood that she worked hard and long. She had sent him a couple of e-mails, but she sounded like she really didn't grasp the gravity of the situation. She had not been to visit him. She didn't have the resources to make it out to Chino. He had not heard a word from his brother Ryan. Not that he expected to. That selfish SOB had never really cared about Michael.

He thought of his latest e-mail from Liz. She said that she believed in him and would support him in any way she could. She said she wanted to visit him. It could not happen if he was in Ad-Seg however, or if he was sent to Modification. She said she was not going to date anyone else. She was focused on her schoolwork, and thought about him all the time. He wondered what her parents thought of him now. Would they still support their relationship if he made it out of here and back home? He doubted it, but he would not give her up without a fight. He was encouraged that she had not just dumped him when he got arrested.

Michael looked at the picture of Liz. He had managed to keep it with his personal property since his arrest. It was the one taken at her graduation party. He recalled the way her smile made his heart leap. He thought of her beautiful, carefree love of life, and her soft skin. He promised himself that he would work harder to get back to her. He made a commitment to himself to talk with Dr. Carson when he got out of Ad-Seg. Maybe he could get through this if he worked hard.

He put the picture on the pillow next to his head as he lay down. He told himself that he could get his head straight and make it out. What was it they said in group? What cannot be helped must be endured! He would endure this, and get back to Liz. The cell seemed a bit less dreary now as he lay there. He thought about how he would overcome being incarcerated.

21

On Michael's third morning in Ad-Seg he awoke to the sound of someone yelling and swearing. Half asleep, he could not make out what the ruckus was all about. He tried to rub the sleep out of his eyes as he rolled out of bed. When he put his feet on the floor they sloshed down into an inch of cold water. He was startled and recoiled from the water. Suddenly he was fully awake. He looked down and saw that his cell was flooded. He looked out and could see that the entire tier was flooded. Then he saw a maintenance worker walk past his cell with a plunger in his hand.

"What's going on out there?" Michael yelled at the maintenance man.

The man ignored him as he disappeared down to the end of the tier. An officer appeared in front of Michael's cell.

"There is an overflowing toilet, Taylor," the officer said as he looked at Michael through the bars of the cell. "Just sit tight. Try not to get any of the water on you because it may be contaminated."

"Great," Michael thought to himself as he reached across to grab a towel off of his sink. He wiped his feet and then lay back on his bunk.

Michael spent most of the morning lying on his bunk because of the flooding. Eventually the cleanup crew reached his cell to mop up the water. Michael found out that toilet overflows were a common occurrence. It was one of the few ways inmates could assert themselves. It made some guys feel important to cause problems for the staff.

After the clean-up was completed, the staff finally served the inmates breakfast. Ad-Seg inmates didn't go to chow hall, so when the morning tray arrived, it was ice cold from sitting on the cart for two hours. Michael ate the toast but passed on the cold oatmeal. He also received his sack lunch with his breakfast tray. He munched on a bag of chips from his lunch to help satiate himself.

Time went slowly in Ad-Seg and inmates only got one hour of program per day. That included showers, medical appointments, and any yard time. Michael was scheduled for yard today. An officer appeared at his cell just as he finished his chips.

"Time for yard Taylor, come over here so I can collar you." The officer said.

Michael stood up and walked over to the cell bars. The officer reached in and put the pulse collar on Michael. Michael closed his eyes with humiliation at being collared like a dog.

"Now strip down to your boxers Taylor, no clothes allowed in the yard."

Michael winced as he removed his clothes. He threw his jumpsuit onto his bunk. He stood there in his shoes and boxer shorts with a pulse collar around his neck. He could feel his anger begin to rise. He clenched his fists as he began to hyperventilate.

"You gonna be able to manage this Taylor?" the officer asked as Michael's emotional state became obvious.

Michael turned and saw the officer staring at him with a concerned look.

"Don't want to have to use that collar now son."

Michael didn't know this officer, but he responded to his concern. "I'll be alright," Michael said as he took a deep breath.

22

Michael walked outside and looked up toward the sun. It felt warm on his face. He closed his eyes and basked in the sunlight.

"Beautiful," he thought to himself.

When he finally opened his eyes, he looked around at the "Yard". He was in a small ten foot by ten foot enclosure. It was surrounded by a fifteen foot high fence topped with razor wire. It had a concrete floor and was completely empty. There was nothing to sit on, no basketball hoop to shoot at, and no weights to lift. Just a showerhead attached to the building.

Michael heard someone singing. He turned around to see who it was. There was an inmate in another enclosure to his right. The enclosures were separated by five feet of open space. The other man was walking in circles singing to himself. He completely ignored Michael. Michael did not recognize him but guessed that he was a not a Darwin. Michael thought it looked like something went wrong. The man was hopelessly muscle bound. He could barely lift his arms above his waist as he circled the yard.

"Twenty minutes remaining," an officer yelled out to Michael.

Michael snapped back to focus on his own situation. Now he began to walk in circles. It felt good to walk, and he could feel his leg muscles strain as he broke into a fast paced stride. With the sun beating down on him he quickly broke into a sweat.

"Five minutes Taylor."

Michael heard the announcement and slowed to a walk. He walked over to the shower and turned on the water. He let it soak his head and body. He lifted his face into the water stream and let it relax him. The water was as cold as ice but it felt great.

An officer appeared at the grill and handed Michael a towel. "Time's up," he said.

Michael took the towel and dried himself off. He entered the sally port ready to go back to his cell. The officer put his hand up to stop Michael, "We need to wait here for a minute Taylor," he said.

Michael could hear someone yelling and crying on the third tier. Then it went quiet. Michael could see a limp inmate being pulled out of his cell. Then he was placed him onto a gurney. Michael felt sick to his stomach as he watched the man be wheeled off.

The other inmates on the unit began to chant and scream as they stood by their cell doors watching. Staff ignored the noise as they methodically went about their business and rolled the gurney down the ramp.

They passed directly in front of Michael as he stood at the grill. He could see the inmate's face as they passed by. It was Flako.

23

At the end of his week in Ad-Seg Michael sat in the administration office across from Sergeant Jack Roberts. He was handcuffed and wearing a shock collar. The office was small with just enough room for a desk and two chairs. A custody officer stood behind Michael. Sergeant Roberts looked at a computer display with Michael's record. A second screen displayed a video recording of Michael's fight.

Sergeant Roberts was a hard-core disciplinarian. He expected others to live up to his standards. His uniform was impeccably clean and pressed. He sat erect speaking loudly and clearly, while making eye contact. His gaze seemed to burn right through Michael as he talked.

"Taylor, the video clearly indicates that you were provoked by inmate Munson. However, your response was violent and out of proportion to the threat. As a result, it is viewed as mutual combat. It is documented as a hostile encounter on your record. Do you understand what I have just told you?"

"Yes sir," Michael said.

"Good. You will be released from the Administrative Segregation Unit today and returned to Unit 9. Your previous cell has been held for you. You will pick up where you left off with the evaluation program. A week has been added to your time at this facility to maintain a three month evaluation process. Provided of course you are not referred to Modification. Do you understand everything I just explained to you?"

"Yes sir."

"Outstanding. Now you will be escorted back to your cell to collect your personals and moved back to Unit 9. Do you have any questions?"

"No sir."

"Good. Thank you for your cooperation in this process."

The Sergeant stood up quickly and looked at the custody officer who was standing behind Michael. The sergeant nodded his head and the officer reached down and grabbed Michael by the arm, standing him up.

Michael was returned to his cell where he collected his property, including his picture of Liz. Then he was escorted down the long hallway and returned to Unit 9. As he entered his cell Billie spoke to him from his bunk.

"Hey Michael, welcome back, dude," Billie said.

Michael smiled broadly.

"So how was The Hole?" Billie asked.

"Boring as can be. The worst part is being forced to wear a shock collar every time you get out of your cell. It made me feel like an animal. I also had to be handcuffed whenever I came out."

"That's so messed up. Did you hear what happened to that moron Munson? The guy you had the fight with."

"No, what."

"He was sent to Modification. He was on Dr. Isaac's caseload, so as soon as he had a fight, zoom-off to Mod."

Michael was quiet for a moment. The realization sunk in that he could have been the one sent to Modification.

"Do you know how long he had been here?" Michael asked.

"Eight days."

"Holy shit, he never had a chance. But he was a total jerk. I saw the video of the fight. I watched it with the Sergeant down in Ad-Seg. They could see he started it, but I still got dinged for what they call mutual combat. They told me if you go to Ad-Seg three times you can be sent right to Mod. I can't believe Munson went on his first offense. By the way, how are you doing with your favorite Doctor?"

"Not so well. I've completed almost all the tests; I.Q., Sex Deviant and all that. I guess I did okay, but he told me he's not too impressed with me. Like I said before, he thinks I'm stupid or something."

"Shit Billie, you need to do something to impress him. Have you talked to anyone? What does Victor say, or Ms. Atkins?"

"You know Victor, he thinks he's funny. He said he will ask for me to work at his shop when I'm a Mod. Ms. Atkins said she tried to speak up for me, but she wasn't too excited about Isaac's response to her."

Again Michael became silent.

"Check this out," Michael said trying to lighten the mood. "This is a picture of my girlfriend Liz. She's still writing to me. I don't think I ever showed this to you."

Michael held it out to Billie. It was the picture of Liz smiling at her party.

"Wow dude, she's beautiful. What does she see in a loser like you?"

"Screw you Cowboy," Michael said as he retrieved the photo. He gazed at her face for a moment. "She is beautiful, isn't she? The truth is everyone wanted to know what she was doing with me. She comes from a lot of money, successful parents. I always felt fortunate to be with her. I just need to get out of here to prove to her that I still deserve her."

Michael placed the picture in an envelope and put it into his locker. Then he wrote her an e-mail.

"Dear Liz, I have been missing you a lot. I got into a little trouble, but it's okay now. Thinking of you helps me make it through the tough times here. I really hope we get to see each other when you come home for a visit. I still have the picture of you that I got at your graduation party. I look at it every day. I want you to know I'm working hard to get back to you. Take care, Love, Michael. XO."

When he finished Michael turned over in his bunk for lights out.

24

Edward Miller, the director of the Modification Center maneuvered his sporty Hover car into his garage. The door shut behind him. He entered his condo and gave a voice command. The living room blinds opened revealing a fabulous ocean view, a lanai, and a hot tub. He gave another command and loud synthesized Techno music began to play. His condo was located on the exclusive Newport Coast of Southern California. It was decorated with the latest designer furniture, fine art, and the best electronics to provide music and entertainment.

The condo also had a walk-in wine cellar. It was stocked with an exceptional collection of fine wines all kept at the perfect temperature, making it Miller's favorite room. His preference leaned toward reds and he spared no expense to acquire them. He felt this was his claim to fame, other than his job. The condo had an antiseptic smell however. Like the feel of a model home. He had no wife or children and worked a lot. He was rarely home.

Miller settled onto his sofa with a glass of wine. He closed his eyes and took a deep breath. Then he took a drink and let his hand caress the centerpiece of his art collection. It was an antique lion sculpture made of Lalique hand blown glass. A very rare nineteenth century piece that he managed to acquire last year. He felt the smooth surface of the glass and admired how the light illuminated the different angles of the glass. He was having another sip of wine when his front door buzzed.

Miller answered the door. He was surprised to see Gavin Jordan, the CEO of Ardent Corporation. Jordan was an imposing man, tall, fit, and athletic. He came from a privileged upper-class family. Jordan pushed himself through the door and entered Miller's home. A small mechanical fly flew in with him. Neither man noticed the fly.

"What the hell are you doing here Jordan?" Miller asked.

"I had to see you!"

"You could get both of us in hot water if anyone sees you here," said Miller. "You know I'm not allowed to socialize with executives of companies who contract for Mods. It's a conflict of interest."

"Don't worry Eddie, it's not a problem," said Jordan.

Jordan poured himself a glass of wine and sat in a chair looking out at the view. The fly landed on a wall out of the way. It flattened itself out, while transforming itself into an audio and video transmitter.

"Nice digs," he said.

"Thank you," said Miller, "and don't call me Eddie."

"Seems a bit above your pay grade," said Jordan.

"Not your problem," said Miller.

"Well it is my problem Eddie, and I'll tell you why." Gavin stood up and got into Miller's face. He stared right through Miller as he spoke. His pulse was rising and blood rushed to his face. His veins bulged and his skin flushed as he began to breathe heavily.

"It's my problem because you're behind in my supply of Mod workers. I'm paying you a ton of money to put me at the top of the list. So if you want to continue to live in this fancy mausoleum, you better come through fast. I have to meet orders for our fall collection. If I can't, then I will be in a shit storm with both the banks and my customers. Understand?"

Miller took a step back and put his wine on the countertop. "Okay, I'm doing the best I can. This is the Federal government you're dealing with after all."

"No Eddie. I'm dealing with you. If you want the gravy train to continue, I will have another fifteen Mods delivered to my LA plant by the end of next week," Gavin said. Then he drew a pulse baton out of his coat and snapped it open with a flick of his wrist. A golden wire charged with fifty thousand pulsating volts wrapped around the entire length of the baton. He swung the baton and it connected with the Lalique lion. It shattered into a thousand pieces. He then pointed the vibrating baton towards Miller holding it under his chin. "Got it Eddie?"

Then Gavin stormed out of the condo, slamming the door behind him. He got into his luxurious Bentley Hover car, and gave an address command. The car engaged and moved off. Gavin did not notice the utility vehicle with the darkened windows sitting at the corner. Inside the utility vehicle an investigator archived the conversation he had just recorded between Miller and Jordan.

Back in his condo Miller was sweating profusely, he was breathing hard, and his hands were shaking. He wiped his brow and took a gulp of his wine. Miller hit the dial up on his coat. He phoned Dr. Louis Brayden.

"This is Dr. Brayden," Brayden said, as his face appeared in front of Miller.

"Braden this is Edward Miller. I just met with Gavin Jordan from Ardent. He says he needs fifteen more Mods by the end of next week."

"What, no way I can deliver that," said Brayden. "I am already pushing the doctors as much as I can. Dr. Isaac is on board, and I have an inmate working to set up other inmates. But the other doctors won't cooperate with us. I don't know what else I can do"

"Well you better figure something out. You and I have both taken his money. We are into this too deep now. Get some new doctors if you have to, but get me those Mods. I will talk to you in a couple of days to see what you've done."

Miller terminated the call, and poured himself more wine. He went out onto his patio, leaned on the railing, and then stared blankly into space.

25

Michael sat in front of Rick. He stared at the picture of Hawaii on the wall, and then looked at the books on the bookshelf. Rick allowed Michael some leeway to familiarize himself with the office. Michael spotted a book with Rick's name on it and pulled it off the shelf. <u>Forensic Evaluations,</u> by Rick Carson, Ph.D

"You wrote this book?"

"Yes I did," Rick said.

Michael turned the book over in his hands.

"What's a forensic evaluation?"

"That's what I'm doing with you Michael. It's the process, the testing, the talks or interviews we have with each other, and the report that I will write at the end."

"So what are you going to say about me Doc?"

Rick looked across at Michael. He could tell he was fishing for help with the process.

"I'm not sure yet Michael. A lot of what I say will depend on you. How you behave when you're here. How you get along with others on the unit and in groups. Also how you do on the tests we give you.   But most of all I will be looking at how you are when we talk."

Michael shifted uneasily in his seat. "So what do you want me to say?"

"I don't want you to say anything," Rick said. "I just want you to be yourself and try to be open."

"What do you mean be open?"

"Well, for example, when I reviewed the video of your fight with inmate Munson, I could see that even though you didn't initiate the trouble, you have quite a temper. In particular it seemed as though you have some issues with bullies. Would you like to talk about that?"

"I don't like bullies, what else is there to say?" Michael crossed his arms and looked down at his feet.

"Do you have a bully in your life?" Rick sat up when he saw Michael react.

Michael continued to stare at his shoes as he mulled over Rick's question. "What do you mean by that?"

"I mean is there someone close to you, in your family perhaps, who is a bully? Is there someone who gets their way through force or intimidation, who pushes other people around for their own amusement, or simply because they can, a person who takes advantage of the weaker people around them? Does that sound familiar?"

"Yeah, I guess so." Michael felt his voice quiver a little as he spoke.

"Who do you think is a bully in your life?" Rick leaned forward towards Michael.

"My brother Ryan, he's a major bully." He looked up at Rick, his jaw clenched.

"He bullies you?"

"My whole life, he's a fucking asshole."

"Do you love him?" Rick sat up straight, startled by the depth of Michael's reaction.

"What?" Michael looked at Rick. He felt confused by the question.

"He's your brother. You've known him your whole life. You lived with him. Do you love him?" Rick asked.

Michael sat back in his chair. "I guess I do. I never really thought about it, but it's true, I do love him."

"And you hate him?" Rick asked.

"Yeah, there are times when I hate his fucking guts."

"Like when he bullies you?"

"Exactly!" Michael said as he slammed his hand on the desk. The blood rushed to his head and he could feel his anger rise just talking about Ryan.

"Excellent," Rick said. "See now you're getting in touch with some of your feelings and emotions."

"That's what you want?"

"Yes, only we have to channel it a little more, so you don't break my desk or get into so many fights."

"Ryan treated me really bad when I was a kid," Michael offered. He became animated, sitting forward in his chair.

"How so?"

"He beat me a lot, cause he was so much bigger than me."

"How much older is he?" Rick asked.

"Ten years. It wasn't only me though. He fucked with everyone. He put neighbor kids in the dryer and kicked cats. He was one of those, sadasts."

"You mean a sadist?" Rick asked.

Michael sat back and laughed. It was really more of a sigh of resignation. "Yeah, a sadist. He is a real motherfucker."

"It sounds like it. Not a very good brother." Rick nodded.

"When I was real little, he would set me in the corner and light matches all around me so I could not move. My Mother set him up once though. She left the house and came back right away. She caught him on top of me, beating me." Michael smiled and let out a little laugh. "She gave him a good beating that time. At the time she told him he was a bad seed."

"Do you often think about what Ryan did to you?" Rick asked.

"Not a lot during the day. I dream about it. Sometimes I worry that I will be like him. I don't want to be a bad seed. Sometimes I try to figure out what I did to make him hate me so much."

"You don't seem to be anything like him," Rick said. "Do you get pleasure out of hurting others?"

Michael shifted in his chair again. "No."

"Then you're not a sadist. And I doubt you did anything to make him hate you. It's not your fault he behaves like he does. You were just a little boy. He is ten years older and should have been a better brother."

"I guess that's why I get so angry and fight a lot," Michael said.

"You think so?"

"Yeah, when I fight…sometimes I see Ryan's face when I'm hitting someone else."

"Have you ever hit Ryan?" Rick asked.

"Not really. I tried, but he's too big and always gets over on me."

"Well maybe I can help you deal with some of that anger." Rick stood and hit a button on the wall. A cabinet opened up and a punching bag made of pliable hard gel came out. Rick gave Michael a pair of heavy gloves. He told Michael to sit back and try to imagine Ryan's face. Rick made a verbal command and a blue beam emanated from the top of the punching bag apparatus. It scanned Michael's head and the gel began to transform into the image of Ryan. "Imagine that is Ryan," Rick said. "Tell him what you want to say and let him have it. You can punch as hard as you want."

Michael smiled and began to hit the bag. "Fuck you Ryan," he said as he hit the bag. "I was just a kid. Why did you have to be such an asshole? Why didn't you help me and protect me like a good brother would have?" Thirty minutes later Michael sat in the chair sweating and breathing hard.

"How did that feel Michael?"

"Great, I really let him have it."

"Now let's try a different tactic." Rick grabbed an extra chair and put it facing Michael. He pushed another button and a hologram of Ryan appeared in the chair, "This time let's use words to let him have it."

26

At the end of the week Edward Miller sighed in disgust after reviewing the latest statistics. He could not believe Dr. Brayden's Mod referrals stayed the same. He hoped Brayden would be able to increase his deliveries after their last conversation

"Jasmine please get Dr. Brayden in Chino on the phone for me," he called out to his secretary in a loud, high-pitched voice.

"Yes sir," Jasmine replied. She quickly contacted Br. Brayden. "Dr. Brayden is on the line for you sir."

Miller hit a button and Dr. Brayden's face appeared on one of his monitors. Dr. Brayden had a large bite of a chocolate covered glazed donut in his mouth. He tried to wash it down with a calorie free cola as he brushed sugar flakes off his shirt.

"Hello," he mumbled.

"Brayden, this is Miller at the Mod Center."

Another drink of diet cola, and Brayden was able to speak. "Yes Sir, Mr. Miller. How are you today?"

"Louis tell me, are you still hitting the Krispy Treat donuts?"

"Yes, I'm afraid so."

Miller shook his head in disgust. "I have that dickhead, Gavin Jordan from Ardent, crawling up my ass again, and I saw that you only sent me ten Mods last week."

Dr. Brayden sat up straight in his chair. "I know how many I sent you. I don't have to be reminded. Trust me. I am doing everything I can at my end."

"Well it's obviously not enough now, is it Doctor? I need you to find a way to send me more people. Think hard. You're a smart guy. Be creative. Put the screws to those two doctors who won't play ball. Whatever it takes, otherwise we will both going be giving some money back, or worse."

"Alright, I have an idea of how to apply some pressure. I will try to light a fire under my Docs."

"Good man Louis. I'll tell you what, if you can get your numbers up to eighteen a week, then I'll treat you to a couple of days at my country club. You can play golf or tennis, go swimming, or have a spa treatment, whatever you want. Does that sound good Louis?"

"Sure, fine, it sounds fine. Like I said, I have an idea."

"Good. I can't wait to see how it works out."

Miller hung up and shook his head as he muttered to himself. "What an ass, this idiot is going to get me smoked."

27

Rick sat in the waiting area outside of Dr. Brayden's office. Nancy Jones, Brayden's secretary was at her desk typing. "So what's going on Nancy?" Rick asked.

"Same old," she said.

Rick noticed a box of chocolate bars sitting on her desk. "How much for the chocolate?"

"Two dollars, how many would you like?"

"I'll take two," Rick said as he handed her the money.

"Thanks," she said.

Rick noticed her biting on her bottom lip, a sure sign of anxiety. This was out of character for Nancy. She was usually cool as a cucumber. In fact Rick had never seen her be out of sorts. At five feet seven she was a human dynamo with brown shoulder length hair and a pretty smile. No, nervous was not a condition he was used to seeing in Nancy Jones.

"Is something bothering you?" Rick asked.

Nancy stopped typing and looked up at Rick. She laid her hands on her immaculately clean desk and leaned forward. In a hushed tone she said, "Yes Dr. Carson, but I'm really not sure what to do about it."

"What do you mean?" Rick asked.

"It's Dr. Brayden. He's been acting very odd lately. This morning he snapped at me for nothing, and that's not the first time. He's been extremely edgy for about a month, and I don't know why. But I do know that I'm starting to feel uncomfortable with his behavior. I don't want to work somewhere where I never know if my boss is going to go off on me. I feel like I'm walking on egg shells. I haven't decided what I'm going to do for sure, but I have already talked to Human Resources about moving me."

Rick looked into Nancy's soft brown eyes and could see the stress she was describing. Lines were forming on her forehead, and she began to nervously rub her hands together.

Just then Dr. Brayden opened his office door. Startled, Nancy jumped and turned to resume her typing. Rick looked up at Dr. Brayden.

"Dr. Carson, good you're here. Please come in," Dr. Brayden said to Rick as he waved him into the office.

Rick rose and walked into Dr. Brayden's office. On the way by Nancy's desk he stole a glance at her. Their eyes locked for a moment, and he nodded reassuringly. Dr. Brayden and Rick entered the office. Dr. Brayden shut the door behind them.

Dr. Brayden walked behind his desk and sat in his desk chair while Rick sat in one of the two casual chairs in front of the desk. It sat low and Rick found himself well below Dr. Brayden's eye level looking up at him.

Brayden's office was sparsely decorated. There were no pictures of his family. He had a few simple pictures of flowers on the walls but nothing on the desk. The idea was not to give a disgruntled inmate something to hit you over the head with.

Rick had worked under Dr. Brayden for thirteen months. Brayden came from a Rehabilitation Center in Northern California. The scuttle butt was that he was removed from that position because he was too adversarial to the overall treatment environment in general. In other words he worked against the process. He undermined the therapists by restricting their resources and interfering with their therapy. He was intrusive and destructive. He was sent to an Evaluation Center so he would not have to be involved in the direct treatment of inmates.

Rick had found him to be dogmatic, myopic, demanding, and easily threatened. Although they had not had any direct conflicts to this point, Rick did not trust him

"Thanks for coming in," Brayden said.

"Sure, what can I do for you?" Rick asked. The hair on the back of his neck bristled at the sound of Dr. Brayden's edgy voice.

"I need to talk to you about some concerns I have about your referral rate," Brayden said.

"What kind of concerns?" Rick asked.

"Well Doctor, it seems you have the highest referral rate to Rehabilitation compared to your colleagues," Brayden said.

"Really, that's interesting," said Rick. "However, I don't see how that would raise any concerns. It was my impression that there was no quota. In fact, Penal Code Section 28569.95 strictly prohibits quotas. That was one of the caveats when the public agreed to the Modification Law."

"Very impressive," said Brayden. "I'm glad to see you are knowledgeable and up to date on the Laws and Regulations guiding our work here Dr. Carson. But meeting a quota is not my concern. My concern is that you are not following the protocols set up to help us make rational and fair recommendations. I would hate to find out that some inmates are referred to Rehabilitation simply because they were lucky enough to be assigned to a bleeding heart liberal, someone who opposes the Modification Law. That certainly would not be fair or equitable to the other inmates who have to go through the Evaluation process."

Rick's back stiffened as he sat up straight. "Are you accusing me of not following the law?"

"No, no, not at all Doctor. It's just that my job here is to make sure that we offer a level playing field to everyone. As a result, I am going to order an audit of your last three months of evaluations. They will be reviewed by the investigations unit to determine if you followed protocol."

"What do you want to know?" Rick asked. "You could just ask me straight out."

"Nothing to worry about really," Brayden said as he pulled on the lapel of his cheap suit. "As I said, I just want to have a level playing field. So if for example, I see your referral numbers to Modification increase, to say the level of Dr. Isaac's in the next month. Then perhaps we could put all this behind us. That would assure me that you are following all the protocols as you should be."

"I make my own determinations. Dr. Isaac is free to make his own. I have nothing to hide, so I welcome your audit," Rick said.

"Okay then," Brayden said. "So that is how we will play this. I will order the audit and you will be contacted by internal affairs. They will need your full cooperation of course."

"Of course, is that all?" Rick asked.

"You know, I've worked with people like you before, when I was at the Rehabilitation Center." Dr. Brayden's face twisted into a contorted mass as he spoke and leaned forward over his desk. "Do gooders who wanted to help cure these scumbags. Let me tell you Doctor, the days for folks like you are numbered. It won't be long before every criminal is Modified. We won't waste any time or money on Rehabilitation."

"That may be," said Rick. "But for now, thankfully, we still try to save some of the good ones. After all, isn't that why we got into this business, to help people? Good day Doctor."

Rick stood up and left Dr. Brayden's office. He shut the door behind him and looked at Nancy who was staring at him.

"Be careful of him," Rick said

Nancy looked at Rick and nodded her head knowingly as he left the office.

28

Rick took a sip of his hydrating power drink as he wiped his brow. An eight mile run always helped him clear his head and wash away the insanity of work. Today it did not seem to be having the cleansing effect he wanted. He was staring out the window when Natalie walked into the kitchen. She was still in her pajamas. He had waited to tell her about Dr. Brayden because he was too upset the day before.

"Good morning dear," she said.

She poured herself a glass of orange juice and sat down across from him.

"Anything interesting out there?" she asked.

"Not really," Rick said as he turned to face her. "Dr. Brayden is having my work audited. He says I may not be following protocols. He wants me to refer more people to Modification."

She sat up straight and looked directly at him. "Wow, that's stressful."

"I'm not too worried about the audit itself. I'm not sure what is going on with him though. Dean and I have been discussing it. He wants us to refer more people to Mod and we aren't sure why. We can't see the big picture at this point. He has been very vocal about it in meetings, and now he called me in and threatened me with this audit. His secretary says that he's been acting on edge, and she is uncomfortable working around him."

Natalie took a sip of her orange juice. "What are you going to do?"

"At this point I have to let it play out. I may talk to the attorney for the Civil Law Office. They are the advocates for the inmates. He may have some insight or be able to pressure Brayden to call off the dogs." Rick sat down and looked her straight in the eye.

"Are you worried about your job?" She asked as she reached out to hold his hand

Rick held her hand and smiled. "I'm not sure at this point. I guess that would depend on how the audit turns out."

"It would impact Ashley's plans to go to Stanford if you got fired."

"I know, I certainly don't want to go down that road. I also don't want to lose our health insurance for your treatment. However, I will not be pressured into condemning people to living life as a drone if they don't deserve it. Some of those young men can still have a decent future." Rick released her hand and stood up. He returned to staring out the window, his frustration was getting the best of him.

"You knew the downside to this position when you accepted it." Natalie got up and walked over to him. She put her hand on his shoulder.

"True, I guess I felt that if the government was going to do this, the Modification program, I wanted to be involved." He turned to face her and put his arms around her waist. "To be a rational voice, I guess."

"It's hard to be a rational voice if the chorus is insane."

"Good point." They stood there for a moment holding each other.

"I want you to know I will support you, your decision, whatever it is. I just want you to remember where your responsibility lies." Natalie hugged him tightly and kissed his face. "Now go take a shower, you stink."

29

Dr. Isaac made a note about how the inmate David Franks' sister was raped and murdered. He also wrote about the inmate's new cellie. The man had beaten a charge of rape, because the victim recanted her story after being threatened by the man's gang. He called the officers' desk and asked for Zack Cole. The officer on duty sent Zack back to the doctor's office.

"Here is the information, Zack," Dr. Isaac said, as he showed him the screen.

Zack read the information and committed it to memory. Then he sneered at Dr. Isaac and made his way back down hallway.

He felt like a bitch having to do the doctor's dirty work. He had no choice though, after they busted him stealing drugs from the prison pharmacy. It was do their bidding, or get sent to Mod immediately. Zack was at the Evaluation Center for selling drugs on the street. It was all he knew. It was his family business, so to speak. His father was sentenced to life after being caught with a truckload of high grade opioids at the Mexican border. Zack was seventeen years old at the time. He never saw his father again.

The next day during dayroom program Zack made his way to David Franks' table. Billie and Michael were at the adjoining table. Zack sat down next to Franks and looked at him out of the corner of his eye. Franks had been on Unit 9 for about a month. He was on Dr. Carson's caseload. Franks was playing dominos with two other inmates. He was an enormous man, at least six feet four inches tall. He was a body builder and had muscles on top of muscles. But he was not known to be the brightest when it came to intellectual pursuits. Too many steroid injections had affected areas other than his biceps and his gonads. He was prone to going into a rage at a moment's notice.

Franks slapped a domino down on the table and looked at Zack. "Something on your mind, Cole?"

"Just a little curiosity," Zack replied.

"About what?"

"Nothing really, I guess I was just a little curious what it was like to share a cell with a rapist, that's all," Zack said as he looked at Franks and raised his eyebrows.

Franks reached out and grabbed Zack's arm squeezing it so hard that Zack thought it might snap. "You want to explain yourself piss-ant?"

"Easy dude!" Zack cried out as he wrestled his arm free. "I guess you didn't know. That's fine, don't take it out on me."

"I didn't know what?" Franks asked.

Michael and Billie were seated at the next table. Billie was sitting the closest to Zack and his ears perked up as he caught wind of Zack and Franks' conversation.

"Alright, I guess I'll have to be the one to break it to you. It's about your new cellie, Roscoe Escobar. He raped a girl a few years back and got off by having his home boys threaten her. She recanted on the stand."

David Franks' face turned red then purple. His jaw clenched so tightly Zack thought it was a miracle his teeth didn't shatter.

"What are you saying? How do you know about this Cole?"

"Don't take my word for it. Go ahead and ask him. You'll know if he's lying to you."

Franks sat up straight and looked Zack in the eyes. Cole looked back at him and nodded his head as if to validate what he had just said.

"Look Bro, I didn't mean to upset you. I just thought you should know who moved in with you, that's all." Zack stood up and stretched. He looked down at Franks and then patted him on the back. "I guess you never know about folks, huh?" Then Zack turned and walked away leaving Franks at the table.

Franks looked across the table at the two other inmates. They had remained silent and still throughout Zack's performance. Nobody wanted to get into the middle of this.

The rumor about Roscoe Escobar spread throughout the unit quickly. By that evening every inmate on the unit was aware of the accusation, and Franks' sister's rape and murder.

At five minutes past six p.m., David Franks entered his cell which was two down the tier from Michael and Billie's. Michael and Billie were sitting on Billie's bunk playing cards at the time. Six minutes after Franks entered his cell, just long enough for him to question Escobar about the alleged rape, Michael and Billie heard a loud thump as Roscoe Escobar was slammed into the bars of his cell door. Roscoe yelled out for help as his face was smashed into the bars. A large gash opened up on his forehead.

Michael and Billie looked at each other as they heard Roscoe scream. There was an odd silence throughout the rest of the unit, as everyone held still to hear the drama played out.

Roscoe yelled again as he took a series of devastating kidney punches while still face first against the cell bars. David Franks was just getting warmed up. He tore off the top of Escobar's jumpsuit and reached around to his chest. He had a razor in his hand that he used to cut Escobar from his clavicle all the way down to his navel. Escobar screamed again as his skin separated and blood flowed from the cut.

"You like to rape, you pile of shit?" Franks yelled. "Well how do you like this?"

Michael and Billie had stopped playing cards and were standing at the front of their cell looking out. They could see the other inmates on the unit doing the same but everyone remained silent.

Finally Escobar's screams were heard by the custody staff. They came running down the tier to Franks and Escobar's' cell. They sprayed gas into the cell but Franks ignored them and continued to brutalize Escobar. They entered the cell and hit him with a pulse baton. After they were able to subdue him they put him into restraints.

The next two hours were a flurry of activity on the tier as Custody removed Franks and Escobar from the cell. The investigations officer examined the cell as a crime scene, and then a team of porters cleaned the cell using Hazmat protocols.

After all the excitement ended, Michael and Billie lay on their bunks.

"That was totally gnarly," Billie said.

"I had never heard anything like that before. He sounded like some kind of animal. That was really disturbing," Michael said.

"Zack Cole is the one who told him Escobar was a rapist. It seems like he is on a mission to get guys sent to Mod."

"How does he get information like that?" Michael asked.

"Good question, makes you wonder about him doesn't it?"

The next morning at chow, Michael had dark rings under his eyes from a lack of sleep. He had disturbing dreams of people being beaten, and kept waking himself up. Victor sat down and dropped his tray on the table.

"Well, that was quite the show last night, eh? Franks was sent to Mod today, and they say Escobar died last night. Loss of blood," Victor said.

Michael and Billie looked at each other and both had the same thought. "Zack Cole's work," they said simultaneously.

"Be careful of that snake," Billie said.

30

Rick was in his office working on a report when he got the call. The audit team was there to perform their investigation. They appeared at his office door and introduced themselves. Dr. Nguyen, the lead investigator, was a tall middle-aged woman. She came across as cold and officious.

Dr. Daniels and Dr. Hill were the other audit team members. No first names were disclosed. Dr. Nguyen explained that they would be reviewing a sample of Rick's cases over the last three months. They would need all the test protocols for the individuals, as well as his reports and recommendations. She would be able to obtain all the information from the data-base, but they would commandeer Rick's office for the greater portion of the day. Rick watched as the team invaded his office and immediately made themselves comfortable.

"I hope you don't mind that we use your office Doctor?" Dr. Nguyen asked.

"Of course not, whatever you need," Rick replied. "In fact, let me know if you need anything else."

"Thank you," Dr. Nguyen said with a slight hint of a smile. "We will let you know when we are finished. It shouldn't take too long. You will be able to get back to work before you know it."

With that she turned her back to Rick and sat down in his chair. Rick stood there for a moment feeling like an outsider in his own office. Then he realized that he had been dismissed. He turned and walked down the hallway to Dean's office.

Dean was looking at a food magazine on his computer when Rick showed up.

"Working hard I see," Rick said.

"Oh, the trials of government work," Dean said. "What's going on? You look like you lost a loved one."

"The audit team just arrived and took over my office. They said they will be in there most of the day."

"Unfortunate," Dean said as he closed the magazine. "And I'm sure they were the epitome of warmth and kindness."

"Of course, an Amazon named Nguyen and her two stooges. She looks like she's wound so tight she could go nuclear at any moment."

"Should we go down to the beach and indulge in some fabulous fish sandwiches for lunch? It might take the edge off."

Rick laughed as he mulled over the idea. Dean was already springing into action as he took Rick by the arm. "Come my liege, the Pescado await."

The two of them skulked out of the office and made it out of the grounds without being spotted by Dr. Brayden. As they walked the one block to the shoot tube, Rick felt better already.

31

After lunch with Dean, Rick felt refreshed. Smelling the fresh ocean air and listening to the waves on the shore always had a calming effect. He was determined to stand up to Dr. Brayden. He would not give in to his demands and refer more people to Modification simply to meet an imaginary quota. It if cost him this job, so be it!

More than that, he questioned Dr. Brayden's motives for pushing that agenda. In fact, the more he thought about it, the more he felt that something nefarious was going on. It could involve more people than Rick was aware of. His talk with Nancy, and Dr. Brayden's behavior at their case conferences, had left him suspicious.

The next day he contacted Henry Smith. Henry was the legal advocate for inmates' rights. He worked for the non-profit group Civil Law Office. They brought legal actions against the government to advocate for inmates. They had vehemently opposed the Modification Law from the onset. It was a major defeat for them when the law passed. They had been working ever since to monitor its implementation. They continued to lobby legislators in the hope the law would be overturned, and they had managed to include their own oversight as part of the agreement with the government. That is why they were in the prisons.

Rick set up a twelve o'clock meeting with Henry at a coffee shop. He did not want to give Dr. Brayden more reasons to question his commitment or neutrality, so he decided to meet off campus. The coffee shop was in an older part of Chino. It was away from the newer restaurants and shopping plazas that were frequented by the prison staff. It was run by a Basque family that had lived in the area for thirty years. They used to own several restaurants, but had been overrun by the major chain restaurants flooding the area. Now they were trying to support themselves with the coffee shop and one carryout sandwich shop. Rick liked to go there because he could avoid being around work people on his lunch break.

He waved to Mr. Zabala, the owner, when he entered. "Doctor Rick, welcome," Mr. Zabala said.

"Hello," Rick replied.

"Can I get you a table, some coffee?"

"Sure, a bagel and a decaf cappuccino please, but I have a table. I'm meeting someone, and I see them sitting in the back."

"Very good, I will bring that right to you."

Henry was waiting for him at a table in the back. Rick did not know him very well. They had met formally one time, and Rick had seen him around the prison on several occasions. Henry seemed to be dedicated to his work. He had a brother who went to prison years ago, before the Modification law. That is how Henry became interested in prisoners' rights. His brother had completed his sentence prior to the Modification law and had been released. Now he was selling real estate in Oakland.

Henry stood up to greet Rick as he approached the table. He was dressed in an old school gabardine suit. He was a short man with thin stringy hair and thick glasses. But he had a big smile on his face that lit up a room. He gave Rick a firm handshake and a warm greeting. Rick took his coffee and bagel, and settled into his chair.

"It's good to see you Dr. Carson," Henry said. "I was a little surprised to hear from you, but I must admit I was pleased you called."

"Really, why is that?"

"Because it's not often that doctors in your position are open to discourse regarding the evaluation process. It's kind of a turf war out there. So what can I do for you? You were somewhat cryptic last night."

"I must admit I'm going out on a limb by discussing this situation with you," Rick said. "However I feel like there is something going on that is very complicated and possibly corrupt. I feel like I'm about to be run over."

"An unenviable spot to be in."

"That's true. I don't like it, but my options are very limited. That's why I am reaching out to you. Sometimes situations can be influenced from outside sources."

"That is also true. Perhaps if you told me your concerns I might be better able to tell you if the Civil Law Office could influence anything, or if it would be inclined to do so."

Rick looked across the table at Henry. He had called this meeting but was reticent to actually follow through by opening up. He took a sip of his coffee. Just then a man walked out of the back room of the shop carrying a box. Rick noticed he had a strange gait. As he looked closer he saw an emerald glow, and realized it was a Mod. Then Rick recognized the man. His name was Eric Stiller. He had been on Dr. Isaac's caseload a few months ago. He seemed like a reasonable person who was convicted of elder abuse. As Rick recalled, it had been a family dispute over inheritance money.

Eric had been caring for his elderly mother for years. After her death, his sister, who had not participated in the mother's care, accused him of fraud. She hired a forensic accountant and high priced attorney to sue him in civil court for squandering the mother's money. She wanted the mother's life insurance payout. The District Attorney was contacted by her attorney and picked up the case prosecuting him for elder abuse. Eric tried to defend himself, but he did not have any money for an attorney. He was not bright enough to allow a public defender to aid him. Rick felt it was a travesty of justice that Eric was sent to prison. He was certain that Eric would be sent to Rehabilitation. He was assigned to Dr. Isaac, however, who said he was a wolf in sheep's clothing. He sent the man to Modification with the blessing of Dr. Brayden.

Rick watched Eric shuffle around behind the counter working to empty the box of cookies he had brought out of the back room. A renewed sense of anger filled him.

Henry had been watching Rick with interest, noticing his face flush as he observed Eric.

"One of yours?" Henry asked.

"No, but I knew him. He came through evaluation some time back. I was surprised he was sent to Modification. In fact, that is what I wanted to talk to you about."

"Go on."

"I feel that I am being pressured to send more people to Modification. Like there is an unspoken quota. It has only been since Dr. Brayden assumed the supervisors position."

"Has he issued a quota to you?"

"Not officially. But he has accused me of not following protocols. He called me a liberal and said that someday there would be no Rehabilitation. That everyone would be Modified. He has put me under investigation. He told me he would end the investigation if my number of referrals to Modification became equal to Dr. Isaac's."

"What does Dr. Isaac have to do with it?" Henry asked.

"I'm not sure. He does refer significantly more people than anyone else in the state. Those are statistics that are easily verified. That man over there, Eric, is a prime example. I know that I have been doing my job correctly. I don't believe the audit will find anything wrong."

"What do you want from my office?"

"I'm not really sure. It just seems like something is off. For some reason there is pressure to refer people to Modification. Some Doctors are complying, and those of us that aren't are being threatened. Ultimately it seems that the inmates' rights are getting trampled. Especially if they are Modified unnecessarily, like Mr. Stiller over there."

Henry looked at his cup as he stirred his coffee. He was silent for a moment and then looked up at Rick.

"You're right Doctor. There is something going on. I am going to share something with you but you must not tell anyone else. Can I trust you to do that?"

"Of course," Rick leaned across the table. Henry had his full attention now.

"We have been concerned about the referral patterns coming out of your office. We have filed an informal letter of protest with the Attorney General's office, and started our own undercover investigation of the personnel. We are monitoring referrals and reviewing files."

"Including me?"

"Yes, including you. The fact you have come to me like this bodes well, but we have limited influence. We can do nothing about your audit and cannot control Dr. Brayden, at least not at this time."

"So I'm on my own?"

"So to speak, we are really more concerned with the larger issues. The general public is becoming more and more comfortable with the idea of modification. There have been some positive reports of economic data recently. People are pointing to the Modification program as the reason. If the trend continues, we may lose the entire war. Someday all criminals may be Modified. I would say Dr. Carson that I appreciate your candor, and your resolve to come to us."

Rick sat there stunned. He was glad they were looking into the office, but essentially Henry had told him he was alone in his fight. The strong smell of Colombian coffee filled his nostrils as he took a deep breath.

"Well, thanks for meeting with me Henry."

"Doctor, please let me know if you find any definitive evidence of wrongdoing. Then we may have something to work with."

Rick and Henry stood and shook hands.

"Good luck to you," Henry said.

Rick turned and left the coffee shop. Eric was outside now sweeping the sidewalk. He worked very slowly and moved like a robot. He looked up at Rick as he walked by and their eyes met, only Rick was looking into a blank slate.

"Hello Eric," Rick said.

In a flat voice devoid of emotion he answered, "Yes, I am Eric." Then he returned to sweeping the sidewalk.

Rick walked away feeling sick to his stomach.

32

Michael had just finished his third week at the Evaluation Center. He was sitting in the chow hall with Billie and Victor. Michael looked at the guys.

"What is a Plethysmograph?" Michael asked.

"Oh boy, are you in for an interesting morning," Billie laughed.

"What do you mean?" Michael asked.

Billie and Victor laughed at each other and shook their heads.

"I hope you enjoy Elsa," Victor said.

"You boys want to fill me in on the joke?" Michael asked feeling left out and somewhat frustrated.

"Today is a big day for you. Today is your sexual arousal and orientation identification test. This is where the rubber meets the road. At the end of this test they can send you directly to Modification," Billie explained.

"Yeah, that is if your peter stands up and salutes if a little boy sits on your lap," Victor said as he looked at Michael with a curious expression.

"What the hell?" Michael said.

Just then the buzzer rang indicating the end of breakfast. Michael shook his head as he headed out into the hallway. He did not have any clearer idea now of what he faced than he did before their conversation.

He headed down the main hallway toward testing station number three. He had not gone far when a fight broke out about ten feet in front of him.

Immediately a loud horn began to blare directly above his head. A voice came over the loudspeakers. "All inmates get down on the floor, now; all inmates lie down on the floor, now."

Michael obeyed the command and got on the floor, face into the ground, flat on his stomach. The two combatants were the only inmates who did not lie down. Michael glanced up and saw them punching each other. Suddenly a gas jet erupted and started shooting pepper spray out of the wall. The fighters were sprayed with the pepper spray, and began to cough and rub their eyes, but they kept fighting. The code one response team was there within moments. The code one team was the group of custody officers stationed in the middle of the long hallway during inmate movements. They were outfitted in full riot gear.

The Custody staff immediately hit the men with pulse batons, quickly ending the brawl. Both men fell to the floor. After their spasms ended, the men were handcuffed and led off.

The pepper spray had migrated throughout the hallway. Some of it made its way to Michael and his eyes began to water and burn. The loudspeaker came to life again this time announcing, "All inmates recover and return to your program."

Michael got up off the floor and rubbed his eyes with his shirt sleeves. All the inmates around him were coughing. There were a lot of custody officers in the area now.

"If you need a water rinse from the pepper spray go to medical shower station two," one of the custody officers was offering to the inmates. Several of the men who were closest to the combatants headed off to rinse their eyes.

Michael felt he would be fine in a minute or two, so he continued on to the testing station.

"Never a dull moment here."

Michael tuned to his right to see who was talking to him. He could not believe his eyes. It was Jason, his good buddy who was responsible for him being in prison.

"Jason," Michael said.

"Yeah, it's me. How you doing, Bro?"

"How do you think I am? I'm fighting for my life in here, thanks to you."

"I know. That was totally fucked up, what happened. I'm really sorry man. I never meant for you to end up here."

"I guess that's it Jason, you never think."

"I see you're still hanging in though. Good for you."

"No thanks to you."

"You're right Michael. I was a dick to get you caught up in that deal."

"Yes you were," Michael said. He was boiling inside. This was the first time he had seen Jason since his arrival. He had thought many times about what he would say to him. But now Jason was being so apologetic. What else was there to say? Michael swallowed hard as his throat was irritated from the pepper spray.

"Who's your Doctor?" Jason asked.

"Dr. Carson."

"Good for you," Jason said. "I have Dr. Isaac. I hear he makes a lot of referrals to Mod."

"I guess there's a lot of that going on, some Docs more than others."

"This is my stop," Jason said. "I have a group in here. Listen Michael, I really am sorry about what happened. I hope you make it to rehab." Jason reached out to shake Michael's hand.

Michael hesitated and then shook his hand. "Okay Jason. I hope you make it to rehab too. Take care." Michael watched as Jason walked into the group room.

"Keep moving," an officer yelled at Michael. He turned and continued down the hallway. Testing station number three was near the end of the hallway.

Michael opened the door and entered. He held his hand out for the correctional officer at the desk, the officer scanned it, and then handed him a brochure.

"Can you read?" the officer asked.

"Yes," Michael said.

"Then have a seat and read that. Let me know when you have read it all. I will answer any questions you have." The officer pointed to a bench where he wanted Michael to sit.

The brochure explained the procedure. They wanted you to be aware of some things before they started so you would not get upset when they attached you to the machine. As far as Michael understood they were going to wrap a strap around his penis. Then hook him up with a bunch of wires while an IV sampled his blood throughout the test. He would experience virtual reality scenarios. His responses to the vignettes would tell them his sexual orientation and what got him sexually aroused. The machine was called a penile Plethysmograph.

Michael let the officer know he understood the brochure and waited on the bench. Eventually a tech called Michael's name and he was led into the testing room.

"Please completely disrobe and put this on," the tech said as he handed Michael a gown. "You can change in there."

The tech pointed to an area that was a nook. It was not a room but an open corner with a four foot high concrete wall around it. It allowed Michael to change while he was still completely in view of the staff.

"Come out here when you are ready Mr. Taylor,"

The tech was a Hispanic man about fifty years old. He was official and professional in his manner. Michael appreciated that, but he was a little uncomfortable knowing what was next.

The tech asked him to sit in a large chair that was somewhat like a dentist's chair. Then the tech began to attach an IV line to Michael's arm. He attached wires to Michael's head and chest and finally he wrapped a strap around Michael's penis. Everything was connected to a computer. The tech handed Michael a bright blue helmet with a crystal face mask. He put it on Michael's head and told him to just relax.

"In about thirty seconds you will experience the first scenario. Just relax and you will forget where you are and become involved in the world of the virtual reality. Do you understand?"

"Yes."

"Good, the test takes twenty-seven minutes. Your doctor will discuss your results with you. We will begin now."

All of a sudden Michael found himself sitting in a park. It was the first Virtual Reality scenario. It was a beautiful day and the sun was shining, kids were playing ball, and families were picnicking. Michael found himself enjoying the setting very much. Then he saw a man approaching him. It was a white man around twenty years old. He was extremely fit and well groomed. He smiled at Michael as he approached and sat on the bench next to Michael.

"Mind if I sit here?" he asked.

"Free country," Michael replied.

"Thanks," the man said. "My name is Russell."

"I'm Michael."

"Nice to meet you, you look familiar, have we met before?"

"I don't think so," Michael said.

Russell took a pack of gum out of his pocket and put a piece in his mouth. He licked his lips as he looked at Michael. "Would you like some, Michael?"

"Sure," Michael said.

Russell gave Michael a stick of gum. It was spearmint. It tasted wonderful. Michael hadn't had anything refreshing in his mouth in months.

"Thanks," Michael said.

"You're welcome. Would you like some more?"

"No, I'm good."

"No silly, I meant would you like some more?" Then Russell laid his hand on Michael's thigh. It startled him and he jumped.

"What the!" Michael said. He took Russell's hand off his leg and moved over away from him. "No thanks man, I'm not like that."

"Really," Russell said. "Well maybe you just need to know who's boss."

Russell stood up and slapped Michael. He was standing in front of him with his hand on his hip.

Michael wiped some blood off his lip and stood up. "Look Pal, you better clear out now before I hurt you."

"My mistake," Russell said. Then he turned and walked away.

"What an ass," Michael said as he sat back down. He realized that now there was a drink of cola on the bench next to him. He picked it up, opened it, and took a long drink. He closed his eyes and tilted his head back to feel the sun on his face.

"Mister," Michael heard a young voice so he opened his eyes. A young child was standing in front of him. It was about five years old. It was a beautiful child, but it looked androgynous, Michael could not tell if it was a boy or a girl.

"Have you seen my mommy?" the child asked.

"What, who are you?" Michael asked.

"Have you seen my mommy, I'm lost," the child asked as it began to cry.

"It's okay kid, don't cry."

"Will you hold me? I'm scared."

Michael looked at the child with tears streaming down its' face. He felt sorry for the kid but did not think it was such a good idea to hold the child. He stood up and patted the child on the head. The child cried louder now.

"Please hold me, I'm scared."

"Hello, anyone know whose kid this is?" Michael yelled out. "Hello, lost kid here."

"I'll help him," a voice boomed from behind Michael. He turned to see a police officer standing there.

"Great," Michael said. "This kid lost its mother."

The officer took the child by the hand and led it away.

Now Michael was in the bar of a hotel. It was a high class hotel, and he was dressed in a fine silk suit. He had a martini in his hand. He took a sip of the drink and looked around. He saw a woman walking into the bar. She was beautiful.

She was about twenty-one years old, with natural blonde hair that fell onto her shoulders. She had on a skin tight red silk dress that was low cut and showed off her voluptuous breasts. She glided up next to Michael and ordered a glass of champagne. Her hair smelled like fresh fruit shampoo, and her perfume made his nose tingle.

She smiled at Michael and laid her hand on his arm. "Are you ready Michael?" she asked as she held up a room key.

"Who are you?"

"Why, Elsa of course, silly." She had big blue eyes that bore right into Michael's heart and a pouty mouth with lipstick that matched her dress. She moved forward while reaching up with her left hand which she used to pull Michael's head towards her where she kissed him. Michael's head was spinning.

"Let's go upstairs," she said.

They took an elevator up to a room. After they shut the door she turned toward Michael. He was standing at the foot of the bed. She was standing in front of the window. The sun was setting behind her and light shone through the window highlighting her figure. Michael stared at Elsa as she reached behind herself and unzipped her dress. It came loose and fell to the floor. She was not wearing any lingerie. Michael gasped.

"What do you want to do Michael? We can play rape, bondage, snuff film, or sadist, whatever you want. Just tell me."

"What?" Michael was confused. He had no idea what half of those things were. "You're beautiful," he said. "I just want to touch you."

She stepped forward so that she was pressed up against Michael. He rubbed his hands along the side of her arms. He could smell her sweetness. He caressed the curve of her back and her behind, and cupped her breast in his hand. His penis was erect and ready to burst. She reached down and caressed him, and he exploded in his pants.

Michael's knees buckled, and he sat on the edge of the bed. The next thing he knew he was swimming laps in a pool. He got out, dried himself off, and headed to the showers. He was exposed to several more scenarios before the end of the test, including at least one that included farm animals that Michael ran from. Finally the tech removed the helmet from Michael's head.

"Please change back into your clothes," he said after he disconnected the IV, and all the wires from Michael.

Michael was in a mild state of shock. He had been on a physical and emotional roller coaster.

"You should not have any other activities scheduled for today. Is that correct?" the tech asked Michael.

"You're right, nothing else."

"Good, take these and then head back to rest." The tech handed him some Benzocarmidone to help with post-virtual reality aftereffects of nausea and flashbacks.

Michael swallowed the pills and drank the water the tech gave him. Then he returned to his cell, and took a nap. When he woke up, Billie was there.

"Dude, what did you think of Elsa?" Billie asked.

"Amazing, now what was that all about?"

"If you let the child sit on your lap and you get a boner, then you are a pedophile and you go straight to Modification. If you do it with the guy on the park bench, you are gay. You don't go to Mod, but they want to know the voyeuristic fucks, because they need a complete profile. If you rape Elsa, or kill her in a snuff scene or fuck her up in general, then you are a twisted fuck and you go straight to Mod, get it?"

"Oh, well the only thing I got off to was Elsa, and that was short and sweet."

"I know what you mean," Billie said. "They could not have made a sexier woman if they tried." The boys both had a good laugh about that as they ate their sack dinners.

33

Rick and Dean settled into a booth at Luigi's for their regular carbohydrate festival. The homey ambiance of the restaurant embraced them as they ordered their usual. Dean took a sip of his lemonade, and leaned back exhaling heavily.

A Mod walked through the restaurant and into the back room carrying a tray of dirty dishes. Dean and Rick watched him go and then turned to each other.

"The longer this goes on, the more we have to adjust to seeing them in public I guess," Dean said. He frowned as he added more sweeteners to his lemonade.

"I saw Eric Stiller working at the Basque coffee shop last week. Remember him? He was on Isaac's caseload." Rick took a piece of pizza.

"It's a new world. What we cannot change must be endured," Dean said.

Rick smiled when he heard Dean's favorite platitude.

"People have reconciled with more state control of their lives for a heightened sense of security and lower taxes. The most recent financial crisis changed a lot of attitudes about the cost of personal freedoms. It's amazing how quickly your values change when you're hungry."

"That's true," Rick said. "But there still has to be a line drawn somewhere. We still have to be vigilant about peoples' rights. We can't just completely give away power, to let others control our lives." Rick sat back and picked at his food.

"How are things going with you and Dr. Brayden?"

"About the same. We don't talk much, the audit is in process. It has only been a few days since they began their review, but I'm not referring more people than I feel is appropriate."

"Good for you. I imagine I may be the next one to be pressured. The truth is I have been asking around, talking to some of the people on our team. Several of them feel that they are also being pressured to refer more people." Dean watched Rick.

"Really," Rick said. "That's interesting. Just so you know, I met with Henry Smith yesterday. I was hoping for some support."

"Did you get any?"

"No, but he told me they think something unusual is going on in our office."

The waitress set the pasta on the table and both men began to eat. A quiet settled over the table for a moment. Dean looked at Rick and then set his fork down. Leaning forward in a quiet tone he said, "I also met with Henry last week. He told me they are doing an informal investigation. I imagine he told you the same?"

Rick began to cough as he choked on his pasta. When he recovered he put both hands on the side of the table and stared at Dean. "Really, he told me the same, but asked me to keep it to myself."

"Exactly," Dean said, "which is why I am whispering."

"What do you think this all means?"

"I think it means we have been doing the right thing. If anything illegal is going on, we have covered our butts by going to them first."

"Good point," Rick said.

"I think our best play now is to simply do our jobs the best we can, and let the chips fall where they may."

"That sounds smart. Say, did you go to Harvard or something to be that smart?" Rick asked smiling.

"Screw you," Dean said.

They spent the rest of their lunch trying to figure out who was playing ball with Dr. Brayden and who was resisting his demands. By the end of the meal, they had a pretty good idea who they could trust and who they couldn't. At the top of the list for those they couldn't trust was Dr. Isaac.

Dean brushed breadcrumbs off of his jacket as he stood up to leave. "The important thing my good man, is to go on with business as usual. We don't want to give Dr. Brayden any ammunition to shoot us with."

"I agree business as usual."

Rick stood up to leave, as he turned around he ran into the Mod that was carrying a pile of napkins. The man had been walking with his head down and did not see Rick get out of the booth.

"Excuse me," Rick said.

The Mod said, "Sorry," and shuffled off into the back room again.

Rick shuddered and shook his head. Dean laid his hand on Rick's shoulder and patted him. "Stiff upper lip Rick," he said as they walked out the front door.

34

The professor stood at the lectern. "Don't forget to do your reading assignment before our next class," he said. "See you next time."

The students all stood up and began to file out of Music Appreciation class. Liz grabbed her bag and walked toward the door.

"What do you think of this class so far?" Asked Ronit, he was one of Liz's classmates.

"I like it," Liz said. "What about you?"

"I find it very interesting. My family has been in the music industry for generations. In a way it is like a genealogy class for me." Ronit laughed as he walked alongside Liz.

"Really, that must be fun, the music industry I mean." They exited the building and walked out into the common area of the campus. There was a slight drizzle of rain falling. Liz took an umbrella out of her bag and opened it.

"It can be. I am the only one that has gone down a different path. I want to be an engineer. My family is a little confused by it, but I must follow my own path." Ronit zipped up his coat and turned up the collar. "I'm heading to the student union, what about you?"

"Me too, I need to get some food before my next class. Want to join me?"

"Sure."

"If you want to be out of music, why are you taking this class?" It began to rain harder. The raindrops sounded like a drummer playing on top of Liz's umbrella. They sped up their pace.

"It is an elective class. I needed the credit and I thought it would be easy for me." Ronit stepped into a small puddle and his shoe got wet. "Darn it, I should have worn my boots today."

They made it to the student union and shook themselves off. Liz collapsed her umbrella and looked around. "I will meet you over by those tables after I get my food," Liz pointed to the corner.

"Yes, alright, I will see you there." Ronit smiled and headed off to the corner.

After getting her food Liz headed over to the corner and sat down with Ronit. She opened her sandwich as Ronit looked at his data pad. She noticed a small table over in the corner where two people were handing out informational pamphlets.

"Do you know who they are?" Liz asked Ronit.

"They are the pro-Modification people."

"What?"

"The pro-Modification people, they are promoting modification for all criminals. They say that it will be a real boom for the economy."

"That's barbaric." Liz put her sandwich down. She had suddenly lost her appetite.

"Yes, it is barbaric," Ronit said as he turned in his chair to look at them. "I can't imagine how someone would be willing to turn someone into a zombie so they can have a nicer jacket."

"Hi Ronit," A woman walked up to their table.

"Hi Neha, please sit down, join us." Ronit said, as he stood up. He pulled a chair out for her. "Liz, this is my friend Neha."

"Hi Neha, it's nice to meet you."

Ronit and Neha kissed and then held hands as they smiled at each other. "Liz and I have music appreciation together."

"How nice," Neha said. "What were you staring at when I walked up?"

"I was telling Liz about the pro-Modification advocates over there."

"I can't believe people will do that to each other," Neha said.

"My boyfriend is in the Evaluation Center in Chino."

"Oh my," Ronit said. "That is very bad. You must get very angry when you see something like that." Ronit pointed to the pro-Mod table.

"Yes, I do. In fact, I think I need to leave now. I can't be here with them. It was nice to meet you Neha." Liz stood up and gathered her things.

"Yes, it was nice meeting you," Neha said.

"See you at class," Ronit said.

"Okay," Liz said. She walked toward the door as one of the pro-Mod people approached her attempting to hand her a pamphlet. Liz began to cry as she tried to push her way past him. He was persistent in trying to hand her one. "No thank you," she yelled at him finally. The man recoiled. Liz ran past him and burst through the door out into the rain.

35

Michael sat with his arms folded across his chest listening to Zack harass Leroy. He was a new inmate in their group. He came from a small mountain town east of San Diego called Descanso. He was arrested for manufacturing drugs. He was a Darwin who had an eighth grade education, and he looked like he had been doing manual labor since the age of ten. He looked hard, and tough.

Michael was getting angry at Zack's bullying, but he found he was able to control it. He decided to use words to confront Zack like Dr. Carson had shown him.

"What's your deal?" Michael asked.

Everyone in the group stopped talking and looked at Michael. The group leader, Susan Atkins, turned to look at Michael. He sat calmly looking at Zack as he spoke again. "I said, what's your deal?"

"Who are you talking to Michael?" Ms. Atkins asked.

Michael looked at her and suddenly felt a sense of empowerment. Instead of wanting to pound Zack like he ordinarily would, he wanted to call him out, to expose him.

"I'm talking to Zack, Ms. Atkins," Michael said. "I want to know what his deal is. He always seems to want to provoke the new guys."

"What the fuck are you talking about, Taylor?" Zack asked.

"Let's watch our language please," Ms. Atkins said as she turned to Zack.

"I'm talking about the fact that you always seem to want to jump on new guys to see if you can get them to go off. To get them into trouble and get them sent to Modification."

"Yeah, he's right," said Jimmie. Jimmie was an inmate who started group on the same day as Michael. He was in for burglary. Jimmie was a Darwin from a middle class family. He got caught up with a home invasion gang to support a drug habit. He was a skinny guy with stringy long brown hair and missing teeth in his smile. "I remember your first day, Michael. You almost jumped on him cause he got you pissed off."

Zack looked around the room with the eyes of a caged animal.

"Are you trying to get me sent to Mod, you little Fuck Head?" Leroy asked, his face flushing red.

Zack looked at Leroy and laughed. "Of course not, why would I do that? I'm just trying to help you get used to the process in here."

"I don't think so Zack," Ms. Atkins said. "What is it you're really doing?"

Before Zack could answer, Leroy erupted. He grabbed Zack by the neck and lifted him out of his seat.

"Leroy no," Ms. Atkins yelled as she activated her alarm.

Leroy threw Zack against the wall. When he fell to the ground he began to kick him continuously as he screamed, "Fuck with me will you?"

Leroy continued to kick him until the custody officers arrived. They did not bother with chemical gas as an intervention but instead went directly to their pulse batons. Leroy stopped the beating and lie on the floor convulsing, face to face with Zack. Zack watched him as he grabbed his ribs in pain.

Later, back in their cell Billie and Michael were playing dominos.

"Nice to have a little down time, don't you think?" Michael asked. "Since group ended early."

"Yeah, but it got a little hairy for a minute. So what was that all about anyway?"

"I just got tired of Zack running his games with nobody calling him on it. You know what he does, we've talked about it. I just thought it should be brought out into the open. Exposed, you know?"

"I know, but now you really will need to watch your back. Zack is going to try to get back at you somehow. That is, when he gets out of the infirmary." Billie slapped down a domino.

36

Rick washed his hands despite the lack of soap or hot water in the staff restroom. He often got frustrated with the deplorable conditions government workers endured. The one-ply toilet paper was the worst. He pulled a sanitary wipe out of his pocket and opened it. After cleaning up he headed to the conference room for his team's weekly case conference. Rick ran into Dean in the hallway.

"Is the light in the men's room working yet?" Dean asked.

"Yes, they finally fixed it late yesterday after a week of darkness. You can put your flashlight away," Rick replied. "But we still don't have any soap or hot water."

"Nice."

"Do you think people at successful corporations have to endure indignities like this?" Rick asked.

"Doubt it."

Dean and Rick entered the conference room and found seats. Rick sat next to Ms. Atkins and Dean sat on his other side. Rick was determined to avoid sitting near Dr. Isaac, and he enjoyed Susan's company.

Rick greeted the other team members in the room and they all engaged in general conversation. Then Dr. Brayden entered the room. Immediate silence ensued as he sat at the head of the table.

"Good morning everyone," Dr. Brayden said. "Okay, let's get started."

Dr. Brayden as went over the statistics for the last period, and Rick let his mind wander to his audit. Dr. Brayden wrapped up his presentation, and was now asking the clinicians for reports on the inmates.

Rick reported on his caseload first. He did not have any difficult cases at the present time, so it was uneventful. At least he didn't think he had any issues until Susan Atkins' report.

"I need to discuss an incident that occurred in my group yesterday," Ms. Atkins said. "Zack Cole was severely beaten by another inmate and was sent to the infirmary."

"That's true," Dr. Isaac said. "The medical report indicates he could be laid up for a week or so. I am requesting that his evaluation time be extended as a result."

"I believe I can approve that under the circumstances," Dr. Brayden said as he and Dr. Isaac stole looks at each other.

"There were a couple of additional issues related to the incident I should mention," Ms. Atkins continued on. "Zack appeared to be baiting the inmate that attacked him. It was not the first time this has happened either. He seems to try to get new inmates to lose their tempers to get them into trouble, which of course could ultimately lead to them being Modified."

"Really, and what possible purpose would that serve for Zack?" Dr. Isaac asked.

"I don't really know, he is on your caseload Dr. Isaac. I was hoping you could tell us."

"The idea is absurd," Dr. Isaac dismissed her with a wave of his hand.

"You said there was more than one issue Ms. Atkins?" Dr. Brayden intervened, distracting the conversation away from Zack.

"Well, yes, as a matter of fact. Michael Taylor is the one who initially noticed what Zack was doing, or rather what he appeared to be doing. He is the one who confronted Zack. But his confrontation was accusatory and aggressive. He was not physically violent on this occasion. But he was definitely aggressive in his posture."

"That individual has already had one fight hasn't he? Dr. Carson, isn't he yours?" Dr. Brayden asked.

"He has," Rick answered. "Yes he is on my caseload. I believe he has been making great strides in controlling his aggression."

"Well it doesn't sound like it in this case. Keep a close eye on him, Doctor. It sounds like he might be a candidate for Modification."

"Of course I will," Rick said. He ground his teeth together as he smiled at Dr. Brayden.

Ms. Atkins moved on finishing her presentation. Now it was Dr. Isaac's turn to take the floor. He reiterated that he would extend Zack's time to accommodate his infirmary stay. Then he began to discuss Billie's case. Billie's image appeared in the center of the table as Dr. Isaac initiated the hologram. His case report appeared in front of Rick on the video screen imbedded in the table.

"Billie Johnson is an individual who presents as very marginal. His IQ score was just above the borderline range. He has not impressed me in individual sessions as someone who would benefit from Rehabilitation. More likely he would simply complete that program and then return to his life just as he is today. I am leaning towards Modification when he completes the testing protocols."

Rick listened intently to Dr. Isaac's evaluation. He knew Billie and Michael were cellies. They had become close friends who supported each other. He believed that if Billie was sent to Modification, it could push Michael over the edge.

"Has he had any disciplinary write ups?" Rick asked.

"No," Dr. Isaac responded.

"Did he fail any of the mandatory benchmarks on the tests, like the sex offender test?" Rick queried further.

"No."

Dean spoke up. "I'm a little curious Doctor. If he hasn't failed any of the protocol items, and hasn't had any disciplinary problems, what exactly you are basing your decision on? Have we been given new guidelines?"

"I'm basing it on my professional judgment, on the time I have spent with him in individual therapy. He just seems marginal, with an inability to benefit from Rehabilitation."

"Gentleman," Dr. Brayden said. "Let's not get off track here. Of course Dr. Isaac's clinical judgment is a significant factor in this process. As it is in all of yours, right?" He asked as he looked at Dean and Rick.

"Dr. Isaac, do you have anyone else to present?" Dr. Brayden asked.

"No sir."

"Okay then, let's end here." Dr. Brayden suddenly stood up and walked out of the conference room.

Rick was astounded at the brazen railroading of Billie by Brayden and Isaac. He left feeling concerned not only for Billie, but for Michael.

37

Michael lie in his bunk scratching his name on the wall with a paperclip. He thought he would leave some evidence of his existence if he was Modified. The paint flakes fell onto his chest, and he brushed them off onto the floor. Satisfied with his work, he thought of his victory over Zack Cole.

"I really got that dick good," Michael said.

"What, what are you talking about?" Billie asked from the lower bunk.

"Zack, I really got him good in group. They said he will be in the infirmary for a week."

"Yeah, you got him good alright. You also got the stupid hillbilly good as well. They shipped his dumb ass off to Modification."

"Really?" Michael asked as he sat up. Suddenly he didn't feel so good.

"Yes, really."

"Shit. I didn't want that. Fuck."

"Maybe you should think shit through then, Dude."

Billie stood up and stretched. Then he hit Michael in the arm.

"Don't worry about it. That dumb shit wouldn't have made it through the month anyway. You just saved the government a whole lot of food." Billie hit him again and laughed.

"Still," Michael lamented. "I guess I do need to be more careful around here."

"And watch your back. Don't think Zack Cole is going to take that shit lying down. Like I already told you, he will try to come after you and he can be very crafty so you need to be sharp."

"What do you have today?" Michael asked trying to change the subject.

"My last test, they call it a projective test. I'm not sure what that means except you have to make up stories to video scenes."

"Sounds weird."

"What about you?" Billie asked.

"I have an individual session with my Doc today."

"Well give him hell."

The door opened and the boys heard an announcement telling them to proceed to chow. In the chow hall they got their food trays and sat down with Victor and Kevin. Michael tried to avoid eating with Kevin because of his bad acne. It made Michael nauseous. Kevin followed Victor around like a lost puppy, however, so they had become a package deal.

"You still here?" Victor asked Michael.

"Of course, why wouldn't I be?"

"I heard you set up Zack Cole to get his ass kicked. I figure his boys get you by now, or you get sent to Mod for being troublemaker," Victor said in his Russian accent.

"I heard it was Bad Ass what you did Michael," Kevin offered.

"I really didn't do anything but ask a question. Ms. Atkins asked the same question so there was nothing Bad Ass about it," Michael said.

He was beginning to worry about what had happened. It seemed to have a much larger effect on the Unit than he first thought. Michael sat quietly for the rest of the meal. When the buzzer rang ending chow he quickly headed down the hallway to Dr. Carson's office.

38

Michael entered Rick's office and sat down.

"Hello Michael," Rick said.

"Hi Doctor Carson, how's it going?" Michael avoided Rick's gaze.

"Well, how's it going with you?"

"Alright I guess. I'm a little confused about an incident I had," Michael said. He picked at his collar with his finger nail.

"With Zack Cole?"

"Yeah, you heard about it?"

"I did."

"What did you hear? Do you think I messed up?" Michael sat upright now and looked directly at Rick.

"Some folks think you did. What do you think? Did you mess up?" Rick asked as he leaned back in his chair.

"I didn't think so at first. At first I felt great. Like I kicked Zack's ass, you know, without actually hitting him. But now I feel like crap because that dumb guy got sent to Mod, and people act like I'm a Bad Ass. I'm not used to this kind of attention as a result of just asking a question." Michael ran his fingers through his hair and crossed his arms.

"Is that what you did, just ask a question?"

Michael sat quietly for a moment and looked at Rick.

"Kind of, but I wanted to out him, point a light on his devious ways, you know?" Michael asked.

"I do know Michael. Did you do that in a productive way?"

"Probably not," Michael said as he looked at the floor.

"In what way did you do it?"

"I don't know, I wanted to hit him for being a bully, but like we talked about, I used words instead," Michael said as he moved his hands about like he was directing a symphony.

"So what did you learn from this experience?"

"I guess that words can be just as destructive as fists," Michael said.

"That's a good thing to learn."

"I guess."

"Someone once said that a good measure of mental health is the extent to which a person is aware of their effect on other people," Rick said. "Do you know what that means?"

"Yeah, if I see what my actions do to someone else, right?"

"Exactly."

"Tough to watch out all the time," Michael said.

"True, it would take a while. Eventually it could become second nature."

"What's that mean?" Michael asked as he leaned forward.

"It means that eventually you may always think of others first, then yourself."

"Why would I want to do that?" Michael asked, frowning.

"When you have the power to impact others' lives, it can be somewhat of a responsibility. Like if you are a parent," Rick said.

"Oh."

"The next step is to learn some ways to better control your anger. You are able to control your physical aggression now. We have to give you some tools to help you control your verbal aggression. Are you game?"

"Sure," Michael said.

"Alright then, let's get to work."

39

The next day, the main corridor was crowded with inmates going to their morning appointments. Michael was walking next to the wall in a path outlined with yellow lines painted on the floor. He was to report to the I.Q. testing room. Jason Kopp was in front of him.

"Hey Jason," Michael said.

Jason looked over his shoulder and saw it was Michael. He slowed down so they could walk together.

"Hey Michael, what's up?"

"Seems like you're making quite a name for yourself around here," Jason said.

"What do you mean?" Michael asked.

"I heard you called out Zack Cole and got him beat up so bad he had to go to the infirmary. That's living on the edge. Rumor is he's connected here. They watch over him if you know what I mean."

"I didn't really do anything, just asked a question."

"Right, just a question, must have been some question."

"This is my stop," Michael said.

"Watch your back bro," Jason said.

Michael entered the I.Q. testing center and extended his hand with the data chip to the officer at the desk. The officer directed him to a holding cell where he found a seat with five other inmates. He recognized Ed Smith from one of his groups. He had been a carpenter on the streets. Ed was twenty six years old with sandy hair, brown eyes, and an average build. He was committed for stealing building materials from a jobsite where he worked. It had been a lucrative side business, until it wasn't.

"Hello Taylor," Ed said.

"Hi Ed, what do you know?" Michael asked.

"I hear this test is like going to Disneyland," Ed said.

"Really, you mean it's fun?"

"That's what I hear," Ed said.

"Cool. I could use some entertainment."

A testing proctor walked out of the back room and addressed the guys.

"Men, I am going to take you back into the testing area in a moment. The entire test takes ninety minutes. It has six sections, and each one is timed. Some of the sections will be done in a group, and some will be done individually. Now please follow me back single file."

For the first test the proctor put the men into two groups of three. Each group was sitting at a kiosk with three chairs around it facing the center. A belly high table top covered the kiosk. It had three video monitors, one in front of each inmate.

"When the test begins, you will see a sentence appear on the monitor in front of you. The sentence will be incomplete; it will have a word missing. Your task is to choose a word to complete the sentence. You will see a three dimensional holograph of words appearing in the middle of the kiosk. To choose a word simply touch the word you want with your glove. The gloves are on the table in front of you. Please put them on now. These are special gloves that act like a computer mouse. When you touch a word with the glove the word will insert into the sentence on your monitor. You will all have different sentences at different times as there are three versions of this test. Each of you will complete a different version so sharing information will not help you. A new sentence will appear on your monitor after you choose a word. The object is to answer as many questions correctly as you can in the time allotted. You have ten minutes to complete this portion of the test. Any questions?"

No one had any questions, so the test began. The monitor lit up and a sentence appeared in front of Michael. Then the 3-D hologram lit up. It was two feet high and thirteen inches across. It manifested in the middle of the kiosk in front of the inmates. Michael thought it was beautiful. It was a cascade of words, each one a different color and all of them constantly moving up, down and around. Michael was hypnotized for a moment and then he heard Ed yell out.

"Booyah."

He had answered his first question. Michael looked down at the monitor and tried to focus on the task at hand.

'If you are hungry you should eat some _____,' the monitor read.

Michael looked up at the cascade of words. "Food." He thought to himself. He reached out and touched the word Food.

Immediately the next question appeared. He smiled, chuckled to himself, and continued. The guys found themselves enjoying the activity, even laughing at times during the test and then as quickly as it began, the hologram disappeared.

The next two tests were also completed at the kiosks. In one test they had to memorize a series of numbers, and in another they had to complete math problems. When they completed all the tests, the proctor took them to another room with large virtual reality chairs. The inmates donned virtual reality headgear, but this time their vitals and blood work were not monitored. Instead they were given another pair of gloves.

The proctor gave more instructions, "In the next two tests you will be manipulating virtual reality environments with your hands. In the first one there are a series of widgets you will use to re-create a design that you will see. In the second you will complete a puzzle by manipulating the pieces."

After a few questions the next test began. Michael was actually enjoying himself taking the exam. He felt he easily completed all the tasks. At the end of the ninety minutes they were given some Benzocarmidone. Michael and Ed headed out of the test area and down the main hallway.

"Not a bad day considering," Ed said.

"Really, I guess now we will know our I.Q., whatever that means," Michael said.

The boys followed the path along the wall and headed back to the unit. Billie was not back yet when Michael arrived, so he decided to lie down and take a nap.

40

Zack rubbed his fractured rib. It still hurt and most likely would continue to for some time. It was difficult to breathe without feeling it. It felt like a knife was being thrust into his chest. He had returned to the unit the day before, but he missed the soft bunks in the infirmary. He had to lie on his back when he slept. He could not lie on his side or the pain became unbearable. He had a broken rib before. His father broke it when he was eleven. Zack had been arrested for stealing. His father was upset that he was caught, and wanted to teach him a lesson.

Zack's cellie was getting ready to shower, preparing his toiletries, getting undressed and wrapping a towel around his waist. Zack was going to skip the shower this evening. He would leave his cell, but he had other business in mind. He swung his legs off the bunk, and onto the floor. Then he readied himself to make it look like he was going to the shower.

Michael's cell was on the same tier as Zack's. That meant they would be let out to shower at the same time. When the inmates went down to shower, their cells were left open. That's when Zack intended to swoop down on Michael's cell, and look for something to help him get even. He would not directly attack Michael. That would be too destructive to his case. His support from Dr. Isaac and Dr. Brayden would immediately evaporate if he did something that brazen. Their agreement was simple and clear. He was to incite other inmates so they acted out and were sent to Modification. Then he would be spared Modification and be sent to Rehabilitation. He could not draw attention to himself. He had been plotting against Michael for days now. He had to reestablish himself on the unit, or he would lose the respect of the inmates who worked with him. They were sheep, but they needed reassurance. He was not sure what he would find in Michael's cell, but that was going to be his first move.

Timing was going to be important. He would need to be quick to stay undetected. Inmates would be coming and going on the tier. Some of the guys liked Taylor and would rat Zack out if he was spotted.

Michael and Billie were preparing to go down for showers. Shower time was always a bit of organized chaos. They had to walk down to the first level where the showers were located. Six inmates at a time could shower, and they were given four minutes. When one group finished another immediately took their place. The first group would then hike back to their cells. One tier at a time would shower, which meant there were thirty guys out at a time walking around in towels and shower shoes.

The staff was efficient and moved the men along, not allowing them to loiter on the tiers or the stairs. They also effectively limited each inmate's time in the shower. If someone gave them trouble they would miss their next shower.

The doors to the cells on the second tier opened, and an announcement was made to proceed to the showers. Billie and Michael moved out of their cell, and headed to the stairs with the other inmates.

Zack's cell was near the end of the tier, at the far end away from the stairs. He hung back a little when they were released telling his cellie he needed to use the restroom before he showered.

Zack walked slowly down the tier watching to make sure all the other inmates had gone down to shower. He stopped in front of Michael's cell looking in to make sure it was empty. He figured he had about three minutes before the first group of six inmates would be heading up the stairs. He quickly ducked into Michael's cell. He looked around to see if anything stood out or came to his attention. Finding nothing he decided to search their lockers. He looked into the first one, but he realized it wasn't Michael's locker so he moved on. He had to move quickly. The first inmates would be returning from shower at any moment.

That's when he saw Liz's picture. Zack smiled as he picked up the picture and looked at it. She was pretty. He had a girlfriend once. She dumped him for a Normal who was enhanced for physical abilities. He was a star athlete at school, and Zack wasn't. He tried to kick the guy's ass, but ended up with a busted lip. He slipped the picture into his towel, and quickly went to the cell door. He knew this would be just what he needed to call Michael out. He checked the tier. No sight of anyone yet. He shuffled out, and made his way back to his cell. His heart was pounding in his chest, and his mind was processing how he could make this work for him.

41

Michael lie on his bunk staring at the ceiling. Billie was washing up at the sink.

"It's almost time," Billie said.

"Yum, I can't wait. What do you think it will be today, green meat or watered eggs?" Michael asked.

"If you're lucky, maybe both," Billie laughed.

Michael swung his legs over the side of his bunk and jumped down onto the floor of their cell.

"Anything exciting on your agenda today?" Michael asked.

"A one on one with Dr. Isaac, he set up a special session with me. I found out about it late last night." Billie looked Michael directly in the eyes. Michael could see concern on Billie's face.

"I'm sure it's nothing," Michael said. "Maybe you need to take a test over or something simple like that."

"You're right, nothing to worry about."

Billie tucked his shirt into his pants and leaned against the wall. Then the cell door began to move and an announcement instructed them to go to chow. Michael patted Billie on the back as they left the cell. He thought about Dr. Isaac's reputation for blindsiding people and sending them to Modification without warning. He was worried that might happen to Billie. How would he handle that? What would he do? What could he do? He could not even protect himself.

Michael walked out of his cell and turned left to head toward the stairs. He thought he heard his name being spoken behind him, so he stopped and turned around to see who was talking about him. He saw Zack Cole and inmate Roberts laughing, and making faces at each other.

"Come on Taylor, let's keep moving." The other inmates on the tier ramp were urging Michael on as they bunched up behind him.

"Sorry," Michael said. He turned and made his way down the stairs. The group from his tier made their way into the chow hall.

Michael and Billie grabbed trays, and stood in line waiting to be served breakfast.

"Zack is up to something," Michael said to Billie.

"What do you mean?"

"I heard him and Roberts talking about me."

Billie leaned back so he could see Zack at the end of the line. Zack and Roberts were still laughing and talking. Billie looked back at Michael.

"Dude, don't let those assholes get you riled up. That's what Zack wants, right?"

"You're right," Michael said as he put his tray out to be served. The man working the food line looked down and plopped a spoonful of oatmeal onto Michael's tray. As Michael looked at him he saw he had a green light glowing on his forehead. Michael was startled and jumped back.

Billie and Michael looked at each other in disbelief. It was a Mod serving breakfast.

"Shit," Billie said. "Just keep moving." He grabbed Michael's arm and pulled him along. Another Mod was working at the next food station serving drinks. He put cartons of milk out for them. They could not help but stare at the Mod and the green light on his forehead. They had never been this close to one before. Feeling a little shaky they made their way through the rest of the food line and headed to a table.

They sat at the first available table and set their trays and lunch bags down. Then they just sat and stared at the Mods working behind the service line.

"How could they bring them in here?" Michael asked. He felt it was the ultimate indignity, not to mention a threat.

Victor sat down at the table. "You boys like workers on food line today?" he asked.

"No, not really," Michael said.

"They bring them from Northern California. Don't want us to recognize them," Victor said.

"Man, this is totally fucked up," Billie said.

The boys picked at their meals while they stared at the Mods who methodically served food. They had completely forgotten about Zack. Until they heard Michael's name being spoken again, amid a cackle of laughter.

They turned to see Zack and inmate Roberts sitting across the chow hall, about two tables away. Roberts had something in his hand, and he was flashing it around the table showing the other inmates. He held it still for a moment and Michael got a good look at it. It was Liz's picture.

"That's Liz, that's my picture," Michael said. He quickly rose and stalked toward inmate Roberts.

"Wait," Billie said, as he tried in vain to grab a hold of him.

"That's my picture," Michael said to Roberts. "Hand it over."

Zack Cole looked across at Michael and smirked as he watched the drama play out. Roberts looked up at Michael and laughed.

"Really,Taylor? It looks like it's mine now. And you know what; I think I'll have her give me a little head." He rubbed the picture on his crotch and laughed as the other inmates including Zack laughed with him.

Michael reached down and grabbed Roberts' wrist. He twisted it as he yanked his arm up and over so that he could take the picture with his other hand. Roberts yelped in pain as his shoulder snapped. Michael snatched the picture away from Roberts and released his arm. Then he turned around and began to walk back to his table.

Billie had been watching all the action from their table. He saw the officers eyeing Michael but no one had moved yet, and no alarm had sounded. Michael had moved so quickly and so efficiently it didn't even look like a confrontation. Now as Michael began to make his way back to his table Roberts yelled and jumped up. He did a bull rush tackling Michael from behind.

Now an alarm did sound. Billie dove to the floor as did all the other inmates in the chow hall. Four custody officers quickly responded and went to the two men wrestling on the floor. Two of them grabbed Roberts and easily restrained him with their superior strength. After Roberts was pulled off of him, Michael offered no resistance. He allowed himself to be handcuffed and a pulse collar was put on his neck. He still held Liz's picture in his hand as he was led down the hallway toward Ad-Seg.

42

The sedative had begun to wear off and Michael opened his eyes. He got a sick feeling in his stomach. He could see the operating room, the doctor, and the medical technicians busily preparing for his Modification. He struggled to move but his body would not cooperate. He was awake, but he could not move at all. He heard a drill begin to buzz and then he saw it. It was headed directly for his forehead. He was screaming inside but no sound came out of him.

Then he woke up. He was lying on his bunk in Ad-Seg. His body was drenched in sweat, and he was panting. He quickly sat up and looked around. It was a nightmare, what a dream. This place was really getting to him. It was his first night back in Ad-Seg after his fight with Roberts, although it really wasn't much of a fight. He felt it was unfair that he was sent here. After all, Roberts attacked him from behind.

He reached into his pocket and felt for Liz's picture. It was still there. He pulled it out and looked at it, her smiling face, and her beautiful smile. That fucking Zack Cole did this, he was sure of it.

Michael got out of his bunk and placed Liz's picture on top of his locker, then he rinsed his face with cold water. He dried off and went to cell front, looking out onto the unit. He was housed on the first tier this time. He could see the officers' station, the showers, and a dayroom. He looked up and could see the three tiers on the other side of the unit. Florescent lighting gave the entire unit a bright orange hue. Sounds of movement echoed off the walls and amplified so everyone could hear anything that went on in the unit.

Several officers were moving about while they escorted inmates in and out of cells. All of the inmates were in handcuffs and pulse collars. Michael touched his neck where he could still feel the cold metal of the pulse collar they had put on him yesterday. It was a humiliating and humbling experience to be collared like an animal.

An officer was approaching his cell, pushing a cart loaded with food. It was time for breakfast. The officer stopped in front of Michael's cell. Without saying a word he thrust a tray of hot food into the tray slot in the cell door. Michael took the tray and set it on top of his locker. The officer handed him a sack of food, Michael's lunch, again without saying a word.

"Good morning," Michael said.

"Good morning Mr. Taylor," the officer replied and then he was gone. He moved off to feed the other inmates.

Michael took his tray and sat on the edge of the bunk. He was still feeling the effects of his dream. What a nightmare it would be to get sent to Modification. His mind was filled with concerns about how his mother would take it. She would still have Ryan, that shit, but losing Michael would be hard on her. What would Liz think, worse yet what would she do? She would move on, forget all about Michael. She would marry some trust fund toad and raise his kids. What would it be like to be a Mod? Would he remember who he was? Would he remember anyone else?

Michael was so preoccupied he didn't even mind the runny eggs and green meat they served him for breakfast. He looked down and his tray was empty, he had eaten everything, but tasted nothing. He set the tray on the floor by the cell door and returned to his bunk. He closed his eyes and flashed on the sound of the drill and the sight of it heading toward him. He quickly opened his eyes again.

In the past he was always able to make the best of a bad situation, but this was different. It could have a devastating outcome. His usual methods of dealing with the world were only getting him deeper into trouble. This was his second trip to Ad-Seg. The Sergeant told him that three trips were an automatic ticket to the Modification Center. What could he do?

He would have to start looking at his behavior. What was he doing to get himself into these predicaments? A commotion out on the tier interrupted his thoughts. He could hear someone crying and yelling at the same time. He got up and went to the cell front to see what was happening. The action was on the second tier on the other side of the unit, so Michael had a ringside seat.

Three custody officers and a nurse were standing outside of a cell. The nurse was putting a hypodermic needle into her bag. The screaming had stopped now, as had the crying. The custody officers entered the cell and came out carrying an inmate who appeared to be unconscious. They picked him up and laid him onto a gurney where they strapped him down securely. They rolled the gurney down to the end of the tier and down a ramp to the bottom floor. Michael could not see who the inmate was. Some of the other inmates on the unit began to yell out. They were calling to a "Charlie," telling him goodbye and that he was going to Modification.

That sick feeling from his dream returned. He could not watch anymore. He returned to his bunk and looked at Liz's picture. He told himself that he could not lose hope. That he would talk to Dr. Carson. He would not come back to Ad-Seg again. He would not be Modified.

43

Michael awoke with a renewed commitment to making it to Rehabilitation. He just completed his second week in Ad-Seg. Time seemed to pass much faster because he knew what to expect, and how to keep himself active in his cell. He was going to be sent back to Unit 9 today. He finished his breakfast tray and got dressed in preparation for his transfer. This last week had given him a lot of time to think about what he was doing with his life. His anger and his fighting could be his undoing if he didn't get it under control.

He realized that he had rationalized getting kicked out of high school. He had blamed the rich kids for being assholes that needed some schooling. He had never really taken responsibility for his behavior in those situations. His sessions with Dr. Carson had helped him see that. He was going to be the master of his own actions from now on.

He had seen other guys be successful in changing in group, so he could do it. Some of them relied on positivity to do it. Their belief in being positive helped them avoid going off on others. Those guys seemed changed in some way after their decisions. More peaceful in a way, like they knew something no one else knew. Michael was never an overly positive person. He relied on his mother's modeling to learn his moral values. She was a good woman, who treated everyone with respect, but life was hard for her, and she could be very negative.

Michael sat on his bunk and closed his eyes. He tried to visualize Liz. He would rely on himself and the people he loved to help get him through this. Realizing that fact made him think of Roberts and how he disrespected Liz in the dayroom. Michael's hands clenched and tightened. He recalled the sneer on Robert's face when he rubbed her picture on his crotch. Michael's breathing quickened, and he could feel adrenalin start to surge through his body.

Michael opened his eyes. He stood up and turned towards his bunk while punching the mattress, once, twice, a third time. Then he caught himself as he realized he was reverting to his old habit of anger and violence right now. "Damn, this is hard," he thought to himself. "How am I going to get this under control? Even if some people deserve to get their asses kicked, I can't be the one to do it." He took four deep breaths as he counted to four. This was one of the anger management techniques they had talked about in group. His breathing slowed and he felt his hands and arms relax. "I guess this stuff can work after all," he thought to himself.

He sat back on his bunk and gathered himself. Then a Custody Officer appeared at his cell door.

"You ready to go Taylor?"

"Yes," Michael replied, as he stood up.

"Rack 22," the officer said into his com system.

The door opened and Michael walked out of the cell. The custody officer escorted Michael to the door of the Ad-Seg unit. That's where an escort officer took over to take Michael back to Unit 9.

As usual the custody officer walked to the side of him and two paces behind. The officers never engaged in small talk. So, Michael just ignored him and enjoyed his walk. Happy to be out of The Hole."

As he left the Ad-Seg Unit Michael could feel a certain tension leave his body. Tightness had manifested in his muscles. He had been unaware of it until now. He felt a little spring return to his step as he walked the long hallway back to the unit. He had a smile on his face as he walked. He looked down the hall and suddenly felt amazement at the design of the building. It was so massive. Somewhat like the airport terminal he had been to when he flew back east with his mother. He was nine years old at the time. It was a magical trip for him. They had gone to visit Michael's aunt and uncle in Missouri. Ryan stayed in California. Michael met his cousins and they played down by a river near their house. They swam, paddled canoes, swung on ropes tied to tree branches, and let go to fly into the river. They also had a cookout down by the river. It was the best barbeque chicken Michael ever tasted. He wished he could have stayed in Missouri to live with his cousins. They were so nice to him. They were nothing like Ryan. But eventually he had to go back to California.

When they reached Unit 9, the officer called in their arrival and the door to the unit opened. Michael entered the unit and climbed the stairs to the second tier. As he made his way down the tier toward his cell, he noticed that many of the other inmates were standing at their cell doors watching him. It made him a little anxious as he didn't know why. Then he noticed that one of the unit staff had followed him up.

He reached his cell and looked in. Immediately he realized what was going on. Billie was gone. His personal belongings were gone and his bunk was stripped down. The realization that Billie was gone and that he was sent to Modification hit him like a ton of bricks. Michael hesitated at the door afraid to enter. His vision became blurred as the blood rushed to his head. He felt his fists clench and his arms and legs tighten up.

"Move in Taylor," said the Custody officer. Michael turned toward him with rage in his heart and fire in his eyes.

"Move in Taylor," the Officer said again.

Michael was panting now.

"Move in Taylor," the Officer said for a third time.

Michael couldn't move. "How could this have happened?" He asked himself. Slowly his mind began to clear. His thoughts focused on the situation at hand. He looked at the officer who had now removed his pulse baton from his belt. It was activated and it pulsated with a dangerous charge of electricity. But the officer was still standing there, he had not moved.

Michael blinked, he saw all the other inmates on the tier watching him. Michael cleared his throat and took a deep breath. Then he took four more deep breaths counting out each one of them. When he got to four, he was more relaxed and calm. Feeling numb he took two steps forward into the cell. He didn't hear the cell door close behind him. He was too focused on the emptiness in the cell.

Michael looked at Billie's empty bunk and his eyes began to well up with tears. He sat on Billie's bunk. He thought Billie was going to be sent to Rehabilitation. What could have gone wrong? Michael began to think of his own situation now. What if Dr. Carson sold him out? He couldn't let that happen. He wouldn't let that happen.

As he lie there he heard his e-mail alert. He sat up and checked his in box. He had a new e-mail from Liz. He smiled as he opened it.

"Dear Michael, I miss you so much now. School is fun but it has been difficult at times. It is a lot to deal with, being on your own, and trying to manage school. I took a heavy load this semester to get a good start. Maybe I shouldn't have done that, ha ha. I'm sure you are dealing with much worse. I saw a group on campus promoting modification for all criminals. It seems to be a hot political issue now. It has to do with the election. I can't imagine what that would be like. I got very upset when I saw them. I have a few new friends but mostly I have been keeping to myself. I am very busy with schoolwork and all. I wish we were together now. I love you and hope to visit you at my first break. Take care for now, Love Liz xo."

Reading her e-mail made Michael feel a lot better, but he wondered what effect the pro-Modification movement would have on his case. He felt a little helpless being unable to communicate with most of the outside world.

44

It had been three days since his return Unit 9 from Ad-Seg. Michael did not have a new cellie yet, and he was not sure if he would get one. He didn't want one. At least not now, that was for sure. He dressed for chow and sat on the lower bunk. He slept there last night. No need to climb up top if he didn't have to. He thought he would stay on the bottom even if someone else did show up. He would not feel right letting them have Billie's old bunk. He was dreading going to chow. He was not in the mood for Victor's sarcasm, and he could not bear to see the Mods serving this morning. It would just remind him of Billie. He wondered if it had happened yet, or if Billie was sitting in a cell at the Mod center waiting, fearful and anxious, about to enter a hole of existence, without emotion or caring.

Michael's cell door opened, and he could hear the other inmates on the tier leaving their cells, heading to chow. Michael forced himself to get up and walk out. He wanted to avoid Zack who would be coming his way. He quickly left his cell and headed downstairs. He sat at a table with three new inmates he didn't know. He ignored everyone and kept to himself during the meal. He felt disconnected. It was kind of like watching himself in a movie. He could see himself moving around, but he was not really aware of what was happening. When the buzzer rang indicating the end of breakfast, he made his way into the main hallway. He headed toward Dr. Carson's office.

When he got to Dr. Carson's office Michael sat with his head down and his arms crossed.

"How are you feeling about Billie?" Rick asked. He leaned forward.

"Horrible, angry, enraged!" Michael said. He did not want to be there. His arms constricted tightly around his body.

"I'm sure it was quite a loss for you," Rick said. "Have you ever lost anyone close to you before?" His eyes widened as he observed Michael.

"My father, but I was just a kid. I'm really angry now, at Dr. Isaac, at the system, at my own situation." Michael began to loosen his grip on himself as he spoke.

"That's understandable." Michael was letting off steam and Rick was letting him do it

"I don't want to talk to anyone, listen to their shit. That's all we get around here is a lot of shit thrown at us. I'm tired of it." Now Michael was waving his arms in the air, pointing his finger at Rick.

"Are you giving up?" Rick asked. He did not retreat. He still leaned forward toward Michael.

"I don't want to, but it seems like there is no way to win here, there's no hope." Michael slumped back into his chair and lowered his head.

"It may seem that way to you now, but I assure you that there is a way to prevail," Rick said.

"Really? Tell that to Billie. He played your game, took all your tests, went to your groups. What did he get for his trouble? A green light where his brain used to be!"

"You're right Michael, what happened to Billie was unfortunate. You are still here however. You still have a chance to save your life. Are you willing to do that? Because you're on the edge of the ledge yourself, your last incident with inmate Roberts was your second strike. I went to case conference yesterday, and my boss was pressuring me to send you to Modification right now. So if you are going to give up I would like to know. I don't need the grief I get for trying to save you if you don't care."

Michael looked up at Rick. He could see the concern on Rick's face.

"I also feel bad about what happened to Billie," Rick continued. "But the fact is, you can't let your grief cause you to suffer the same fate. Sometimes life isn't fair. That's messed up. But that's the way it is. If you've lost all hope you might as well write your girlfriend right now. Tell her to have a nice life without you."

"I don't know what to do," Michael half screamed and half cried. "Nothing I do seems to work. I get into trouble no matter what I do."

"Good, that's a start. Admitting there is a problem with your approach to life is something that we can work with. The same way we worked on different ways to deal with your anger. You're not a Mod yet. So use the brain you have to work on getting out of here alive."

"I can do that," Michael said.

"Then we need to come up with a plan. First of all, what is the single thing that you believe will undermine you in the future, going forward? In other words, what will be your biggest problem, or most difficult situation to deal with without getting into trouble?"

"Zack Cole." Michael looked directly at Rick as he spoke.

"Tell me about Zack, what do you mean?" Rick asked.

"He is the reason I got sent to Ad-Seg."

"How was he involved, I thought the incident was with inmate Roberts?"

"It was, but Roberts is one of Zack's boys. He was just the fool that got used by Zack."

"Can you prove that?" Rick asked.

"No, but I'm pretty damn sure. Someone took Liz's picture out of my cell. Roberts had it, but I have been watching Zack. He seems to want to try to set guys up to get into trouble so they get sent to Modification." Michael shifted in his chair, trying to judge whether or not Rick believed him.

"Right, you called him out on that in one of your groups, didn't you?" Rick's eyes lit up as he looked at Michael.

"Yes." Michael said, as he felt relieved that he was acknowledged.

"So how is he going to be a problem for you?" Rick leaned back in his chair as he pursued Michael's line of thinking.

"I want to get even with him. I want to do something to him, to punish him for setting me up, and for messing with my personal property." Michael became animated as he talked about his plans.

"So what would you ordinarily do to get even?"

Michael felt like Rick was supporting him, but he suddenly felt on the defensive. "I don't know, in the past I would probably fight him, try to beat him up. But after you showed me how to deal with people with words I might try to mess with him in group again. I'm not sure right now."

"Do you always get even?"

"Not always, like with my brother Ryan, but most of the time with other people." Michael felt ashamed as he realized just how much power Ryan had over him.

"Have you ever let something go, just move past it, decided to focus on other things, set different priorities?" Rick leaned forward toward Michael.

"No," Michael said, as he leaned in toward Rick. "How could I?"

"Here's the problem. If you focus on getting even, then you are giving the power to Zack. He can control your life, and maybe your destiny. If you shift your focus to something different, like your own self-control, then you are the one who will control your destiny. Right now your goal is revenge. It should be getting sent to Rehabilitation. Don't let Zack be in charge of your focus."

"Right, I think I understand." Michael sat back as he considered what Rick had said. Was it possible for him to see the world differently? Could he do it in time?

"So let's work on some ways to control your anger, diminish your need for revenge, and stay focused on your most important goals."

"Alright, so how do we do that?"

"Well, the anger management training is fairly straight forward. It is basically an extension of many of the things we have already been working on. We just need to incorporate some more methods of diverting your emotions into positive actions. Setting goals is an ongoing process. Naturally the first goal at this point is to make it to Rehabilitation. If you can manage to stay out of any more fights then we may be able to reach that goal."

Michael smirked and looked away as he realized how silly he had been acting by fighting all the time.

"The tricky part is to diminish your need for revenge. Revenge is a very powerful human emotion." Rick said. He watched Michael nodding his head in understanding.

45

The cockroach measured about two and a half inches long and one and a half inches wide. It moved up the wall in measured staccato-like increments. It scanned the environment sensing the air, hunting for food and wary of predators.

Michael watched the roach in amazement. He marveled at the rich caramel colored armor encasing the bug. Its symmetrically spaced legs provided perfect balance and incredible mobility. The roach was making its way up the wall near the front of his cell. Michael leaned over his bunk and picked up his shoe. He launched it at the cockroach. The roach moved to the right just as Michael released the shoe, so it did not hit it flush. Instead it glanced off the roach and sent the bug flying through the bars of the cell where it landed onto the tier walkway, essentially unharmed. The shoe bounced off the cell bars and landed on the floor. The roach turned in a circle as if to check on all of its parts. Then it scurried off down the walkway and out of Michael's sight.

Michael sat up and checked the time on the digital clock built into the bunk's data reader. It was almost eleven o'clock. Today was a special Saturday for him. He was going see Liz. She was home from college for the weekend and promised that she would visit him. Michael had not had a visitor since he arrived in Chino six and a half weeks ago. He was excited and anxious.

He pulled her picture out of his pocket where he kept it at all times now. He looked at it and felt his throat tighten up, and his eyes filling with tears. It had been almost five months since that night at her graduation party. Things seemed so simple then. They were in love and had a bright future. Now he was on the verge of being Modified and they could only see each other in the prison.

Michael's cell door began to open and he heard an announcement telling him he had a visitor. His heart leapt as he jumped up and headed toward the stairs.

Visiting was held either inside a large hall, or weather permitting, outside in a grassy area with picnic tables. Since the weather was nice, it would be held outside today.

Both the inmates and the visitors had to endure full body scans. The inmates were scanned both before and after their visits, and they had to strip down. The visitors were limited to what they could bring into the visiting area. Most of them brought only digital vouchers to buy food out of the vending machines. To inmates, that food was a real treat.

Michael got in line to have his body scanned. He stripped down and put his clothes into a box. They went through a separate scanner. He walked through the scanner and retrieved his clothing. There was a staging area where the inmates redressed prior to being released to the visiting area. Kevin was in the staging area. He evidently got visits from his family. As with everything else in prison, it seemed to take forever to be released to the visiting yard. At last a custody officer called his name. Michael went to the door.

"Taylor, table twenty-five," the officer said.

Michael walked outside into the sun. He closed his eyes and lifted his face to feel the warmth of the sun. He remained still for a moment and took a deep breath. Then he opened his eyes and looked around the yard. The tables were arranged in four long rows of twelve tables each. There were people everywhere, talking, and hugging. He deciphered the numbering system and headed down the middle row. As he neared the end of the row, he spotted her.

Liz rose from her seat and smiled at him as their eyes locked. She looked beautiful. She was dressed casually as required of visitors. Black slacks and a sweatshirt, with her hair pulled back. Michael felt numb as he went to her and put his hands on her shoulders.

"Hello Michael," she said.

"Hi Liz."

They hugged each other, and then sat on opposite sides of the picnic tables as was required. They held each other's hands. Her hands felt warm and soft. Michael could not take his eyes off her, nor could he stop smiling.

"Thank you for coming to see me," Michael said.

Liz smiled at him and squeezed his hands. Michael had a million questions, but felt content to just hold her hands. Her presence always had such a calming effect on him. Finally he spoke up.

"How's college?" he asked.

"It's okay, it takes some getting used to, you know. As I told you in my e-mails I'm living in a dorm."

There was a question burning in his mind about whether or not she was dating anyone, but he promised himself he would not ask that. "How are your parents?" Michael asked, while what he was really thinking was, "Do they want you to stay away from me? Are they freaked out you are coming into a prison to see me?"

"They're okay, you know, mom is busy with her charity work, and dad with his business. I don't really talk to them much now because I am away at school."

Michael looked at her as the sun reflected off of her auburn hair, and her blue green eyes were shining. She was smiling at him, looking right into his eyes, trustingly. She seemed like the same Liz he always knew.

"I'm sorry you have to come here, to see me like this," Michael said.

"Don't worry," she said. "I just hope you make it to Rehabilitation. The Modification program has been in the news a lot lately. You know they want to expand, it and some people want to do away with Rehabilitation altogether."

"That would be bad, if they expanded it," Michael said. "Have you seen a Mod up close yet?"

"Yes actually," Liz said. "My parents got one to help around the house. I saw him when I came home yesterday. He was only recently Modified. His name is Billie."

Michael could not believe what he was hearing; he thought his head was going to explode. It couldn't be.

"Billie, what does he look like?" Michael asked as he almost jumped out of his seat.

"What do you mean?" Liz asked as she was startled by Michael's dramatic reaction. "He looks like a guy. I don't know. What does it matter?"

"It might matter to me." Michael had become animated. He noticed a custody officer taking notice of him. He gathered himself and leaned forward now speaking in a measured but somewhat strained voice. "The cellie I had, that I wrote to you about. His name was Billie. I never told you his name because they don't allow us to talk about other inmates in our letters. My cellie was Billie and he was recently sent to Modification."

"Oh no," Liz gasped. "Michael, I'm so sorry."

"Is he a white guy, about five feet eight or so, muscular, with blue eyes, and tattoos on his neck and arms?"

"Maybe, I only saw him once. He kind of fits that description Michael. I'm so sorry about your cellie. You hadn't told me."

"It just happened when I was in lock-up last week. He was gone when I got back to the unit."

Michael looked at Liz. He was upset now. He knew it wasn't her fault, but he was confused about what to do. He tried to lighten the mood. He didn't want his time with Liz to be completely ruined. Michael took some deep breathes and counted to four. When he gathered himself he smiled at Liz again.

"Let's talk about something else, okay?" he asked. "Tell me more about life at college."

"Well, I like my classes. The teachers are dedicated and the other students are all serious about learning. It's not like high school were you have half of the students sleeping, and the other half texting their friends." Liz smiled at Michael.

He could tell she was trying to lighten the mood, but he was having trouble getting Billie off his mind. The rest of the visit was like a dream for Michael. The moment he had anticipated for weeks had been spoiled. Finally the visit was over. Michael and Liz hugged each other goodbye.

"Keep writing if you can," Michael said. "It means a lot to me."

"I will," Liz said smiling. "Don't quit on me Michael Taylor. I'm counting on you."

"Of course not."

Michael watched Liz until she was completely outside the gate. Then he headed back to the inmate staging area. On the way he passed by Kevin and his family. It looked like both his parents and a brother had come to visit him. Liz's comments about no more Rehabilitation came to mind as he watched them interact. They looked just like any other family spending time together. He wondered what Billie's family was doing now.

After clearing the second scan he headed back to the unit. Michael was angry. He decided he was not going to end up as someone's house zombie or serving eggs on a prison steam line. He was hoping his visit with Liz would lift his spirits to give him some motivation. It had not gone exactly as planned, but he was motivated. He decided he was going to get tough, to be resilient and adaptive, like the cockroach.

46

The world seemed a little different this morning, a little colder. Michael was still reeling from the realization that Billie was a Mod in Liz's home. He did not sleep much and barely touched his breakfast. His sack lunch sat on top of his locker. He had not bothered to check the contents. He was supposed to report to group therapy in twenty minutes, but he could barely get himself motivated. His resolve to be like the cockroach was already dissolving, he was depressed.

In his head he knew he could not afford to be depressed. He was on the bubble as it was. Non-participation in group could be the last straw. Feeling sorry for himself was a lousy reason to allow himself to become a Mod.

As he lie on his bunk trying to talk himself into getting up his cell door began to open. Surprised, he sat up. A man appeared in the doorway carrying a bag of personal items. He entered the cell and looked down at Michael.

"My name is Tyrone," the man said. "I've been assigned to this cell."

Michael blinked his eyes in disbelief. He was totally taken off guard. He had no idea they were going to give him a new cellie, especially so soon.

"Hi, my name is Michael. The top bunk is yours, and the locker on the right." Michael pointed out Tyrone's locker.

"Okay Michael," Tyrone said. He threw his bag into his locker and turned to watch the cell door close behind him. For a moment he stood and stared out, surveying the unit. Then he turned and looked at Michael, somewhat expectantly.

Michael watched Tyrone with curiosity. He was a young black man of medium build with short hair. He had fine features and was muscular. He looked worried.

"Did you just arrive in Chino?" Michael asked.

"Yeah, I just got off the bus an hour ago."

Michael stood up and extended his hand to Tyrone.

"Then, welcome to the party," Michael said.

Tyrone shook his hand. He had a firm grip but he didn't try to crush Michael's hand. Michael smiled at Tyrone, then turned and put on his shoes.

"I have to go to group now," Michael said. "Did they give you a lunch?"

"Yeah, it's in my bag."

"Your first day you don't do much, you will just be hanging out here in the cell until tomorrow morning. You will get a schedule every morning. It will show up here on the data reader. They feed us dinner in the cell, which will come later, another sack meal, just chill for now. Like I said, I have to go to a group."

The cell door began to move again and an announcement on the P.A. system told inmates with ten o'clock appointments to come out of their cells. Michael walked out of the cell and headed to group. He had completely forgotten about being depressed for a moment. As he headed to group, he decided it didn't make a lot of sense to bring himself down. The arrival of Tyrone had energized him. His presence had made Michael get out of bed and face the day. He was ready to fight on again, but he would not forget.

He arrived at the group room ahead of most of the other inmates so he found a seat and waited for their arrival. Victor and his shadow Kevin came in and sat on Michael's right. Victor was next to Michael. He reached out and put his hand on Michael's shoulder.

"Sorry about Billie," Victor said.

Michael felt himself begin to tear up, but he stopped himself.

"Thanks," Michael said. "I got a new cellie today, his name is Tyrone."

"Wow, that was quick," Kevin said.

Zack Cole entered the group room. He sneered at Michael and took a seat on the opposite side in the circle of chairs.

"Make sure to warn him about that snake," Victor said as he glared at Zack.

Michael nodded to Victor as he returned Zack's sneer. The rest of the group members arrived and took their seats, and then Ms.

Atkins arrived. She made Michael smile as she burst into the room in her usual energetic style.

"Good day everyone," Ms. Atkins said as she took her seat and waved to the custody officer to wait outside.

"Good morning Ms. Atkins," the men responded as a group.

"Now let's see who's here today. It doesn't look as if we have any new people today so we can forego the introductions. Who would like to go first today, any volunteers?"

On impulse Michael decided to speak up. "I would just like to let everyone know that Billie was sent to Modification. I just thought we should say something about that."

"You are referring to Billie Johnson? He was your cellie, correct Michael?" Ms. Atkins asked.

"Yes, Billie Johnson, my cellie."

"That was very unfortunate, I was sorry to hear about it. I thought he was doing well," Ms. Atkins said.

"I guess not well enough," Victor said.

"Well then, what is well enough?" Kevin asked. "Didn't get into no fights or nothing, he got along well. What are we to think of that? What did he do to get sent to Modification?"

"It's a difficult process and a difficult decision," Ms. Atkins said.

"He had Dr. Isaac, that's what he did wrong." It was Charlie Smith speaking up now. Charlie had been on the unit as long as Michael, but had been assigned to a different group until last week. He was in for check fraud and assigned to Dr. Isaac's caseload.

Everyone looked at Charlie after he spoke up. He was a heavy white guy with long greasy hair and a scraggly mustache. He had some trouble with one of the guys in the other group and went to Ad-Seg for a week. That is why he was moved into Michael's group. He was pretty quiet the first week, and he surprised everyone by speaking up now, especially by pointing a finger at Dr. Isaac.

"Now, we are not here to talk about staff. Let's keep focused on ourselves," Ms. Atkins said.

"I am focused on myself," Charlie said. "I'm afraid I will be the next one Dr. Isaac has sent to Modification, especially since I just went to Ad-Seg. Everyone knows he sends more people to Modification that anyone else."

Michael was watching Zack as the conversation went on. He seemed to be squirming in his seat but he remained quiet.

"Billie told me Dr. Isaac felt he was not smart enough to benefit from Rehabilitation," Michael said.

"I know it is difficult to see someone sent to Modification," Ms. Atkins said. "Especially someone you know, or someone you feel close to. The truth is that everyone, even myself, must come to terms with it. Blaming Dr. Isaac is not going to bring Billie back. It will also not help you stay out of Modification. Only focusing on your own program can do that."

"That's bullshit," Charlie said. "Working my program won't mean shit to Dr. Isaac. He will still ship us off to Modification." Charlie had become agitated and was now standing up with his fists clenched. His face was red, and he was spitting as he talked. The two inmates on either side of Charlie tried to move away from him by leaning in the other direction in their chairs.

Ms. Atkins pushed her alarm and the custody officer entered the group room. He looked at Charlie who looked like an over-inflated balloon, ready to burst. The officer asked Charlie to return to his seat. Charlie looked at the custody officer and then squealed like a banshee. He lowered he head and ran full speed at the officer.

The officer was a blur he moved so quickly. In the blink of an eye Charlie was thrown to the floor and hand cuffed. Then the code one response team showed up. They instructed all the other inmates to lie on their stomachs on the floor while they removed Charlie from the group room. After they left Ms. Atkins told the men to recover to their seats.

"Well, I guess this is a very emotional topic," Ms. Atkins said. "Who can tell me a relaxation technique Charlie could have used instead of losing his temper like that?"

"I can," Zack Cole said.

47

Rick sat in his office. He was looking at Runners' Update Magazine on his computer. He enjoyed reading about the latest training techniques and nutritional supplements. The older he got, the more he was interested in the supplements. However, he didn't think they stopped him from getting older and slower. His only consolation was that his marathon times were comparable to other runners in his age group. That lessened the blow a little bit. He reviewed the local marathon schedule for Southern California and noted several runs of interest. The knock on his door startled him.

"Dr. Carson," Ms. Atkins stood in the doorway.

Rick stood up, "Hello Susan," her smile lit up the room. "Come on in, have a seat. What can I do for you?"

Ms. Atkins took a seat and crossed her legs. "Well, we have a few minutes before case conference, so I thought I would talk to you about Michael Taylor."

"Sure," Rick sat down.

She leaned forward talking quietly, almost in a whisper, she said, "I'm a little worried about him. He seems like such a genuine guy, not really antisocial. I'm worried his cellie Billie being sent to Modification might put him over the edge. Cause him to do something that will get him sent to Modification himself."

"Has something happened?"

"Not yet, but in my group he brought up what happened to Billie. He seemed upset, and then the group members started to blame Dr. Isaac for having Billie Modified. They accused Dr. Isaac of sending people to Modification unnecessarily. Michael actually seemed somewhat disassociated, he said he thought we should talk about the fact that Billie was sent to Mod. Maybe I'm making too much of it, I don't know. I know you've been working with him so I thought I would let you know."

"Thank you, I appreciate your concern. I will meet with him soon. We haven't really had an opportunity to completely process what happened yet. What do you think about what they said regarding Dr. Isaac?"

"I think they have a legitimate concern, and they're angry about it. In fact I had to call custody to remove one of the guys from the group because he got so angry talking about it. He actually charged one of the officers and was taken down. He's on the Doctor's caseload and said he felt hopeless trying to do well. He believed Dr. Isaac would send him regardless of his behavior."

"Do you think Michael instigated something?"

"No, initially he seemed genuinely interested in talking about Billie. I think the inmates' problem with Isaac has a life of its' own."

"Yes it does, doesn't it? In fact I think the whole issue of how many inmates we send to Modification seems to have taken on a life of its own."

"I heard Dr. Brayden ordered an audit of your work."

"Yes he has. I'm not concerned, but the purpose of the audit seemed related to a whole undercurrent of pressure to refer more people to Modification."

Just then Dean appeared in Rick's doorway.

"Knock, knock," Dean said.

Rick and Ms. Atkins both looked up at him. As usual he was dressed impeccably. He had a smile on his face like a Cheshire cat. Dean always perked up around Susan Atkins. He had a schoolboy crush on her.

"Hello Susan," Dean said.

"Hello Dean," Ms. Atkins said.

"We're talking about Susan's group," Rick said. "The group members got upset today because they think Dr. Isaac is sending men to Modification, regardless of how well they do in the evaluation process."

"Really?" Dean asked, as he looked at Rick with a raised eyebrow.

"One inmate got so angry, he attacked a custody officer," Ms. Atkins said. "Now he's almost surely going to be Modified."

"Nasty business," Dean said. "What do you think is going on with Dr. Isaac?" Dean asked while looking at Ms. Atkins.

"I don't know for sure, but I have been uncomfortable in our case conferences on several occasions. I felt like Dr. Brayden and Dr. Isaac were pushing cases through to Modification, you know, without giving the guys their due process."

Dr. Brayden walked past Rick's door and stopped briefly to look inside at the group. They all stopped talking and stared at him.

"Time for case conference," Dr. Brayden said. Then he turned and walked down the hallway toward the conference room.

Rick, Dean and Ms. Atkins all looked at each other apprehensively.

"Perhaps we should go to our meeting," Dean said.

"Right, let's go," Rick said. They all headed out the door and made their way to the conference room.

When they entered the room, they found seats next to each other. Dean managed to push his way past Rick so he could sit next to Ms. Atkins.

Dr. Brayden opened the meeting with his usual dryness while reviewing statistics. What should have been a banal exercise had taken on new energy and significance lately for Rick.

"Dr. Carson, it appears your referral rate has stayed relatively stable over the past six weeks," Dr. Brayden said as he looked at Rick with a cold stare.

"Evidently that's true from the data you just read," Rick said. "I would imagine that shows consistency in my work. I believe that's a good thing, don't you think?" Rick asked as he returned Dr. Brayden's stare.

"I guess we'll have to wait and see what the audit says before I respond to that comment," Dr. Brayden said. Then he moved on to case reviews.

Rick sat back in his chair and stole a glance at Dean. They both remained quiet as they listened to Dr. Isaac review his cases. He was talking about the report he just received on the incident in Ms. Atkins group. He said he was sending Charlie Smith to Modification.

48

Liz rolled over in her bed and gazed toward the window. The curtains were drawn but the sun shone brightly behind them illuminating her room. She threw back her comforter and rose to shower and dress. Her visit with Michael yesterday had not gone quite like she expected. She had been looking forward to seeing him, and had been anxious about how he would receive her. She didn't know what life in prison would do to change him. Would he still be her precious Michael? She had always enjoyed the way he kept upbeat despite his challenging life. She loved his handsome smile and the attention he showered on her, even though she didn't require it. She was upset that the tone of their visit had been colored by the news about Billie.

The whole issue of Modification had not felt real to her before that. She always assumed that Michael would come back to her and they would move on with their lives. Now she had serious doubts.

As she stood in the shower with hot water spraying her face, she made a decision. She would look into the anti-Modification movement. They had been on her college campus passing out literature, but she had not paid attention. Now she got it, she understood what they stood for. They had family or friends turned into robot slaves, and they were attempting to save others from the same fate.

After her shower she went downstairs to have breakfast. It was Sunday and both her parents were home. She knew they were waiting for her in the dining room. As she walked down the hallway she glanced out a window and saw Billie. He was outside by the pool helping the gardener. He was dressed in blue clothes and moved methodically, planting shrubs along the fence. She paused to watch him, recalling Michael's description of him. How he loved country music and his upbeat attitude. None of that was evident as he robotically dug into the soil. Then he turned and faced Liz. The green light on his forehead blinked and his vacant eyes locked onto hers. Liz opened the patio door and walked outside. She walked over to Billie and stood in front of him.

"Hello Billie," she said.

"Hello," Billie replied in a monotone voice.

"My name is Liz. I'm a friend of Michael Taylor's. Do you know Michael?"

"Hello Liz." Billie did not respond to the question about Michael.

The gardener noticed Liz talking to Billie. "Can I help you with something Miss Liz?" he asked.

"No thank you," Liz replied.

The gardener shook his head and turned back to trimming the bush he was working on. He kept a wary eye on Liz and Billie.

"I hear you like country music Billie. Would you like to hear some?" Liz asked.

Billie continued his blank stare.

Liz manipulated the sleeve of her smart wear sweater and country music began to play from the speaker on her sleeve. At first there was no response from Billie. But then the second song began to play. "Mama don't let your sons, grow up to be cowboys," the music played.

A small smile began to form on Billie's face, and Liz could swear she saw a flicker of light in the back of his eyes. Then just as quickly as it appeared, the smile disappeared. Billie turned away from Liz and began to rake the dirt at his feet. Tears began to form in Liz's eyes. She put her hand on his shoulder and gave him a squeeze. Then she turned and went back into the house. She shut the patio door and took a last look at Billie.

Liz realized that the Billie Michael had told her about no longer existed. She turned away and moved toward her parents who were in the dining room.

"Liz sweetheart, there you are. Are you alright? You look a little pale?" Liz's mother gave her a hug. "It's so good to have you home."

"Good morning Elizabeth," her father said as he lowered his data pad.

Liz went over and kissed him. "Good morning Dad," she said.

Liz took a seat with her back to the window, so she could not see Billie. She began to serve herself some food from the platters on the table. Her father folded his newspaper and set it down turning his attention to Liz.

"So tell me, how's college life?" He asked.

Rosie the kitchen maid entered the room and looked at Liz. "Good morning Miss Liz," she said. "Would you like something to drink?"

"Orange juice please," Liz said. "College is fine Dad. There is so much going on, it can be a distraction, but I try to stay focused."

"Good girl," her father said.

Just then the family butler entered the room. "Sir, your guests have arrived," he said.

"Good, thank you," her father said. Then he rose to go meet his guests. "Duty calls," he said. He kissed Liz's mother and Liz, and disappeared through the dining room door to the front of the house.

When they were alone, Liz asked her mother about Billie. "Mom, when did you decide to get a Mod? Did you know that he was Michael's cell mate?"

Her mother put her fork down and stared at her plate. Quietly she spoke, "It was your father's idea. I am not very comfortable around him myself. And, no, I didn't know Michael knew him, that's horrible. Does he know he's here?"

"Yes, I accidently told him during my visit yesterday."

"This whole Modification business is getting very contentious. Your father is one of the people who want more prisoners Modified, anyone who commits a crime in fact. He believes the free labor they will provide can reinvigorate the economy. That's why he wants a Mod here. It's to show his support for the program. The people he's meeting with right now are also in favor of that idea. They've formed a political action committee to support politicians who are pushing for comprehensive Modification of all criminals. The next election will be between the pro-Modification and anti-Modification candidates. The outcome will have a significant effect on the country and anyone who is convicted of a crime."

Liz gripped her cutlery hard and sat back in her chair. She felt nauseous. "How could he support that?"

"He feels very strongly about it. He says that Rehabilitation puts an unnecessary financial burden on taxpayers."

"But it's just like slavery was in the 19th century. It's horrible! Look at Billie, he's like a robot." Liz angrily pointed out of the window toward Billie who was now raking up dead leaves.

Her mother nervously bit her bottom lip as she looked at Liz. "I'm sorry dear, but your father is adamant about this."

Liz could see a look of resignation on her mother's face. For the first time she realized the sacrifice her mother had made to be with her father. To be subservient, to make his needs and wants take precedence. Her mother would not speak up against him, but Liz could.

"Well maybe I will also be adamant about it, but I'm against it. I can't stay here with him in the house. You can let Daddy know. I'm going back to school."

Liz stood up, as she stormed out of the dining room she ran smack into Gavin Jordan, the CEO of Ardent Corporation.

"Whoa there little lady," Jordan said. "Slow down a little."

Liz just looked at him, and then turned and ran up the stairs to collect her things. Her father watched her go. "Sorry about that Gavin," he said. "Come on into my study, and let's have a drink, I have some very good brandy I would like you to try."

49

Rick sat in his office reviewing the video of Ms. Atkins' group session. It showed Michael talking about Billie's Modification. Rick wanted to see how Michael handled himself. He was out on a limb with Michael. He wanted to be sure it was the smart thing to do. Rick was pleased with what he saw. It appeared that the inmate who attacked the guard had his own issues that set him off.

Rick got a call from the desk officer telling him that Michael had arrived for their session. He told the officer to send him back and then turned off the video. Michael appeared at the door.

"Good morning Dr. Carson."

"Come in Michael," Rick said, as he met him at the door. "Have a seat."

"Thanks Doctor," Michael said.

"I'm glad we're meeting today. I know a lot has gone on recently. I wanted to see how you're doing."

Michael took a seat. He crossed his arms and looked at Rick.

"Honestly Doctor Carson I'm not sure how I'm doing. A lot has happened in the last week. It's been confusing."

"You want to tell me about it?"

"My girlfriend Liz finally came to visit me. It turns out her family has Billie working in their home as a Mod."

Rick's eyes got big as he leaned across the desk. "What?" Rick's mouth dropped open and he put his hand over his mouth. "Are you sure?"

"Pretty sure Doctor. I described him, and she was fairly certain it was him. She was surprised when she came home from school. She didn't know they had a Mod until she saw him." Michael clenched his jaw and gripped the arms of the chair.

"Oh Michael, I'm so sorry."

Michael continued to look directly at Rick. "Thanks, but it is what it is. Right now I'm confused. I can't afford to get emotional and all stressed out, but I'm really angry at Liz, and angry at Dr. Isaac, and I didn't want a new cellie."

"That's understandable, Michael." Rick nodded in agreement.

"I feel that I need to focus on my survival." Michael's jaw began to relax, and he released his death grip on the chair. He sat upright and took a deep breath.

"That's true. It's not going to help you to get angry about everything and go off on someone. You are learning how to control your anger. It's done nothing but cause you trouble most of your life." Rick acknowledged Michael's progress.

"I know, at first I was depressed, but then out of the blue a new guy showed up to take Billie's place as my cellie. It shocked me out of my fog. I realized that time marches on and I need to march with it." Michael's arms were flailing about now as he became animated.

"What are you going to do about Liz?"

"I don't know. I need to wait and see if I make it out of here. I don't want to make any rash decisions about her. I may never see her again. If I get dragged off to Modification tomorrow then she will go on with her life. I will stay in contact with her while I can. She has been my source of inspiration the whole time I've been here. I know it wasn't her who Modified Billie, and it wasn't her who brought him into her parent's home." Michael quieted again.

"That's true Michael. Did she say how she is dealing with having a Mod in her home?" Rick urged Michael to continue on despite Michael's obvious discomfort.

"She was upset, especially when she found out it was Billie. She is kind of naive, sheltered, but very sweet and good hearted. She comes from a wealthy family and hasn't seen much, except what her parents have wanted her to see." Michael calmed himself again as he thought about Liz and how much he cared for her.

"So you are still going to write to her?" Rick seemed determined to get the whole story.

"Sure, I still love her and want her to write to me. I feel like I'm going to have a different sense of motivation now. I want to survive for me, and then I can worry about being with her. I was not too concerned about myself, like I should have been. I was reckless and often got myself into trouble. But you knew that, you've seen it firsthand." Michael slumped back into his chair.

"Yes I have. It's good to hear you say this Michael. It could not have come at a better time. To be honest with you, I've taken a lot of heat by not sending you to Modification already. My boss has been pushing for it as I told you before. So it's important that you don't get into any more trouble. If you do, it could be the end for you." Rick looked at Michael, with his brow furrowed.

"I guess I was lucky to be assigned to you Doctor Carson. If I had been assigned to Dr. Isaac, I would have been Modified a long time ago. Thank you for what you've done for me." Michael laughed at himself.

"You're welcome. But let's not be too premature. You aren't on your way to Rehabilitation yet. You still have a lot of work to do and I have a feeling that there will still be some difficult challenges." Rick said, as he smiled at Michael.

"I know. I know that there are people who don't want me to go to Rehabilitation. There are guys who seem to be trying to get others sent to Modification. I will be careful."

"Good for you Michael. I will be here for you if you need anything." Rick stood up to signal that their time had ended.

Michael stood up and extended his hand to Rick. They shook hands, and then Michael headed back to the Unit.

* * * * * * * *

Dayroom program was in progress when Michael got back to the Unit. He went over and sat down with Kevin and Victor. They were playing dominos as usual.

"How much time do you have left in the process Victor?" Michael asked.

"Seventeen days," Victor said. "Testing is done, mostly group and individual meetings now."

"What do you think is gonna happen to you?" Kevin asked.

"I will go on to be rich and famous, of course," Victor laughed.

"At least you have a chance," Kevin said, "being on Dr. Cooper's caseload. And you have one too Michael cause you're on Dr. Carson's. I got fucked. I got put on Dr. Isaac's caseload. He told me right out he didn't have much confidence in my abilities."

Michael and Victor both stopped playing for a moment and stared at Kevin. He had tears in his eyes and was turning a domino over and over in his hand.

"Sometimes I feel like I would rather be dead than to end up as a Mod," Kevin said.

"Don't talk like that Kevin. You are going to make it out. Dr. Isaac doesn't send everyone to Modification. Last week he had two guys go to rehab. There's still hope."

"Not when he tells you outright that you're lame and he doesn't have hope for you. That's what happened to Billie."

"Billie's working as a Mod in my girlfriend Liz's home," Michael blurted out.

"What the fuck!" Victor said. "Are you shittin me?"

"It's true. She told me at her visit. Her parent's brought him into their house. She didn't know because she was away at school. She didn't realize it was Billie until we started to talk about him."

"What are you going to do?" Kevin asked.

"There's not much I can do. I just need to stay focused on my own program, and on getting the fuck out of here in one piece. And that's what you need to do too Kevin. Quit talking that bullshit about being better off dead. Don't quit. There's still hope."

Kevin laid down a domino and looked at Michael. "Sure Michael, there's always hope."

50

Liz sat at the desk in her dorm as she worked on a school assignment. It was a small room that was just large enough for a twin bed, dresser, and desk. She shared a bathroom with the room next to her. Her mind wandered as she thought about how she liked the comforts that having money bought, but she only recently realized the price her mother paid for that lifestyle. Now she had to ask herself if she was willing to go without the luxury her parents' money afforded her. Could she survive on her own if she was to stand up for what she believed in? Her e-mail alert buzzed, and she picked up her data pad to check it. It was from Michael.

As Liz read Michael's e-mail, tears formed in her eyes. She wasn't sure how Michael was going to react to Billie being a Mod in her parents' home. She was glad he wrote to her, but her hands trembled as she read it. This was their first contact since she returned to school.

"Dear Liz," Michael wrote.

"It was great to see you on your visit. I really appreciate you. It has been very hard and painful going through this. Knowing you are there for me has kept me going, kept me alive. I cannot thank you enough for that. I have kept your picture close to my heart, and it has helped me get this far. Knowing Billie is a Mod in your house threw me hard. I'm sorry if I seemed angry at you. I know it was not your doing. But it made me realize there are events in this world that we have no control over, and they can influence our lives. Since I saw you, I have been trying to take more responsibility for myself. To do well for me, not just for you. People tell me I seem different now. I'm not sure exactly what they mean, but I think it is a good thing. I hope you will continue to stick by me. Your support means a lot. Love Michael. xo"

Liz wiped her eyes and laid back sinking into her down pillows. She looked at the ceiling of her dorm room and gazed at the poster of the movie star she had taped there. She felt silly and petty for focusing on such mundane things. Michael was fighting for his life. Meanwhile her father was conspiring with other captains of industry to send him and many other young men to their doom. Just so they could have a free labor force. She must do something.

She felt resolve enter her body like a rapidly flowing river. Her dedication to Michael rose like waves surging upon the shores. She balled her hands into fists and threw back her comforter as she stood up and quickly dressed. She paid no attention to fashion as she grabbed the first slacks and blouse she found. After brushing back her hair, she put on a baseball cap and rinsed out her mouth with mouthwash. Then she ran out of her dorm room and onto the quad.

She knew exactly where they were. She passed the table every day on her way across campus to her second period class. The Anti-Modification League is what they called themselves.

She felt she was moving in fast motion, like a movie sped up to achieve comic effect. She got a couple of curious looks from other students on the quad. She was afraid to slow down because she didn't want to lose her nerve. She just kept moving. Then she started to have doubts. Should she go against her father? What will he do when he finds out?

There were two people sitting at the folding table with a video screen showing Mods at work. Liz stopped in front of the table and breathed heavily as she paused to catch her breath. The man and woman sitting in the folding chairs stared at her wide eyed. He had a full beard and long dark hair, and was dressed in older clothes, a hoodie jacket and jeans. The woman looked older than most students. She had long blond hair and was dressed in the latest data wear. She had sad eyes, but an engaging smile.

"Can I help you, dear?" the woman asked.

Liz stared at her. She looked down at the table and picked up one of the brochures. She opened it and read it. It had a picture of a Mod. The caption read, "What if this was your son, your husband, or your brother?" Liz noticed the green light on the Mod's forehead and his blank eyes. He reminded her of Billie.

"His name is Martin," the woman said. "He is my nephew."

"Sorry," Liz said sheepishly.

The woman walked around to the front of the table and longingly looked at the picture of her nephew. "We don't know what happened to him. We aren't sure where they sent him. After someone is Modified, the family is cut off. They don't want anyone trying to rescue them or getting crazy with the owners. All you get is this picture to verify they have gone through the process."

"How horrible," Liz said. She put her hand over her mouth, disgusted by what she heard.

"We're trying to put an end to all that," the man spoke up. "We're working toward changing the law. We think there are better ways to lead the country back to economic health."

Liz looked at the man, curiously, "How will you do that?"

"We're a ground roots organization that is supporting politicians who are actively against Modification. We also organize demonstrations and distribute literature like that handout," he said as he tipped his head toward the handout Liz was holding.

"Do you know someone who was Modified?" the woman asked.

"Yes," Liz said quietly as she stared at the picture of the Mod.

"My name is Alice. Would you like to join our organization?" the woman asked.

Liz looked at the woman and smiled, "Yes, I think I would."

"Good for you dear," the woman said. She reached out and hugged Liz. Liz grabbed onto her and squeezed her as though her life depended on it, or Michael's life did.

51

The next morning after chemistry class, Liz made her way off campus to a small house on Bradbury Street. She knocked on the door and waited. Alice O'Neil, the woman Liz met at the anti-Modification table opened the door and greeted her with a smile.

"Hello Liz," Alice said as she stepped aside and waved Liz inside.

Liz entered the foyer of the small home and immediately felt a sense of comfort. It didn't have many of the new technological trappings like most modern homes. Pictures of Alice and her family adorned the walls of the foyer. The smell of freshly baked bread wafted through the home like a morning fog. Liz had immediate flashbacks to her grandmother's home. The scent of freshly baked bread always permeated her home. Her mouth watered as she recalled the taste of her grandmother's pumpkin bread with allspice and walnuts. Liz's grandmother had passed the summer before Liz started high school. Her mother did not bake, so she had not smelled such aromas in years.

Alice led her back to a kitchen area where there was a small table pushed against the wall with three chairs around it. "Have a seat Liz."

Liz took a seat and looked up at several photographs hanging on the wall. She recognized a picture of Alice's nephew Martin, the boy who was Modified. It looked like it was from a couple of years ago based on his age. He was smiling and waving, playing with his dog, an Irish Setter who appeared to be chasing a ball.

"You might recognize Martin," Alice said. "Those were happier times obviously. It's a heck of a price we are paying for the economy."

Alice set a plate of freshly baked and cut French bread on the table, along with some apricot jam that looked homemade. She placed plates and cutlery on the table for herself and Liz.

"Would you like some tea?"

"Yes, thank you," Liz replied.

Alice served cups of hot chamomile tea, and then sat down next to Liz as she placed a dispenser of honey on the table. "So tell me about yourself Liz?"

"What would you like to know?" Liz was feeling comfortable with Alice, but she wasn't sure what she would be doing for the group.

"Well, I'm assuming you're a student since I met you on the campus, correct?"

"Yes, I'm a student. I'm a freshman." Liz took a sip of tea and served herself a piece of bread and apricot jam. She took a bite of the bread and jam, the warmth of the bread and the flavor of the fruit caressed her tongue, "This is delicious."

Alice watched her and patiently waited while Liz enjoyed her snack. "I believe you said your boyfriend was at an Evaluation Center?"

"Yes, his name is Michael. He's at the Chino center. He's been there for a couple of months now. His former cellie, Billie, was Modified and my father has him working in our home. It's terrifying and disgusting at the same time. I can't bear to be there while he's in the house." Liz put her cup on the table, suddenly she lost her appetite. "Talking about it is very upsetting."

"Really, you have a Mod working in your home?" Alice sat up straight. "Your father must be an important man. I understand only a select few have been given Mods in their homes."

"I guess so," Liz said.

"What does he do?"

"He's a banker. He is also active politically with the Total Modification group. You know, the people who want all criminals Modified. So no one would have any chance of Rehabilitation." Liz looked directly at Alice as she spoke. Alice looked amazed at what she was hearing.

"Wow," Alice sat back. "So what would he say if he knew you were working with our group?"

"I'm sure he would be very upset." Liz stared into her cup of tea, "He would be very upset." She had never defied her father. She had not even had the courage to tell him how upset she was about Billie.

Alice watched her struggle with her thoughts and took a drink of her tea. "Are you sure you're up to this?"

Liz looked up at Alice. She could see Alice was having doubts about her. It made sense, after all, she was having doubts about herself. "Yes, I'm sure."

"Alright," Alice said. "We can start you out with something simple like working the table on campus, and handing out fliers. We'll see how you do and how that feels for you." Alice stood up and walked over to a table in the corner of the room. She returned with a stack of anti-Modification information fliers which she handed to Liz. "Here, take these and pass them out on campus. I will check the schedule and e-mail you the times you will work the table. I will also need your class schedule. What's your e-mail address?"

Liz wrote down her e-mail address and then took the fliers. She sat back looking at them. She looked up and saw the picture of Alice's nephew glaring back at her. He reminded her of Billie. "Okay," she said. "I will wait to hear from you."

"I have another meeting soon, so I have to go now Liz, but I want you to know that I am glad to have you on board with us." Alice stood up and Liz followed suit. Alice gave Liz a hug and then gently guided her toward the front door.

As she left Alice's home and made her way back toward campus, Liz felt a new sense of purpose. She was glad she was going to help Michael and the other people who faced Modification.

* * * * * * * *

Alice watched through the window of her den as Liz walked away. Alice turned away and touched her sleeve to make a vid phone connection. The face of a man appeared in front of her. It was Frank Capreti, the leader of the Anti-Modification movement in the southern part of the state.

"Hello Alice," Frank said.

"Hi Frank, I wanted to let you know that I just had a very interesting chat with one of our new recruits. She told me her father is an influential banker, who actually has a Mod working in their home. She said her father is also connected to a political group working to get the total Modification candidate elected."

"Wow, that's huge."

"I know."

"Are you sure she's not a spy?"

"Pretty sure, but I will check her out. In the meantime, I plan to groom her for something much bigger than handing out pamphlets."

"Good thinking Alice. She might be able to get us some Intel on her father's group."

"I will keep you apprised Frank, gotta go now, talk to you later." Alice touched her sleeve and the hologram of Frank disappeared. Then she went to her computer and started an information search on Liz and her father.

52

The next morning as Liz made her way to her class, Alice watched from across the street. When Liz disappeared from sight, Alice made her way into Liz's dormitory. Alice had already searched the university files to determine the location of Liz's room.

Alice carried a box of pastries so as not to draw undue attention to herself. She avoided eye contact with the young women walking through the hallways of the dorm as she made her way to Liz's room. She made a special effort to avoid the floor supervisor as she let herself into Liz's room by picking the lock. It was a skill Frank taught her. He said you never knew when such a talent might come in handy.

She shut the door behind her and quickly scanned the room to be sure she was alone. Then she shut the curtains so she would not be seen from outside the building. She also shut the door to the bathroom Liz's room shared with an adjoining room. She did not want the student from the other room to disturb her, so she also jammed a chair up against the bathroom door.

Alice noted that the room was tidy but sparsely decorated. Students did not devote much energy to sprucing up dorm rooms because they were usually moved to a new room at the end of each term.

Alice quickly examined the contents of Liz's desk and notebooks that were accessible. She found nothing remarkable. She found Liz's data pad and turned it on. It was password protected. She plugged a thumb drive into the data pad. It contained a pass code decoder program. She started the program and waited for it to do its magic. In a few minutes the screen lit up as the password was decoded.

She spent about thirty minutes going through the data pad. When she finished she removed the thumb drive and replaced the data pad where she found it. She put the room back in order and let herself out, taking the pastries with her. After she had made her way back to the street, she tossed the pastries and pulled out a cell phone. She did not want to use a vid phone because she wanted the conversation to be private. She did not want to chance anyone overhearing her. She rang Frank and he answered immediately.

"Well, what did you find?" Frank asked.

"She appears to be genuine," Alice answered. "And her father is who she said he is. I think our Ms. Liz can be a huge asset for us."

"Interesting," Frank said. "Okay, get close to her while we figure out how to work this."

"Okay."

"Are you sure you're alright with this plan?"

"Yes, I just think of my nephew when I have any doubts. Besides, her heart is in this. I am just helping her find her voice."

"Okay Alice, but be careful."

Alice hung up and made her way to the University commons area.

53

Over the next two weeks Alice rarely left Liz's side. She kept Liz very busy handing out pamphlets, attending rallies, and meeting members of the inside circle of the anti-Modification movement. Frank told Alice he was very pleased with how close they had become.

Today was going to be a big day for the movement. The governor was going to be in town and the movement had a protest rally planned. Liz was excited about being there. She was scheduled to be one of the speakers. She was going to talk about her experience with Billie, and about how Michael was fighting for his life.

Liz sat at a card table in a warehouse and reviewed her notes for the speech. All around her people busied themselves as they prepared for the rally. They readied pamphlets and signs, and prepared a microphone for the speeches. Frank advertised the rally on social media sites. Alice walked up to Liz and put her hand on her shoulder.

"Are you ready?" Alice asked.

"I think so. I'm a little nervous, but I'll be okay."

"Good, just remember that I'll be right next to you. If you need anything, just let me know."

Liz stood up and hugged Alice. She squeezed her tightly. Alice was nine years older than Liz, and had become the big sister Liz always wanted. She had become very attached to her.

"Let's load up, people." Frank yelled out. He waved his arms to indicate they should all begin to head to the rally.

Liz rode with Alice and Frank. They carried some microphone equipment with them. Liz sat in the back. She looked out the window of the hover car as they made their way downtown to the Governor's hotel. She wondered if her father would be at the hotel meeting with the Governor. His friends used money and business influence to make their point. The anti-Modification group was short on both of those. The Governor had not committed publicly on the issue of Modifying all criminals. That is why they were having the rally. They wanted to show him that there was a lot of social support against the idea.

They reached the hotel, parked and made their way to the demonstration site. The police had set up an area to use for the demonstration. It was across the street from the hotel. Alice grabbed Liz's hand as they made their way to the stage. Liz squeezed it and smiled at Alice.

There was a good-sized crowd which pleased Frank. "It looks like a great turnout," he said as he began to walk quickly to the stage. He smiled and shook the hands of supporters. Liz began to feel overwhelmed by the size of the crowd.

The three of them made their way onto the stage and waved to the crowd. Frank spoke first. He had a way with words and got everyone worked up. Then it was Alice's turn to speak. As she went to the microphone, a group of men entered the demonstration area with large sticks. They began to beat the demonstrators, and people began to scream and run. There were far too few police present to contain the scene or to stop the beatings.

Liz had never seen anything like it before. She froze as she watched the brutality of the men beating unarmed and helpless people. Then two of the men made their way onto the stage. They headed straight for Alice while she was at the microphone. One of them swung his stick and hit her in the stomach. She screamed and doubled over. Frank ran forward and grabbed the man so he could not hit her again. That is when the other man hit Frank in the back with his stick. Now Liz sprang into action. She rushed forward and leapt onto the back of the man hitting Frank.

As the five of them wrestled, the police finally arrived. They broke up the fight and ran off the attackers. Alice laid on the stage crying and wincing in pain. Frank was able to stand up and appeared to be okay. Liz felt her bleeding lip, and then rushed to Alice's side.

The police called for an ambulance, and Alice was taken to the hospital. Liz rode with her in the ambulance, and Frank took his own vehicle to meet them there. Paramedics gave Alice a sedative to help ease the pain. Liz held her hand as she looked at her friend and cried.

Frank and Liz sat in the waiting room staring at the news reports of the incident on a vid screen. Frank was Alice's age and always very well groomed and dressed in the latest data wear. Liz was not sure what he did other than coordinate the anti-Modification group, but she found him to be intelligent and a persuasive speaker. He was also always a perfect gentleman. Liz and Frank watched themselves being attacked by the men with sticks, and then at the police who stood by at the start of the incident.

"You realize those men were most likely paid to do this by people like your father, don't you Liz?" Frank asked.

Liz lowered her head in shame as she replied. "I thought of that already." She said.

Frank put his arm around her. "That's not you though, Liz."

"I know," Liz said.

"Maybe you can help us prevent something like this from happening again." Frank said.

"How could I do that?" Liz asked. She looked up at Frank with renewed hope in her eyes.

"I have some ideas," Frank said as he gave Liz a hug. "But we can talk about it later, okay?"

Just then the doctor came out of the emergency room. "Are you folks here for Alice O'Neil?" He asked.

"Yes." Frank said.

With a concerned look, the Doctor took a quick glance at the chart in his hand and then spoke. "She will be alright. She has a lacerated spleen and will have to spend a few days in the hospital, but she should heal in time."

"Can we see her?" Liz asked.

"You can see her tomorrow. She is asleep now."

"Thank you Doctor." Frank said.

The Doctor smiled and then turned to walk back through the doors of the emergency room.

"Come on Liz." Frank said. "Let's go home."

He put his arm around Liz as they turned to leave.

"I will do whatever it takes to stop this from happening again." Liz said.

"I know you will, little sister," Frank said.

54

Gavin Jordan touched his sleeve and a hologram of Eddie Miller appeared.

"Miller, I'll be there in five minutes. Are you there yet?"

"Yes Gavin, I'm here. I'm sitting in the back."

Jordan touched his sleeve again and the hologram disappeared. He reached into his coat pocket and pulled out a blue pill which he placed onto his tongue. It was Zylapheron. He felt a rush of euphoria overcome him, then he spoke an order and the accelerator on his hover car engaged. Three minutes later he was walking into the dining room of the Organic Veggie Bowl.

Before he got out of his vehicle, he touched his sleeve again. This time no face appeared, but he heard a voice on the line. "Talk," the voice said.

"This is Jordan. I'm meeting with Miller now." Jordan fiddled nervously with his shirt collar.

The voice on the other end said, "Call me when you're done. If you feel he's jacking us around, we'll initiate the appropriate measures to remedy the situation." Then the line went dead.

Jordan took a deep breath and exited his vehicle. He entered the restaurant and looked around. He walked to the back of the restaurant and spotted Edward Miller, the man in charge of the Modification Center. He was drinking an iced tea. Jordan took a seat across from him at the table.

"I don't think this is a good idea," Miller said. "I told you before we shouldn't be seen together." Miller glanced around the room.

"Don't worry about it," Jordan said. "So what have you got to tell me? Something good I hope." Jordan moved forward into Miller's space in an attempt to intimidate him.

"Nothing new really," Miller said as he leaned backwards. "As I told you on the phone, we are sending you as many Mods as we can. This new policy of providing Mods to work in citizens' homes is killing the supply line." Miller took another sip of his iced tea.

"What can you do about it?" Now Jordan gave him a little sneer as he narrowed his eyes.

"My hands are tied Gavin." Miller seemed un-phased by the intimidation tactics. "I have only so much leeway. You know how the government works. I have very little authority, and all of the responsibility. I have been working with Dr. Brayden, but he has been unable to increase the number of inmates he is sending me." Miller held his hands up in a gesture of futility.

"What's holding him back?" Jordan was feeling frustrated now.

"Not all the doctors want to play ball. He's been trying to pressure them, but he said he can't do too much. Remember he still has to deal with the Civil Law Office. He thinks some of the Docs have been in contact with their man there at the Evaluation Center to complain about Brayden's pressure tactics."

"I don't think we are going to need to worry about the Civil Law Office much longer. After the election we should have the votes we need in Congress to expand the Modification Law. Soon there will be no Rehabilitation, and then the Civil Law Office will have nothing to monitor. But in the meantime you promised me Mods to work in my manufacturing plant, and you haven't delivered. I need those men to meet my numbers for the upcoming quarter." Jordan slammed his fist down on the table and almost toppled Miller's iced tea.

"I told you already, I'm doing the best I can." Miller remained cool and took another drink of his tea, this time avoiding Jordan's gaze.

"Fuck you Miller," Jordan said as he sat back frustrated. "I told you I'm tired of you fucking me on my Mod deliveries. I have quotas to meet and you've taken my money along with that fat fuck doctor at the prison, and you haven't delivered as promised." Jordan could see that this line of inquiry and intimidation was going nowhere. He began to run alternate scenarios through his mind as he squirmed on his chair.

"I told you, there are a lot of government regulations and monitors we have to deal with. It's not as simple as sending you every third inmate." Miller finished his tea and gestured to the waiter.

"You think I don't know what's involved. I do. I'm very involved in this process. I give a lot of money to important people to make sure that the Modification law stays intact. In fact I'm spending a lot of money to try to increase the scope of the law. What I need from you is to do your fucking job and send me the Mods you've promised me." Jordan watched Miller and was beginning to feel that he had been played.

A waiter approached and gave them menus. "Can I get you something to drink?" He asked looking at Jordan.

"I'll have a green tea spritzer," Jordan said. "And give me a Number Three."

"I'll have the Special," Miller said.

The waiter scurried away and Jordan faced Miller again. "Look Eddie, I don't mean to bust your balls, but like I've told you before, I have serious production quotas and I need Mods to meet them."

"I'll contact Dr. Brayden today and see what more he can do," Miller said. "Maybe you can get some of your important politician friends to stop the distribution of Mods to citizen homes. That would help a lot. I would have no problem meeting your needs if that happened."

The waiter quickly returned with their food and the men stopped talking. After he left, Jordan stuck his fork into a carrot and thought for a moment. "That idea might have some play in it," he said. "I'll see what I can do. I might be able to come up with an angle that can be used to stop that for the time being. Some safety issue perhaps, I'll make some calls. But in the meantime I really can't stress to you enough the need to send me Mods at every opportunity." He took another bite of his food, it was tasteless to him.

"I understand, believe me, I understand. It's not like I've run off to some foreign land or somewhere. You're at the top of my list." Miller smirked again as he took a bite of his meal.

Jordan put his fork down and spit his food into his napkin. "How can you eat this stuff?" he asked. "I've had enough. I have another meeting. I'll be in touch later next week." Then he stood up and put some money on the table. He put his hand over Miller's hand squeezing it so hard it made Miller's eyes water, and looked into his eyes. "I'm counting on you Miller," he said, "Don't let me down."

Then he walked out of the restaurant. Miller continued to eat, and then he got a video call. He touched his sleeve and a hologram of a face appeared.

"Miller, is that you? It's me, Stevenson from Atlas Shoes."

"Hello Mr. Stevenson, what can I do for you?"

"Well Miller, I'm calling to check on that delivery of Mods you promised me. It seems it was a few bodies short. You know, I paid you in advance for some consideration on this matter. I just want to find out what happened."

Miller repeated the same story he gave Gavin Jordan to Mr. Stevenson. Behind him an antenna twitched on a metallic fly that had attached itself to the wall of the restaurant. Outside the restaurant the man in the utility vehicle with the darkened windows recorded Miller's conversation.

55

Mr. Black sat in the back of the bar as he drew a long drag off his cigarette. He held the smoke in his lungs for a moment, and then blew out a long steady stream of grey smoke. It created a cloud that acted as a prism reflecting the amber lights of the bar. He tapped his fingers on the table at the booth, and motioned for the waitress to bring him another drink. He caressed his empty glass, and then tipped it into his mouth. It was a futile attempt to get another drop of the cheap scotch.

A blast of light illuminated the dingy bar as the front door opened. Gavin Jordan entered. Gavin was always leery about meeting Mr. Black. Mr. Black was an imposing man who took care of "problems." They only met when Gavin had a problem, as he did now. Gavin looked around the bar and then headed back toward Mr. Black. Mr. Black took his second drink as the waitress set it on the table.

"Do you want something sir?" the waitress asked as Gavin slid into the booth across from Mr. Black.

"No thank you," Jordan said. "I won't be here that long." He waited for the waitress to leave and handed a data card to Mr. Black. "This is the information. As we discussed I want it to look like the Mod lost control. No citizens seriously hurt. Any questions?"

Mr. Black reached across the table and took the data card. Then he took a long drink emptying his glass. "No problem, do you have my money?"

Jordan reached into his pocket and retrieved an electronic pad. He handed it to Mr. Black who punched his account number into it and handed it back. Jordan then completed the money transfer and showed the readout to Mr. Black.

Mr. Black nodded, and stood up. He placed the data card into his pocket as he stared at Jordan with blank eyes. "You take care of the bill," Mr. Black said. Then he quickly disappeared out the back door.

56

Three days later, Gavin Jordan sat in his office at Ardent Corporation's main headquarters watching news feed about an assault by a Mod. The Mod attacked a family pet and mutilated it, leaving the carcass in the homeowner's pool. The Mod then suffered a brain hemorrhage and died. The Mod was found with the animal's blood all over him.

A slight smile began to form at the corners of Jordan's mouth, and his beady eyes lit up with delight as the story continued. It stated shipments of Mods to residences were being temporarily halted pending an investigation. He immediately hit his vid phone to contact Edward Miller at the Modification Center. Miller's face appeared as he answered the call.

"Miller this is Jordan."

"I can see that. I have asked you not to contact me, Mr. Jordan. Your allotment of Mods is not under my control."

"Never mind that, listen. I saw on the news that they are suspending shipment of Mods to residences. I think you can read between the lines. I expect to get some good news from my warehouse manager very soon."

"I can't comment on any shipments Mr. Jordan. You are allotted your workers just like everyone else," Miller said. He was always cautious about discussing details when his conversation might be recorded.

"Right," Jordan said. "Sorry to have bothered you." Gavin Jordan could read between the lines.

"Okay I must go now," Miller said as he terminated the connection.

Jordan growled to himself as he made a second call. The face of his warehouse manager Johnny Beefson appeared.

"Hi Mr. Jordan," Johnny said as he saw Jordan's face on the vid phone.

"Johnny, listen. I'm expecting some more Mods to be delivered in the next week."

Unit 9 - 205

"Alright sir." Johnny seemed to snap to attention when he answered.

"I want you to keep me informed. I want a daily report from you on whether or not they arrive. Understand?"

"Yes Mr. Jordan," Johnny said. "I will contact you daily with an update."

Gavin Jordan terminated the connection without another word. Then he sat there stewing. He had a feeling Miller was going to fuck him again. Then he was going to be forced to have Mr. Black deal with him. "Nobody fucks me over," he said under his breath.

Gavin got up and made his way outside. He walked toward a shoot tube. He decided not to use his hover car in case he was being followed. The tube deposited him outside the Hotel Grandiose downtown, San Francisco. He made his way inside and took the elevator up to the eighth floor. He went to room 814 and knocked three times and then twice more. The door opened and he went inside the suite. There were five men sitting in a circle of chairs. They all had drinks in their hands.

Gavin went to each and shook their hands.

"Good evening Governor," Gavin said, as he smiled.

The Governor smiled and nodded.

He shook Mr. Hansen's hand and smiled again, "How's that lovely daughter of yours?"

"She's fine Gavin," Mr. Hansen replied as he shook Gavin's hand.

Gavin finished his greetings and took a seat in the circle. Mr. Hansen surreptitiously positioned his data pad to record the festivities. He always covered his own ass and wanted some leverage if he needed it in the future.

The Governor stood and raised his glass. "Here's to us gentlemen, may this work be profitable to all of us, you through your business dealings and me through your donations." Everyone laughed and raised their glasses to toast the governor.

"Seriously though, I must say that your tactics with the last anti-Modification rally were deplorable. We can't have any more of that, right?" The Governor raised his glass again as if to get agreement from the other men in the room.

The other men in the room half-heartedly raised their glasses toward the governor as if in agreement. Then Gavin stood up and patted the Governor on the back. "Thank you sir for that inspiration, now men shall we get down to business. We need to plan our strategy to win some more support at the national level."

The Governor smiled again and took his seat. Gavin sat down and proceeded to pull an agenda out of his pocket. "Alright then," Gavin said. "The first item is funding for the Senator from Montana. Any ideas on how we should approach this?"

57

It was a brisk fall day, and the cool air was energizing to Liz. She was on her way to meet her parents at the Bon Vivant Restaurant in the city of San Luis Obispo. It was located just off the campus of Cal Poly. She had decided to walk there since it was close. She hoped the walk would clear her head.

It was a surprise visit. Her mother had called last night and asked to meet. Liz's father was on a spur-of-the-moment trip. Liz had not told her parents she had joined the anti-Modification group. She planned to tell them today.

Liz had become more involved working the recruitment table since Alice was injured at the rally. Now, however, she had been asked to do something dangerous. Something devious that worked against her father. Frank gave Liz a cloning patch to attach to her father's data pad. It looked like a piece of tape. Once she attached it to his data pad, it would transmit all his data to a remote computer. The anti-Modification group wanted as much information about her father's political action group as possible. Liz was nervous and conflicted about her task.

She neared the edge of campus where a rose hedge marked the boundary to the outside world. She recalled simpler times when she helped her mother tend their rose garden. Her mother took great pride in her roses, crossbreeding and nurturing them to create stunning and unusually colored blossoms. Liz loved to help her take care of the roses by trimming and watering them. More important though, was the time she spent with her mother. Liz passed by the roses as quickly as her childhood passed her by.

Bon Vivant was a high-class steak house. Exactly the type of restaurant her father favored. Liz had given up eating red meat two years ago when she became a vegetarian. She found meat nauseating now. She made the change after watching a documentary on a meat processing plant.

Her parents were already seated when she arrived. The hostess led Liz to their table in the bowels of the restaurant. It was dimly lit as she made her way between tables covered with white linen tablecloths and populated with people in business suits. Smooth Jazz music combined with the chatter of the patrons.

Liz momentarily thought of the Humanities test she should be studying for. She had basically been summoned to visit with her father. She felt obliged because he was paying for her college expenses.

Her mother's smile guided her through the final paces of her journey. She rose and they embraced. Her father extended his hand, and Liz walked around the table to embrace him.

Liz sat down across from her parents and looked at her father. He was using his hand held data pad. He finished his work and set his data pad on the table. Liz realized that she loved her father but she hardly knew him. He was always a peripheral figure in her life, moving in and out of his business deals. He was kind, but distant, self-involved, and officious.

"It's so wonderful to see you darling," Liz's mother said. "Thank you for coming. I know it was last minute, and you must be very busy."

"I always have time for you and Father," Liz said.

Her father motioned to the waiter who immediately came to the table.

"I'll have another Cognac please," her father said. The waiter nodded to him acknowledging his request.

"Would you like a beverage Miss?" the waiter asked Liz.

"A lemonade please," Liz said.

"I think we're ready to order," Mr. Hansen said.

After the waiter took their order and departed, Mr. Hansen turned to Liz. "So Elizabeth, how is school going?"

He always called her by her given name. That thought suddenly bothered her. Most fathers had some type of affectionate pet name for their children, especially fathers for their daughters. Not her father. To him she was always Elizabeth. He didn't even call her Liz like everyone else.

She felt a small surge of adrenalin as she looked at him. Emboldened by that she said, "Well Father, it has been very interesting, especially since I joined the Anti-Modification Movement."

Her Father's face turned red, and then purple. His breath sounded labored and raspy as his eyes widened and he said, "You what?"

"I joined the Anti-Modification Movement, you know, to support Michael."

He looked toward Liz's mother now and demanded, "Did you know about this?"

"No she didn't," Liz spoke quickly to deflect his anger from her mother. This was her fight. She didn't want her mother to suffer because of her ideals.

"You realize that I am spending a lot of time and money in support of the Modification Program? We are trying to expand it. That is the purpose of this trip."

Liz just looked at him. She had never been in a direct confrontation with her father before. She realized he could be quite intimidating.

"Do you hear me Elizabeth?"

"Yes," Liz said. "I guess I feel differently about the matter than you do."

"That's unacceptable," her father said. "I will not have you working with those criminal-huggers, to undermine my efforts."

"I thought one went to college to learn how to think for themselves." Liz said. "That's what I'm doing."

"Well you need to do that in a different area. I cannot tolerate this activity." Her father was looking very stern, and his stare felt like it could burn a hole right through her. He leaned forward and Liz found herself recoiling from him.

Liz realized now why her mother had given in. He was an imposing man. The moment of truth was at hand, she knew her future self-worth was at stake. She felt numb all over. The adrenaline that had fueled her initial thrust had disappeared and now all she felt was a void. A void where she floated alone, cast off from those she had loved her entire life.

"Is this how it needs to be?" Liz asked.

"What?" her father asked.

"Is this how it needs to be?" She looked up at him and realized she had a choice. "I was wondering, is that how things will be if I don't agree with what you want?"

"What are you talking about?"

"What if I don't agree to drop out of the group? What if I continue to work against the Modification program? Because that's what I want to do, that's what I believe in."

Tears began to form in her eyes as she spoke. Her parents stared at her. Liz had always been their good little girl.

Their food arrived and the servers put down their plates. A hush fell over the table as they waited for the server to leave.

"Let's stop all this talk about Mods," her Mother said. "Let's just enjoy this lovely lunch."

Liz looked at her Mother as she stuck a fork into her salad.

"Here, have a roll dear," her Mother said as she handed Mr. Hansen the roll basket with her other hand.

He took a roll and broke it into two pieces shoving one half into his mouth, like a gag.

"Where are we staying tonight?" her Mother asked.

"La Mirada," her Father replied.

"Oh, I love La Mirada," her Mother said.

Liz watched in amazement as her Mother managed to babble for what seemed like an eternity about the La Mirada Hotel. "So this is how she does it?" Liz thought to herself as she picked at her salad. "Denial, avoidance, and distraction, and he probably thinks she will take care of this."

No one mentioned Mods for the rest of their time together. Liz was not going to back down, but she felt she wasn't sure how it would play out. This was new territory for her.

When he finished eating, her father got up to go to the restroom. "I'll be back in a minute," he said. He put his napkin on his chair and headed off.

Liz looked at the data pad sitting on the table where he left it. She knew this was her chance to apply the cloning patch. Her heart was beating so hard she felt the blood rushing through her body. Her ears felt like bass drums pounding.

She glanced at her mother who was staring out a window munching on her dessert. Liz casually reached out and knocked the data pad onto the floor. "Oops," she said. "How clumsy of me."

Liz bent over to retrieve the data pad while applying the clone patch. She set it back onto the table then looked over and smiled at her mother. Her mother smiled back at her and reached out to caress her hand.

"You know we love you, Liz."

"I know Mom, I love you too."

Her father returned to the table and announced that he was ready to leave. He bent over and kissed Liz on the cheek as he retrieved his data pad, then left to pick up their hover car from the valet.

Her Mother rose from her chair, gave Liz a hug, and then she left. Liz made her way to the restroom where she splashed cold water on her face. She was confused about what would happen next, but she was certain she would not give up the fight to stop Modification.

58

Michael lie on his bunk with his eyes closed. It had been several weeks since Liz's visit and the revelation about Billie. The time had gone by quickly as he focused on his therapy groups and the final tests. He had less than two weeks left, and he felt good about how things were progressing. He was hopeful he would finish his time at the Evaluation Center and move on. Michael had been spending most of his free program time by himself trying to avoid any entanglements that might go wrong and cost him.

One such problem was brewing with his cellie. Michael winced as he heard Tyrone sobbing. He'd been like this for an hour now. Michael hoped he would stop, but it didn't seem as though any let up was in sight. Finally Michael opened his eyes and spoke up, "What's going on Ty?"

Tyrone sniveled and blew his nose. "It's my wife. She told me she is going to divorce me. She said she can't be married to a robot."

Michael had seen this before, right after his arrival to Unit 9. Sal Monroe was an inmate who bunked on the third tier. His wife sent him a letter telling him that she was leaving him. Sal took a nose dive from the top tier and his head splattered on the bottom floor like a smashed Halloween pumpkin.

Michael cringed as he recalled the sound. Sal had actually jumped from just above Michael and Billie's cell. He walked up to the third tier to ensure he would have terminal velocity on his journey. Michael saw him fly by to his death. Michael had run to the railing and looked over in time to see Sal's brain matter lying next to his body as it spasmed involuntarily.

"You can't let this kind of thing get you down," Michael said. "You have to stay focused on your goals here. Then when you're done here, you can straighten out all that shit."

Tyrone moaned again and rolled over, smashing his face into his pillow. "Don't have no damn goals if she leave me."

Michael shook his head and leaned forward to use the data pad at the foot of his bunk. He punched up the medical request program and asked for an urgent mental health intervention for Tyrone. He knew Tyrone would not do it for himself. Besides, he didn't want Tyrone offing himself and getting Michael caught up in an investigation. Michael had enough of his own issues jeopardizing his program. Ultimately he felt bad for the guy, and maybe the shrinks could help him.

Michael laid back and listened to Tyrone cry some more. The intervention team arrived and the cell door opened. "That was fast," Michael thought to himself. The team quickly removed Tyrone from the cell and then the door closed again. "He will thank me later."

Since his visit with Liz, Michael had become much more assertive. He felt confident taking charge of his own life and doing things that he believed in. In fact, he was much more adept at even knowing what he believed in, like calling in Tyrone's crisis. The thought of Billie being a Mod in Liz's home seemed to bring the world into focus. He realized that he must take responsibility for himself, and the more he did, the more confident he became.

He wanted to see Liz again, to share his life with her. He still loved her, but he did not feel so desperate for her affection now. The things he was going through made him realize how important his decisions were. He had to focus on himself if he was going to be any good for Liz. He was developing long-term ideas of how they would spend their lives together. He wanted to get married eventually, have children, and a good job. He could go to school like Liz to figure out a career. That is, if he made it out of here without being Modified.

Dr. Carson had warned him to watch his back. He could not do much more to save him if he got into trouble again. Looking back, Michael got upset with himself when he thought about how careless he was, fighting over stupid things. In some ways he felt he was being self-destructive, like Sal when he jumped from the third tier. Maybe at some level Michael really did not care what happened to him back then. He was too busy feeling sorry for himself.

Now it was different. He realized he needed to survive this ordeal. To do that, he needed to focus on being smart. Not let his emotions control him.

His data pad beeped, and he realized he had an e-mail from Liz. He opened it and began to read. He was happy to hear from her. He was surprised to hear that she had joined the Anti-Modification movement at her university. "Alright!" Michael thought. "She is fully behind me now."

Michael leaned back and smiled. He realized that would cause problems with her father. She may need his support now. He was ready for that. He had to make it out of here.

59

Michael walked down the main hallway. He was headed toward testing room six to take his last psychological test. The testing battery that all inmates endured culminated with a projective test. Projective tests presented an individual with visual stimuli, or an image. The person's verbal interpretations of the images were used to assess their personality. It was an ancient process that first became formalized in the nineteenth century with the advent of the inkblot test. Like many elements of the evaluation process, there was no right or wrong answers. That is what Michael had found the most frustrating. He always felt like he was clueless about what was expected of him.

He was not afraid of taking the test today because he had heard a lot about it from the other inmates. He knew he should just do his best, and be honest.

The hallway was crowded as he made his way. He finally reached the testing room and showed his data hand to the desk officer. He took a seat and waited. Finally a tech came out and asked him to go back into the testing area.

"Mr. Taylor, my name is Ms. Swenson. I am going to administer your test this morning. It is called a projective test," the tech said as they headed back. She was a short blonde woman with green eyes. Michael guessed she was in her late thirties so she would be a Darwin. It was always nice to have the opportunity to interact with the female staff. It got old being around stinky guys all the time. Michael was amazed at how many females worked in the Evaluation Center. He could see that it had a negative effect on them. The women that worked there the longest seemed to have developed a harsh edge.

The testing room was small. It had a small desk and a chair. The desk had a viewing monitor on it with a built in microphone.

"Please have a seat here, Mr. Taylor," Ms. Swenson said.

Michael took a seat at the desk and looked at the monitor. It was dark but erupted into a bright blue image of the ocean when Ms. Swenson turned it on.

"You are going to see a series of fifteen images Mr. Taylor. When you see the image I would like you to tell me what you see. For example what do you see in this image?"

"The ocean," Michael responded.

"Very good Mr. Taylor, now tell me what else the image might be?"

"What else?" Michael asked. He was a little confused.

"Yes Mr. Taylor, what else, look very closely at the image, can you see anything else in this image?"

Michael was a little amused and confused, but he took a stab at it. He looked more closely at the image on the screen. As he did he noticed that he could see fish swimming in the water.

"Okay, I see some fish here, they are swimming," Michael said.

"Very good Mr. Taylor, tell me what else you see?" Ms. Swenson said.

Again Michael looked at the image. It took him a moment but when he focused on the details of the image he saw someone swimming. "Here," he said. "Someone is swimming over here."

"Very good Mr. Taylor, now we are going to start the test. I would like you to give me at least three responses for each image, okay?"

"Okay."

The next image appeared on the screen. At first it looked like nothing more than a smear of black paint. Michael focused on it as Ms. Swenson had showed him with the first image. As he looked more closely things began to appear. He offered his three responses, "I see a cat, and this might be a pizza, and this is a hammer." The tech nodded and they moved on to the next image.

Eventually they completed the test and Michael was released back to his cell. He knew better than to ask the tech for any feedback on his performance. They never told you anything. They always said you would get your results from the doctor.

Michael felt a sense of relief and accomplishment at finishing the testing phase, but he knew that did not guarantee him a ticket to

Rehabilitation. He remembered that Billie had completed the testing phase.

Thinking of poor Billie made Michael felt very lucky to have been assigned to Dr. Carson. He was sure he would have been Modified if he was put onto Dr. Isaac's caseload. When Michael got back to his cell he settled back onto his bunk and ate his lunch. He had dayroom program later so he would rest until then.

60

Michael lay on the blanket next to Liz. It was a warm sunny day and they were enjoying the park. He rolled over onto his back and closed his eyes. She dug her fingers into his side and tickled him. He squirmed and laughed. She continued to tickle him, now she dug her fingers into him more aggressively. It no longer felt pleasing to Michael.

"Alright already, that hurts Liz," Michael cried out.

As he twisted his body to get away from her, he woke up. He realized he was lying on his bunk. Then he felt the pain in his side again. He looked down to see what was happening and saw a mouse gnawing on his shirt. He jumped up and flung the mouse across his cell.

The mouse landed onto the floor. It shook itself and then ran under the cell bars onto the tier walkway. Michael threw a shower slipper at the bars and scared the mouse away. It disappeared down the walkway out of Michael's sight.

He examined his side and saw that he had a hole in his shirt, and some small bite marks on his side. He would have to go to medical for treatment. He brushed potato chip crumbs off of his shirt. He realized he must have fallen asleep while eating and the mouse helped him finish his lunch.

While he rinsed his wound in the sink, Michael heard the announcement for dayroom program. He decided he would go to medical after dayroom. He hated to miss any opportunity to get out of his cell. He could use the medical appointment to get some extra program time later.

His cell door opened and he headed down to the dayroom. When he entered he realized he did not see any of the usual guys. He took a seat with a couple of new guys who were recent additions to Ms. Atkin's group.

"Hey guys," Michael said as he sat down.

"Hey Taylor," the men responded.

"I was looking for a couple of my regulars, but I don't see them today," Michael said.

"Who's that?" One of the men sitting next to Michael asked. He was playing dominos and did not even look toward Michael when he responded.

"Bang," the domino made a loud sound as it hit the table. Michael could never understand the significance of slamming down a domino. He recalled that Billie used to do that and yell out at the same time.

"Victor and his sidekick Kevin," Michael said. "Have you guys seen them?"

"Nope," the man next to him replied. "And you won't see them anymore either."

"What do you mean?" Michael asked.

"Victor was transferred to Rehabilitation this morning. Lucky fool, and Kevin got gaffoed up by Dr. Isaac, poor bastard."

"Yeah, I saw Kevin right before it happened," the man on the other side of Michael offered. "He knew it was going down and was refusing to go to the doctor's office. They had to restrain him here on the unit and then take him over to see Isaac."

Michael sat there in disbelief. Kevin had been right all along. He never had a chance. No matter what he did, he was still doomed. Victor made it though. That clever SOB knew how to get out of here.

Suddenly Michael did not feel like socializing any more. He raised his hand to get the attention of the officer in the control station. He was given clearance to head to the door where he asked to go to medical to treat the bite wounds.

As he headed to medical he thought about the other guys, two very different outcomes and two very different lives. It was amazing to Michael how life could change course in a moment.

61

Michael sat in his chair and watched the other inmates arriving for group therapy. They all took seats and then Ms. Atkins burst into the room in her usual high-energy fashion.

"Good morning everyone," Ms. Atkins said.

"Good morning," the guys responded.

Michael felt that this would be one of his last groups. He was near the end of his three months. He wanted to make a good impression today. He never knew exactly what would happen in group, but he was determined to make the best of it. He noticed that Zack Cole was not in group today, so that could help him.

"It doesn't look like we have any new arrivals today, so let's get started," Ms. Atkins said.

"I would like to know exactly what we are supposed to be doing in this group?" It was Eddie Haskins who spoke up. He was one of the guys who told Michael that Victor and Kevin were gone. "I am still not sure how this works."

"Well," Ms. Atkins replied. "This is called a process group. So we don't have a specific topic, such as anger management. We just talk about ourselves and our lives. It's a place to try and learn about how we deal with each other, and the world around us."

"That sounds weird," Haskins said.

"What's weird is that just saying it's weird can change your entire life," Michael said.

"What?" Haskins asked.

"Sure," Michael said. "I've been in this group for almost three months, and I have seen a lot of things happen in here. It sounds innocent enough but you can be sure that it is very important. I learned that something as simple as getting angry and losing your temper can have you turned into a Mod. So if anger management is one of your problems, you should watch out. I used to have that problem, and it cost me two terms in Ad-Seg. I learned to control it partly in here, in this group."

"Thank you for your input," Ms. Atkins said.

"You're welcome," Michael said.

"Well, what are we supposed to say about ourselves?" Haskins asked.

"Why don't you start by telling us about your family? Who were your parents and your brothers and sisters?" Ms. Atkins said.

Haskins started to talk and it turned out he was very chatty. The rest of the group time was spent talking about his family and how he was the black sheep. Michael made his best effort to join in and be positive. When the group ended, he felt good about his participation.

Michael headed back to his cell and sent Liz an e-mail. He told her he was very proud and thankful for her participation with the anti-Modification movement. He was thinking about what kind of life they could have together, with children, and how he wanted to go to school to decide on a good career. He missed her, loved her, and wanted to be with her. She was his main source of friendship now. All of the guys he started the evaluation process with were gone, Billie, Victor, and Kevin. He missed Kevin and felt badly for him, even though he was usually annoyed by his presence.

Michael finished his e-mail and opened his dinner bag. He emptied the bag out onto his bed and examined the contents. A bag of chips, a bag of carrots, two slices of bread, a packet of mustard, and a packet of green meat. Michael smiled to himself as he tossed the meat into his trash.

62

Zack Cole sat in Psychology department holding cell. The harsh florescent light made his eyes hurt and the stench of the other inmate in the holding cell made him nauseous. He couldn't wait to get out of the shit hole called Unit 9. By his estimation it shouldn't be much longer. He had done everything the doctors had asked of him. He felt personally responsible for at least twelve inmates being sent to Modification. That was their arrangement, he gets inmates to act out and sent to Mod, and they send him to Rehabilitation. He had been here well over ninety days. Perhaps Dr. Isaac had called him down to give him the good news that he was being transferred to rehab. That must be it.

Meanwhile, he was gagging from the stench of the inmate sitting next to him. Zack scowled at the stinky inmate. Ordinarily he would have said something to the other man, tried to draw him out, to bait him into assaulting Zack. This inmate looked strong, however, and he didn't look too bright. Zack did not want to get hurt. Being locked in the holding cell with him might be too dangerous. What if it took custody awhile to get there? Zack noticed muscles ripple on the inmate's arms as he stretched. He didn't recognize stinky guy, so he must be new. Besides, Zack had suckered in more than enough inmates already. He didn't need to take any more lumps. He had been to the infirmary three times.

The correctional officer opened the door to the holding cell and looked at Zack. "He's ready for you Cole."

Zack got up and headed down the hallway to Dr. Isaac's office.

"Come in Zack," Dr. Isaac said. "You know Dr. Brayden."

"Yes," Zack said.

Dr. Brayden stared at him but did not acknowledge him. Zack noticed what looked like a piece of donut stuck to his shirt. Zack sat in the empty chair and looked expectantly at Dr. Isaac.

"Zack, I wanted to talk to you today because we are a little disappointed. We're concerned that you haven't been able to get Michael Taylor sent to Modification yet.

Zack tensed as he listened to Dr. Isaac. He could not believe it, that fucking Michael Taylor.

"I understand Sir," Zack said. "He's very smart, not like most of the other guys. He's also on to me. He knows what I'm doing. He even called me out in group and got me beaten up. I was backing off him, so we wouldn't be exposed. "

"We are aware of Mr. Taylor's actions. We are also concerned that he is aware of you working for us. Our concern is that he might make it to Rehabilitation and shoot his mouth off. We can't afford that," Dr. Isaac said.

"We need you to take him out," Dr. Brayden said. "One more problem out of Mr. Taylor and I can send him directly to Modification myself, regardless of what Dr. Carson says."

"Do you understand Zack?" Dr. Isaac asked.

"I think so," Zack replied.

Without another word Dr. Brayden stood up and left.

"If you expect to make it to Rehabilitation, this needs to be taken care of," Dr. Isaac said. "That's all for now."

Zack left Dr. Isaac's office and headed back to the unit. He was angry and frustrated. "That fucking Taylor," he mumbled to himself.

63

Michael felt like he was making some headway because he'd gotten good feedback from Miss Atkins after his last group session. However, like everyone else in the Evaluation Center he was constantly on edge. He was also worried about his most recent e-mail from Liz when she told him how deeply she was becoming involved with the anti-Modification group. Michael's e-mails were screened by the authorities. So she was smart enough to skip a lot of details, but he could read between the lines. She was risking her relationship with her family, and her ticket to college.

He was flattered that she would do that for him. No one had ever gone out on a limb for him before. He knew that he had to do his part now and not mess up. He needed to get to Rehabilitation.

Michael hoped a shower would make him feel better. The inmates got to take showers two times a week. The rest of the time they kept themselves clean with birdbaths. It was only moderately effective, but it was better than nothing. Michael sat on his bunk waiting to be released from his cell. Tyrone had not returned from the psych ward yet. Maybe he was even worse off than Michael thought when he made the crisis call.

Michael was stripped down except for the towel he had wrapped around his waist. The towel was almost bath sized, white and as soft as medium grade sandpaper. He could feel the graininess against his body as he sat there. He had his shower shoes on, and held a bar of soap in his hand. Michael had grown accustomed to the process during his time at the Evaluation Center. He also knew not to waste any of the brief time they were allotted to shower, which is why he was sitting on his bunk waiting.

Michael's mind wandered for a moment as he thought about how Billie used to sing cowboy songs in the shower. A sad smile crossed his face. He doubted Billie would ever sing again. Billie had been a good friend to Michael. It didn't seem fair that a guy like Billie was Modified. Michael never even got to say goodbye.

What if the same thing happened to him? Michael made a fist as his blood began to boil and his temper rose considering that possibility. Suddenly he heard the announcement for showers. The door to his cell screeched from the sound of metal scraping on metal as it slowly rumbled open. Michael closed his eyes and took a deep breath counting to four very slowly trying to calm himself before leaving. As he reached the count of four, he heard someone at the front of his cell. He looked up and saw Zack Cole and two of his stooges. Zack had a sneer on his face and he was laughing.

"Look at this boys," Zack said. "What's the matter Taylor? Have you been crying over your boyfriend Billie?"

Michael's anger flared again as he stood up and walked to the cell door. Zack and his boys were blocking his exit. Michael stared at Zack with cold steely eyes.

"Move out of the way," Michael said.

Michael looked at the two other inmates. He recognized them as two new guys. One had arrived three days ago. Ed Sands, a large guy who did not seem too bright who was most likely a Darwin. He would easily be manipulated by Zack. Easily pumped up to prove himself, and dangerous to Michael. Michael figured that if anything went down it would be Sands that would come after him. Michael noticed that they had not entered his cell. They were just outside on the tier walkway. That could work to his advantage.

Michael was looking for a way out of this situation. It was three on one and Michael thought back to his high school judo class. He tried to remember the training he had for situations when you were outnumbered. Zack moved to his right allowing the other two inmates to position themselves in the doorway while he was on the side. Michael saw Sands' eye twitch and his muscles tighten. Michael dropped his soap on the floor just as Sands took a swing at him. Michael ducked and grabbed Sands' right shoulder as his arm passed by Michael's head. He stuck his foot out blocking Sand's foot and pushed with all of his strength. Sands fell to his left tumbling on top of the third inmate. As they scrambled to right themselves, Michael grabbed his cell door by one of the bars and jerked the door to his left. The door slammed shut and the door latch clicked as the cell door locked. Michael stepped back as the three men looked at him with surprise.

"Look here, Sands," Michael said. "You're new here so you don't know me well. But if you let Zack pump you up to assault people, you're going to end up as a zombie working in a sock factory. Now why don't you boys move along?"

The three men looked at each other quizzically.

"Don't worry about him," Zack said. "He's nothing to us."

Zack turned to leave just as a correctional officer appeared.

"What's the hold-up down here?" the officer asked. "Move along."

The three men moved down the tier to the showers. The officer looked into Michael's cell.

"What's up Taylor? I thought I racked you out to shower?"

"I'm going to skip it today, Boss," Michael said.

The officer shook his head and moved on as Michael picked his soap up off of the floor. Michael turned to his sink, put the plug in, and began to fill it with water. He wondered if anyone would review the video of what had just happened. Would they try to use it against him? Now he would have to be extra careful as it was obvious that Zack was out to get him. Michael splashed water onto his face, cold as usual.

64

After the incident with Zack and his boys, Michael's anxiety level spiked. He knew they were out to get him. He was proud of himself for fending them off and controlling his anger, but he was still concerned that someone could twist the facts if they reviewed the video. Then he got the call to report to Dr. Carson's office. His heart leapt into his throat as he listened to the officer instructing him to get up and report immediately to the Psych Unit.

He did not have an appointment. Could he be gaffoed-up today? Sedated and dragged off for Modification. His cell door opened, and Michael took a deep breath to steady himself. The officer stood on the tier walk looking at him. He was expressionless and erect. He quietly waited for Michael to gather himself.

Michael stood up and then strode out of his cell heading toward the stairs with the officer in tow. His mind was racing and his senses were extremely alert. The drab colors of the unit appeared even more lifeless than usual as he made his way down the stairs. The stench of all the bodies warehoused in cell after cell permeated his nose and he almost gagged. It seemed to him that everyone was staring at him.

He made his way to the front door and stood on the yellow line while the officer opened the door. They moved into the main hallway with Michel leading the way. Michael felt like a trapped rat. He looked around for a possible escape route but he knew there was none. He obediently walked across the hall to the Psych Department. The officer opened the door and Michael walked into the office area. The florescent lighting was extremely bright and hit him like a lightning bolt. He winced and blinked his eyes to adjust. The officer at the desk greeted him as the escort officer stepped back into the main hallway and shut the door behind Michael.

"Have a seat in the tank, Taylor," the desk officer said.

Michael went into the tank and sat on a bench. There were two other inmates with him. He didn't recognize either of them. Michael did not have to wait long.

"Taylor," the desk officer said.

"Yes," Michael said.

"Room eleven, Dr. Carson, go on down."

Michael stood up and slowly walked down the hallway. He passed the offices of the other clinicians as he went. He noticed some of the staff had inmates in with them. He wondered how many of them would end up being Modified.

Michael reached Dr. Carson's office and knocked on the door. It was open and Dr. Carson sat at his desk facing his computer. No one else was in the office. Michael thought that was a good sign; no nurse, no custody officer. Dr. Carson turned around when he heard Michael knock.

"Michael, come in, have a seat," Dr. Carson said.

Michael sat down and looked across the desk at Dr. Carson, trying to read his face, his emotions. Dr. Carson leaned on his desk and looked directly into Michael's eyes.

"Michael, good morning, thanks for coming in on such short notice. I called you in to tell you that I am recommending that you be sent on to Rehabilitation."

"What?" Michael asked. He was shocked.

"Rehabilitation."

"Rehab, really?" Michael was ecstatic. He had made it. Tears began to well up but he fought them back. "Thank you Dr. Carson. Thank you so much."

"You earned it Michael. I saw a video of what happened with you and Zack outside your cell the other day. You handled yourself well. Congratulations. Now I don't want you going to any more groups or dayrooms. You will be cell fed until you leave. Those are precautions to help you avoid contact with the other inmates. Sometimes they get jealous and try to hurt guys when they know they have made it through. I can't tell you exactly when you will be transported, but it will be soon."

Michael felt a great sense of relief overcome him. He took a deep breath and let himself relax.

"This means an awful lot to me Dr. Carson. Thank you for all of your help."

"You're welcome Michael, I know you will do fine."

A custody officer appeared at the door and Dr. Carson stood up and extended his hand. Michael shook it and then went with the officer to his cell. The walk back was like being in a dream. He was barely aware of his body but when he got into his cell he let out a yell.

"Yes!" he yelled. Then he sent Liz an e-mail telling her the good news.

He lied down and fell asleep, sleeping soundly for the first time in a very long time.

PART III

65

Liz knocked on the door to Alice's home. She pulled a scarf tightly around her neck protecting herself from the cold blustery day. Colored leaves from the large oak tree in front of the house blew past her face. She knocked again and Alice opened the door. Alice used a cane and moved slowly since her release from the hospital.

Liz entered the house and the aroma of freshly baked bread filled her senses. "Should you be baking in your condition?" Liz asked, as they walked toward the kitchen.

"Probably not, but I'm not going to let those bastards dictate my life." Alice looked Liz directly in the eyes as she spoke.

"Okay," Liz said. She was always surprised by Alice's high intensity.

Liz removed her coat as they entered the kitchen. Frank was sitting at the table munching on bread and jam, and staring at a data pad.

"Liz," Frank said without looking up.

"Frank," Liz replied as she glanced at Alice who was shaking her head at Frank.

"We have only begun to scratch the surface with the information from your father's data pad." Frank said. "But I can tell you it is definitely going to change the political landscape when we begin to release it to the public." He sat back in his chair and smiled at Liz.

"Wow, I had no idea it would mean that much. Remember though, you can't do anything with the information that is going to hurt my father," Liz said as she leaned forward toward Frank.

"We are not going to purposely hurt Daddy, Liz. But you need to face facts. There are videos of him with powerful people making plans to do illegal acts, all to help pass the total Modification law. He is even responsible for the attack at the rally." Frank softened his voice as he told her about this part.

"What are you talking about?" Liz began to cry.

Alice walked over and comforted her. "It's true Liz. I saw the video myself. If you wish we can play it for you."

"I don't care. Our agreement was that you could use the information, but you could not destroy my father. Now I expect you to keep your word." Liz stopped crying and slammed her hand on the table. "I will not be responsible for destroying my parents any more than I want my father responsible for destroying others' lives. So you need to find a way to make this work."

Frank stood up and walked away while throwing his cup into the sink. "Damn it Liz. This information can make all the difference. Your father taped all of the meetings. For whatever reason, I don't know. But all we have to do is feed the tapes to the news media and his group will be finished. That includes the governor and other politicians they have paid off."

"Maybe we can track the money now that we know where it came from and where it went. Expose them that way." Alice said.

"Or we can set them up and make our own tapes," Liz offered.

"What do you mean?" Frank said. He turned around suddenly interested again.

"Now that we know who they are and how they meet, we can follow them and record them ourselves. That way it will not be obvious it was my father who recorded them." Liz said as she looked hopefully at Alice and Frank.

"We could do that," Frank said. "But your father may still be implicated."

"Let me worry about that," Liz said. "I could not bear it if he knew I had betrayed him."

"We still have time before the election," Alice said as she sat at the table. Liz thought she looked exhausted. "There is no need to do anything today."

"You're right Alice. Let me make some calls to help us with the money trails, and we can talk to the tech team about setting up surveillance." Frank came over to Alice and put his hand on her shoulder.

"Frank, we should go now so Alice can get some rest." Liz said.

"Good idea," Frank said. "Liz, I want you to know I am very proud of what you did to get us this information. I promise we will do our best to protect you and your father."

"Don't worry honey," Alice said.

66

Zack Cole paced back and forth in his cell. He made two requests to see Dr. Isaac this morning and got no response. He had a new plan to get that asshole Taylor to engage in a fight. He wanted to let the doctor know he wasn't giving up. He knew Taylor had been staying in his cell since last night and was avoiding contact. That usually meant you were being transferred to Rehabilitation.

That infuriated Zack even more. How could he be going to rehab? Zack should have left weeks ago. Instead they kept him there to do their dirty work. He stopped pacing to look out through the cell bars. There was no activity on the living unit. Most of the guys had gone to appointments after chow. Zack was not in any treatment groups at this time. He had completed all his testing, so he didn't really have any reason to leave his cell.

Then he heard the wheels of a gurney coming down the walkway of the tier. He could hear the muffled conversation of several staff becoming louder. They finally came into his view and he could see it was an inmate removal and transfer team. He saw the nurse with a bag and three officers pushing the gurney. "Who could they be for?" he thought.

Then the realization hit him. He was the only one up here right now. It had to be for him. Panic set in and he began to look for some type of a weapon as the removal team came to a stop in front of his cell.

He heard the officer call to have his cell door opened. Zack rushed the staff trying to push his way through, but was immediately restrained by the three men. The nurse's hand moved like lighting as she administered the sedative.

"But I helped them," Zach said.

Those were his last words as he succumbed to the sedative and was placed onto the gurney for transport.

67

Rick closed Michael's report on his computer and sent it on with his cover letter outlining his recommendation. Then he sat back and looked out of the slit that was his office window. His vid phone alarm sounded and he clicked answer.

"Dr. Carson?"

"Yes."

"This is Dr. Nguyen. I just called to inform you that your audit has been completed, and we found no irregularities in your work."

"Thank you," Rick said.

"As of now the audit investigation is considered completed and your case is closed," Dr. Nguyen said.

"Thank you," Rick started to say, but before he could complete his thought she had disconnected.

"You have to love that bureaucratic efficiency," Rick thought to himself.

Rick clicked his vid phone again and his wife Natalie's face appeared.

"Hello Darling," she said.

"I just heard from the audit team. I was cleared and the investigation is closed."

"That's wonderful," she said. "What did Dr. Brayden say about that?"

"I haven't spoken to him. I don't know if he has been informed."

"Well, try not to rub it in too badly. You wouldn't want to antagonize him."

"Good advice, I'll think about that." Rick said. "I love you. I'll see you tonight."

Rick disconnected and sat back in his chair. He smiled to himself. Then he walked down to Dean's office. Dean was sitting at his desk reading a report.

"In the mood for some good news?" Rick asked.

"Sure, what do you have for me?" Dean said.

"I just heard from Ms. Nguyen of the audit team. I have been cleared." Rick smiled and Dean applauded him.

"So what's next?

"Celebration of course. Luigi's for lunch?"

"Excellent idea, and by the way, I never had any doubts." Dean said.

"See you later," Rick said as he turned and headed back to his office.

68

Gavin Jordan threw his glass against the wall of his office. He had just finished a vid phone call with Edward Miller. Miller had blown him off again, not coming through with the Mods he had promised to deliver. Jordan stood up and paced back and forth in front of his desk. Finally he stopped pacing and returned to his seat. He was done fucking around, if he was going to go down, so was that asshole Miller. Jordan clicked his vid phone and a voice came across the audio feed. The video feed was blocked.

"Speak," the voice said.

"Mr. Black, this is Gavin Jordan."

No response was offered.

Jordan realized he wasn't going to be acknowledged, so he continued on.

"I want you to initiate the Plan-B we discussed regarding Mr. Miller," Jordan said.

Still no response, finally Mr. Black responded. "Can you process the funds transfer?" "Yes, of course, hold on," Jordan said.

Gavin Jordan quickly put a money transfer into action through his data port.

"The job will be completed within 24 hours," Mr. Black said.

The connection was terminated and Jordan called to his secretary.

"I broke a glass in here. Call janitorial to come and clean it up."

* * * * * * * *

The next morning Gavin Jordan was reviewing the daily news feed when he saw a story regarding the untimely death of Edward Miller, the director of the Modification Center. Jordan grimaced as he heard it. "What an asshole," he thought. "He got what he deserved."

As he sipped his morning coffee, his secretary called to him. "Mr. Jordan there are some people here to see you."

"Who are they?" Jordan asked. "I don't have any appointments scheduled. Please ask them to schedule an appointment."

Gavin Jordan was cut off in mid-sentence when four uniformed officers strode into his office. They were accompanied by a man in a suit. The man in the suit showed Jordan a badge.

"Gavin Jordan, I am Smitty Wilson, an officer of the Attorney General's office. You are under arrest for bribing a public official, and conspiracy to murder."

Jordan jumped over his desk and tried to run but was stopped in his tracks when one of the officers zapped him with a pulse baton. He fell to the floor and began to urinate on himself. His secretary stood in the office doorway and screamed when she saw the drama play out.

Officer Wilson turned to look at her and then asked one of the officers to take her into custody for questioning. Gavin Jordan and his secretary were given to a transport team to be taken to the adjudication center. Then Officer Wilson looked at his data pad and barked out some new orders to his team.

"Alright let's get moving. We have three more stops to make today. It looks like we have a couple of doctors on our schedule, very interesting."

69

The day began much like any other day at the Evaluation Center. Rick got to work and made his way to his office. He turned on his computer, read his e-mails, and reviewed his schedule for the day. He spoke to Dean and made lunch plans. Then he began work on a report for an inmate whom he was sending to Modification.

It became a different kind of day around 9:45 am when Dean came rushing into his office.

"You are not going to believe what is going on right now," Dean said. He was so excited he could barely catch his breath.

"What are you talking about?" Rick asked.

"Officers from the Attorney General's office have arrested Dr. Brayden. The Regional Administrator is here. He wants to meet with all of us in a few minutes," Dean said.

"What the hell," Rick said. "He wants to meet with whom?"

"All of us, the entire staff of the evaluation unit."

"Wow," Rick said. "What did they arrest Dr. Brayden for?"

"I'm not sure. Maybe the Regional Administrator will tell us."

Ms. Atkins appeared at Rick's door and looked at Dean.

"Do you know what the heck is going on here?" she asked.

"The Attorney General's office arrested Dr. Brayden. They want to meet with all of the staff in a few minutes," Dean said.

An officer from the Attorney General's office walked up to Miss Atkins and they all stared at him. He was a tall man dressed in a navy blue uniform and had a data patch on his temple similar to the patches worn by their custody officers. He was expressionless and his voice was measured and emotionless. Ms. Atkins looked up at him, but she kept her ground as he towered over her.

"Your presence is requested in the conference room please, all of you," the officer said as he motioned toward Rick and Dean.

They all looked at each other and Rick shrugged. "Of course," Rick said. "Shall we?"

They entered the conference room which was already filled to capacity with other staff, including the custody staff. They found no available seats. The Regional Administrator stood in the center of the room. He was dressed in a cheap version of the new data-wear business suit. He raised his hands and asked for quiet.

"My name is Hani Nordquist. I am the Regional Administrator for the department. I am here today acting with the direction of the Attorney General's office. They have recently concluded an investigation into criminal activities in this department. As a result of their investigation Dr. Brayden and Dr. Isaac have been arrested on charges of conspiracy, taking bribes, and criminal negligence. Additional arrests are being conducted simultaneously in the community. Dr. Dean Cooper is being appointed Acting Administrator of Clinical Services for this facility. Dr. Cooper I will meet with you in your office in ten minutes to discuss this appointment."

Rick and Dean looked at each other in astonishment. Dean's back straightened as he straightened the lapels on his Harvard Jacket.

"That is all," the Regional Administrator said. "Please return to your jobs and continue to work as usual."

The Regional Administrator turned and went out the side door of the conference room. Everyone in the room was in shock as they looked around at each other and began to talk about the recent events.

Rick and Dean made their way out of the conference room and ducked into Dean's office, which was the closest.

"Congratulations Boss," Rick said.

"This is unbelievable," Dean said. "Those snakes Brayden and Isaac finally got their due."

"I guess lunch is off for today," Rick said.

"A true state employee, keeping focused on the important issues," Dean laughed. "Yes, I imagine I will be tied up."

"Keep me up-to-date," Rick said as patted Dean on the back. "And congratulations."

70

Rick kissed Natalie goodbye and headed to work. He was in a decent mood today. A lot had transpired in the last twenty-four hours. He was hopeful that all the changes would be a good thing. He was confident that Dean would not change much even after being thrust into a managerial position. He was glad they gave it to Dean. Rick certainly didn't want anything to do with being a boss. That's all supervisors were in a bureaucracy, bosses. They never really had any opportunity to manage anything. Everything was determined by policy, procedures, and laws. All the responsibility and no authority, that's what Dr. Brayden, used to say. He likened the job to being in a kayak going down a category five rapids, while wearing a straitjacket. Maybe that's why he did what he did, frustration and disillusionment, and a touch of greed for sure.

Rick approached the gate but had to wait for a transport bus to pass. It was on its way to the Rehabilitation center. As Rick looked in the window of the bus he recognized a familiar face. Looking out at him smiling and waving was Michael Taylor. Rick smiled back and waved goodbye to Michael.

"I hope he makes it," Rick thought to himself

PART IV

71

Michael woke up and looked around. He was unaware of Zack's modification, or the arrests of Dr. Isaac and Dr. Brayden. Michael stretched and rubbed his neck. He had been on the bus for almost four hours. It was a ten hour trip from Chino to Redding where the Rehabilitation Center was located.

This bus was more comfortable than the one that took him to the Evaluation Center. It was large and spacious with padded seats, and it had heating and air conditioning. He still had to wear chain restraints on his legs, waist, and arms, but he had a large seat to himself. There were only ten inmates on it. Two transport officers sat in the front of the bus with a barrier between them and the inmates.

Michael looked out the window. Cotton fields, almond groves, and grape vines stretched all along the sides of Highway 99 which ran the length of the San Joaquin Valley in Central California. The Valley was the breadbasket of the west coast of the United States. Large agribusinesses had taken over most of the farms. Small communities dotted the highway and the bus was coming to a stop in one of them now. It was time to give the inmates lunch and a bathroom break. Tulare, California, was a small community. The government had a contract with the Palmer farm located on the outskirts of town to provide a way station for the transport buses.

Michael and the other inmates were unloaded at the Palmer farm and herded into an outside pen that had picnic tables and outhouses. After relieving themselves, the men were seated at the tables for lunch.

Michael sat down and looked around. The house was a large two story structure that was surrounded by oak trees. They provided shade from the triple digit temperatures of the summer months. It was a beautiful morning and Michael took a deep breath of fresh air. He was seated at a picnic table with one of the other inmates. Michael didn't recognize him.

"I'm Taylor," Michael said to the other man.

"Fredrickson," the other inmate replied.

"I don't recognize you. What unit were you on?" Michael asked.

"Seven," Fredrickson said.

A young woman entered the pen and began to serve plates of food. A white golden retriever followed her and began to smell the inmates. It had been a while since the inmates had been outside in the fresh air. They all sat and stared at the young lady as she performed her duties.

When she got to Michael's table she set down two plates. "Thank you," Michael said.

The woman looked at Michael and smiled. She had big brown eyes, dark hair, and beautiful white teeth. "You're welcome," she said. Then she turned and walked away.

Michael looked down at his plate. It was a turkey sandwich with fresh fruit and nuts on the side. He took a piece of fruit and bit into it. It was the juiciest and freshest food he had ever had in his life. Michael must have made a funny face because Fredrickson laughed at him.

"Haven't you ever had farm fresh food before?" Fredrickson asked.

"No I haven't," Michael said. "It's fabulous."

"Nothing like it, I grew up on a farm." Fredrickson said. "Once you've tasted food like this, you are spoiled for life. Try the tomato on your sandwich."

Michael lifted the bread and pulled the tomato slice off his sandwich. It was an odd orange color. "This is a tomato?" he asked. He popped it into his mouth and bit into it. The sweetness made his mouth explode with delight. "Wow."

"They're called heirloom tomatoes."

"Amazing," Michael said.

Michael felt something cold and wet rub up against his hand. He was startled and pulled his hand back. Then he saw it was the dog. He reached down to pet the dog on his head and scratch his ears. The dog nuzzled into Michael's leg.

"You're a friendly fellow aren't you?" Michael said.

Michael pulled some turkey from his sandwich and gave it to the dog. He gobbled it up in an instant.

"His name is Oso,"

Michael turned to see who was talking to him. The woman stood there smiling at him.

"It's very generous of you to share your lunch with him." She said.

"He's a great dog. I never had a dog of my own," Michael said.

"Oso means bear in Espanol," she said.

"Well Senor Oso, I am happy to share my lunch with you," Michael said as he pet Oso on the head and rubbed his back. Oso happily snuggled up against Michael as he pet him.

"Looks like you made a new friend," Fredrickson said. They both laughed.

The inmates finished their lunches and boarded the bus to continue the journey to Redding. As they pulled out of the compound Michael watched the young woman clean up after them. Oso followed closely behind hoping for some table scraps. For the first time in a long time Michael felt like a normal human being.

72

After making one more rest stop near Modesto, the bus finally reached Redding. All the inmates stared out the windows as it pulled up to the gate of the Rehabilitation Center. Michael was pleased by what he saw. Other than the fence with the razor wire, it was a beautiful college campus.

The Rehabilitation Center was located on the former campus of Sampson University. It had been a liberal arts college. It was located on 92 beautiful acres of land in northern California.

The bus entered the campus and pulled up to one of the six large residence halls. Michael and the other inmates were unloaded, unshackled, and then ushered into a large group room where they met the director of the center. He stood on a podium surrounded by seven staff members. They were outfitted with the same type of data and communication enhancements that the custody officers at the evaluation center wore. The difference was the staff here dressed in civilian clothing, not uniforms.

The director had on the latest Data Wear suit. He addressed the new arrivals.

"Welcome gentleman, my name is Director Jesse Winters. You will address me as either Director or Sir. You are at the Rehabilitation Center. You are enrolled in a nine month program that is geared to make you productive members of society. As you may have already noticed, the tone of this facility is much different than that of the Evaluation Center. But make no mistake. You are still considered incarcerated, and we have the best electronic surveillance system watching every move you make. So please don't entertain any notions about escaping. You will not be successful, and you will be sent to Modification immediately. I know you have had a long bus ride so I will not keep you any longer. You will be assigned to a residence hall and escorted to your rooms. In the morning you will attend an orientation. The data chip implanted in your hand at the Evaluation Center will continue to be used here for means of identification and information. Thank you for your time, and good luck."

The Director then turned and walked out of the room through a side door. One of the remaining staff addressed the men.

"My name is William Peyton. I am the Assistant Director. We are going to take you to your rooms now, so listen up and go with the person who calls your name."

One by one each of the staff called out two names and escorted the men to their rooms. Finally Michael's name was called along with Fredrickson's. They followed the staff member on a journey up staircases and down hallways. It was a clean building with rooms on both sides of the hallways. It had carpet on the floors and looked freshly painted. Michael wondered if this is what Liz's dorm looked like. They finally reached their room and the staff opened the door to let them in.

"This is your room men," the staff said. "Taylor you are assigned to bed one, which is over there," he said pointing to the back of the room, "Fredrickson you are assigned to bed two, in the front here. My name is John Shaw and I am the supervisor for this floor. My room is at the end of the hallway to the right. The showers and bathrooms are at the end of the hallway to the left. It's lights out at oh nine thirty hours. If you are found out of your rooms after lights out you are penalized. All of that will be explained tomorrow. For now get cleaned up and hit the sack. It's almost lights out. Clothing and personals have been provided for you in each of your sizes. They are located in your dressers, any questions?"

Michael and Fredrickson looked at each other and then looked at John Shaw.

"No, I'm good," Michael said.

"Yeah, me too, I'm good," Fredrickson said.

"Okay then, see you men tomorrow." Shaw turned and walked out of the room shutting the door behind him.

Michael and Fredrickson watched him go and then looked at each other. Then they broke out into laughter.

"By the way, what's your first name?" Michael asked. "I'm Michael."

"Stewart, glad to meet you Michael Taylor." The guys shook hands.

"Can you believe this?" Fredrickson asked. "After putting up with that shithole in Chino, this is fucking awesome."

Michael walked over to his bed and sat on it. It was a real twin size mattress. He felt the blanket and sheets. They were soft and clean. "Amazing," he said to himself.

Fredrickson was busy going through his dresser. He was pulling out clothes and hygiene supplies. "This is unbelievable," he said.

Michael stood up and went to his dresser. "I'm going to shower and get ready for bed. I don't want any problems my first night. Let's try to beat lights out."

They both looked at the large digital clock on the wall above the door. They had twenty minutes.

"That should be no problem," Fredrickson said. "Considering we can shower in under three minutes."

"Not tonight we don't," Michael said.

73

Mr. Hansen entered the hotel room and saw the concerned faces of his fellow conspirators. He made his greetings, got himself a stiff drink and took a seat. He was the last to arrive so the meeting began.

A man in an expensive suit made of the most advanced data conductive materials stood up to address the group. "I'm sure you all heard about Gavin Jordan. He was arrested and charged with conspiracy to murder and bribery. He was stupid and jeopardized all of us with his reckless behavior. I hope that we can learn from his situation."

"Do you think he implicated any of us?" Mr. Hansen asked.

The man in the expensive suit spoke again. "It is highly doubtful. I have people in the Attorney General's office. They told me that he was charged because he was pressuring the director of the Modification Center. He even took out a contract to have him killed. They had it all on tape. The surveillance did not extend to our meetings with him thankfully."

The other men in the meeting began to talk among themselves expressing relief and gratitude at their continued anonymity. The man sitting directly to the right of Mr. Hansen spoke up. "Has anyone been approached by our political candidates about the situation?"

"The governor contacted me but it was mostly to give me a heads up on Gavin. He knew all about it already and wanted to express his concern for our discretion in the future." Mr. Hansen said.

The man in the expensive suit sat down and took a drink. He addressed the group again. "None of this is going to change our plans. We lost Gavin but things like this are to be expected. There are casualties in any conflict. He was careless, and we will not be. Our funding continues to expand and our candidates are very anxious to have our support. So that is the bottom line. Now what is our next move?"

Another man in the group stood up. "Our next move is to approach Senator Castillo from Nevada. He is facing some stiff competition in the election and could use the financial support. He has been on the fence regarding the Modification law, but has not come out against it. That could be very helpful in winning him over."

The men continued to make their plans for another ninety minutes. They were not aware of the fact that the Anti-Modification group was recording the entire meeting thanks to Mr. Hansen.

74

The sun warmed her face as she crossed the campus in the mid-day crush of students. Liz was not headed to a class however. She was very excited because Michael had made it through evaluation. He was at the Rehabilitation Center in Redding.

Liz wanted to check on Alice and her recovery. She left the campus and made her way to Alice's home. Liz was beginning to love this time of year. It was the beginning of Fall and everything smelled so fresh. The seasonal change was much more pronounced in northern California than in southern California where her parents lived.

She also noticed all the older homes. They gave a certain character to the area. All the homes in her parents' neighborhood were relatively new, by housing standards. It felt so sterile to her. She had gone back East to visit her aunt in upper New York once. She recalled how the area looked so genuine. Trees and shrubs were random, and streets and driveways were not so neatly organized and maintained.

As she approached Alice's home, Liz came across a little girl playing in her front yard. She had a doll house and a small table with two chairs. The little girl's face lit up when she saw Liz.

"Hello," the little girl said.

"Hello," Liz said.

"Would you like some tea?" The little girl held up a toy tea cup and smiled.

Liz hesitated as she did not see any adults nearby. The girl looked to be around five years old and was very cute.

"Where's your mommy?" Liz asked. She looked around while she walked up onto the lawn.

The little girl became very sad all of a sudden and sat down on one of the chairs. Then she began to cry. "Mommy is a robot."

Liz was startled by her statement. "What?"

"Her mother's a robot," a man suddenly appeared on the porch of the home. "She was Modified for causing a car accident while under the influence of alcohol. I'm her uncle. Her father is at work now."

"Oh my," Liz said. "That's terrible. Is it alright if I sit with her for a moment and have a cup of tea?" Liz asked the uncle.

"Sure, that would make her happy, thank you. What is your name?"

"Liz."

"Her name is Ellie." The man turned and walked back into the house.

Liz took a seat next to Ellie and put her hand on the girls shoulder. Ellie's crying stopped and she sat upright. She picked up the small teapot that was sitting on the table and pretended to pour Liz a cup of tea.

"Here you go Liz," Ellie said.

"Thank you."

Ellie put the teapot down and picked up a doll that was lying on the grass. She began to hug the doll and sing to it. Liz pretended to drink some tea.

"What's her name?" Liz asked.

"Molly, she's my best friend."

Liz imagined this poor little girl felt so alone going through life without her mother. Worse yet, the idea of having to think of her mother as a robot was horrible. Liz spent about thirty minutes at the tea party with Ellie. Then she gave her a hug before continuing on her journey to Alice's house.

After letting herself into the house, Liz found Alice resting upstairs in her bedroom. She walked over and gave Alice a hug.

"How are you doing?" Liz asked.

"I'm actually doing much better," Alice said. "I do find that getting plenty of rest helps a lot."

"Have you talked to Frank lately?" Liz asked. She took a seat in a chair that was located in the corner of the bedroom. It was a small accent chair that Alice used as a clothes dump. Liz had to relocate the clothes to the dresser before she sat down.

"Sorry about that," Alice said. "Yes I talked to him this morning, why?"

"Because I just had the most unsettling experience and it has changed my mind about using the information from my father's computer. I think we should let Frank know as soon as possible. We cannot let this Modification thing go on any longer." Liz had tears in her eyes as she spoke.

She related the story of Ellie to Alice, the little girl whose mother was Modified.

"I'm sorry Liz. I can tell her story has really upset you. Are you sure this is what you want to do?" Alice sat up in her bed.

"Yes it is. I'm not sure what will happen with me and my father. Maybe he won't know what I did, but we have to take that chance. If he figures it out I will have my mother help me deal with his anger. She knows how to handle him." Liz stood up and anxiously paced around the room as she spoke.

Alice reached out to her and Liz went over to her. They hugged and Liz sat back. "I know it's a big risk, but I am ready to take it now." She said.

"Okay then, I will call Frank right now." Alice picked up her phone and made the call.

"I will go downstairs to get us some fresh tea and something to eat," Liz said.

As Liz made her way to the kitchen she could hear Frank and Alice talking about the plan to use her father's recordings against his group. She knew she was doing the right thing. She realized that being an adult was hard. The right thing was not always the easy thing. She thought about Michael, she was hoping to be able to visit him soon. She took out her data pad and wrote Michael an e-mail as she waited for the water to boil.

"Dear Michael, I hope this finds you doing well. I miss you a lot and wish we could be together. I have been very busy with school and the anti-Modification group. My activities with the group have taken me down paths I never imagined I would travel. It has been an emotional roller coaster, but I think I can handle it. If not, I guess we will find out. I am hoping to be able to visit you soon. It has been a long time, and the last time we saw each other was not exactly what we hoped for. I know you are facing a lot of challenges, and I want you to know I still support you and love you, so hang in there! I will let you know the date I am coming to visit later. Love, Liz, XOXO."

75

Michael was sitting at the desk in his dorm room. He had a data pad and was reading the latest e-mail from Liz. He was excited that she was supporting him by participating in the anti-Modification movement. Her e-mails had become more emotional however. He wondered what was going on.

His data pad had restricted access so he was unable to view any news from internet sources. Michael was only permitted to have information approved by the administration. He did not know about the activities of Liz's group, or the attack on them at the rally.

Michael wrote his own e-mail and told Liz about the Rehabilitation Center and his new roommate Stewart. He was feeling upbeat about his situation. After he sent the message, Michael began to review his orientation packet.

The program had several phases. The first was a testing and evaluation phase where Michael would be given vocational interest surveys and academic achievement tests. In the second phase he would participate in an educational program that was classroom instruction, and a vocational training program which could include hands on job training. Counseling and psychotherapy would be the third phase to ensure his emotional stability before release. His testing and evaluation would begin immediately.

Stewart entered the room. "Taylor," he said.

"Hey," Michael replied.

"This place is quite a change of pace." Stewart threw his orientation packet onto his desk and flopped onto his bed.

"I know, have you looked at this material yet?" Michael asked as he stood up and stretched.

"No, I just know what they told us at the meeting."

"The thing they didn't cover is what gets you sent to Mod." Michael walked over to Stewart's side of the room.

"True, but I guess it would be similar to Chino, fighting, stealing, you know." Stewart said as he sat up with his back against the wall.

"Those things are obvious. The not so obvious things are staff like Dr. Isaac. Did you know him?" Michael crossed his arms. He was curious about Stewart since he really didn't see him at Chino, and that didn't make a lot of sense. Stewart looked to be around twenty-two years old. He looked like he was a Normal. At least his physical attributes looked engineered. He was very fit and good-looking, with blonde hair and perfect teeth and features.

"Dr. Isaac?"

"Yeah."

"Okay, yeah, I think I knew him." Stewart said

Michael suspected Stewart was lying. Stewart stood up suddenly. "I need to go to the restroom. I'll be back in a few minutes."

He walked out of the room and turned left for the bathroom. Michael peeked out of the door to watch him go. Stewart walked right past the bathroom and headed down the stairs.

"Damn," Michael said to himself. "What the hell is going on?"

76

The information splashed across the news services like a tsunami: a cabal of politicians and business men were conspiring to push through total Modification. Frank wasted little time in releasing the tapes once Liz gave the go ahead.

Liz was viewing an internet news service and watched in horror. She saw her father and his group talking about the attack at the anti-Modification rally. Her father's face was the only one that could be seen, and the voices of the other men sounded altered to hide their identities. It was certainly different than the tape she saw at Alice's home. The attorney general held a press conference and made a statement about his office launching a full investigation.

Liz called home to assess the situation. Her mother answered.

"Hello honey," her mother said.

Liz thought she sounded stressed.

"Hi Mom, I just called to see how you are. Have you been watching the news?" Liz held her breath.

"Yes, yes we have. Your father is worried. He seems to think someone put a chip on his data pad to steal his personal information. Now some recordings he made are all over the news. People are accusing him of horrible things." Her mother was wringing her hands as she spoke to Liz.

Liz hardly knew what to say. "Your father thinks we should take a trip out of the country dear." Her mother began to cry.

"Are you scared Mom?"

"I'm not sure. I don't really know what's going on. You know how your father is. He keeps all of his business dealings to himself. But if that is what he thinks is best, then we should probably do it."

"Is he at home now?"

"Yes, he's holed up in his office talking on his business phone. He's been in there for two hours. I really wish he would come out and talk to me. Let me know what's going on." She started to cry again.

"I'm so sorry Mom. I wish I could be there to help."

"Oh, don't you worry honey. I'm sure it will work out. Now you just focus on doing well at school. I will let you know if we leave, okay?" Her mother forced a smile for Liz and blew her a kiss. Then she disconnected.

"How can I focus on school when my family is blowing up?" Liz sat down and began to realize the damage she had caused by releasing the tapes. What if her father got arrested? What if he got Modified? If her parents didn't pay for school, she would have to drop out. Now she began to cry.

She decided to call Alice. Alice answered right away.

"Liz, are you alright?"

"Not really. I just spoke with my mother. Everything is going crazy. I don't know what to do."

"It's alright Liz. I know you are confused and upset. Can you get over to my house?"

"I'm not sure, I'm just so worried right now. What if I caused my father to get Modified? It looked like the tapes were modified to hide the identities of the other men. The only one who you could see and hear clearly was my father."

"Alright Liz, I'm going to call Frank and have him pick you up at the dorm."

"I guess that would be alright," Liz said very softly.

"Good, now just sit tight. He will call you when he gets there so you can meet him downstairs. Do you understand?"

"Yes."

"Good. I have to hang up now to call Frank. Do you understand?"

"Yes."

"Alright, I'm hanging up now and will see you in a little while. So just wait for Frank."

Alice hung up and Liz lay down on her bed. She could not stop thinking that she had caused her father to get Modified.

Five days later the men met at the Hotel Grandiose for the last time. Liz's father was not present. He and Liz's mother left the country for a location without an extradition treaty. Liz was told they would continue to pay her tuition and living expenses from there.

The Governor took a long drink from his cocktail. "I can't believe he taped our meetings. What the hell was he thinking?"

"Better yet, how could he let his data pad be compromised?" The leader of the group spoke up. "Has it been confirmed that his daughter was on the stage at the anti-Modification rally? Was it her who was involved in the incident on the stage?"

"Yes sir, it has been confirmed." One of the group members stood up as he spoke and walked toward the window. He looked out over the park fifteen floors below. "We had our suspicions before this. We have her under surveillance. We also have eyes on her boyfriend. He is in the Rehabilitation Center in Redlands."

The governor set his glass on the table and sighed. "Alright, so this is what's going to happen. The attorney general is going to work with us. Since we have a member who fled the country, the focus will be on him. The recordings cannot be authenticated. They are also not good quality thanks to our friends in the media. You can't see any of our faces. Therefore we can easily deflect this incident. Once the media frenzy dies down, we will be fine."

"We will continue our work, but we can't meet like this anymore. We can't risk someone else trying to put a camera on us," the leader said. "We will continue to monitor the situation and work toward our goal. The election is in six weeks and we are positioned well. Let's not allow this to get away from us."

The men all shook their heads in agreement and then ended the meeting. One by one they left the hotel by different exits.

Michael made his way to the dining hall. He was alone because he had been wary of getting too close to Stewart. He did not trust him after the night he watched him lie about using the restroom.

During Michael's first week at the Rehabilitation Center he completed all the evaluations and tests that would determine his program. He was scheduled to start academics today and the vocational program next week. He had qualified for the elite program at the Rehabilitation Center, which was tech training. Michael was surprised and pleased when he found out.

He entered the dining hall, which as usual, was organized chaos. He got a tray of food and looked around hoping to find a seat. He hadn't made any real friends yet, so he always sat alone. The dining hall had long tables with chairs on both sides. They were arranged in six rows that ran the length of the room. It was a well-lit room with a steam line at the front and beverage dispensers along one side. The walls were adorned with beautiful murals of farm life in California. They were a holdover from the old university days. Michael saw an available spot and walked toward it when he heard someone call to him.

"Hey Taylor, you lost?"

He turned around and saw Victor smiling and waving to him. Michael walked over to him. "Victor, how's it going?" Michael asked.

"Is good, how about with you?"

Michael saw there was an open seat across from Victor so he set down his tray and took a seat.

"How long you here?" Victor asked.

"Almost two weeks. Listen, I was sorry to hear about Kevin. That asshole Dr. Isaac sent him to Modification." Michael looked Victor in the eye as he spoke.

"Thanks," Victor said.

Michael was hungry and dug in enthusiastically to devour the food.

"You seem to like food here much better Taylor. No green meat, eh?"

"Yeah, I think it's actually food. So what do you make of this place?" Michael asked.

"Is okay so far, not so much like a prison, but I still feel like walking on eggshells." Victor said while eating his meal. They were only allotted thirty minutes to eat so they could not afford to just sit and chat.

"I know what you mean." Michael said. "I had a weird moment with my roommate and quite honestly I don't trust him."

"Smart thinking, I heard politicians are trying scam to get everyone Modified. Then we would have to work in factories as free labor. Election soon, no guarantee we safe. If still here and law changed we get sent to Mod." Victor kept his voice low while he spoke and looked around to ensure no one was listening in on their conversation.

"That would truly suck," Michael said. "After everything we had to do just to get here."

"Exactly, would suck. We not out of woods yet. I had visit last week and brother told me big scandal in news. Issue is heating up out there, and we are tinder." Victor took a long drink of his beverage and nodded his head as he stared at Michael.

"We need to stick together in here Victor in case anything goes down. What residence are you living in?"

"Scudder Hall, room 234, good idea Taylor. We should make sure to have breakfast with each other every day to share information, but not meet too often to raise suspicion. Where you live?"

"Simpson Hall, room 331, alright, let's meet here every morning." Michael stood up and picked up his tray. "Oh, I forgot to ask you. What's your major?"

"Fuck you, that's what Taylor."

Michael laughed, turned and walked away. Sitting two tables away his roommate Stewart bit off a piece of a Danish as he watched Michael bus his tray.

79

Michael spent his first week of classes working hard to get into student mode. After three months of life in the Evaluation Center where it was a daily battle for survival, he had to worry about things like math and science. It was quite a challenge to become studious again.

He spent every evening doing homework and every day in classes.

The third week he started his vocational program. That required him to spend eight hours a week in the tech lab, in addition to three hours of classroom instruction. By the end of the third week, he finally started to feel comfortable in his new role.

Michael adopted a polite but distant posture with Stewart. He did not trust Stewart and did not spend any of his free time with him. The guys were allowed half of Saturday and all day Sunday to themselves. Many of the guys received visitors on the weekends. Michael had not had a visit since his arrival. His mother wrote to him occasionally, but he never heard from Ryan. Liz was planning a visit but she was busy with school. She seemed to be having a hard time lately, so he did not want to pressure her.

Michael and Victor would meet every morning for breakfast. Victor was Michael's information network to the outside world. His brother visited every weekend and gave Victor updates on what was happening.

It sounded like the elections would be closely watched by everyone. The outcome could affect the future of everyone at the Rehabilitation Center.

Victor was also taking vocational training to be a mechanic. He told Michael that he had access to tools and other materials that could be used as weapons if necessary. Michael was attempting to study the surveillance and security system of the facility during his training in the tech department. He hoped he might learn to disable it, if need be, without much luck so far.

Michael and Victor were not taking anything for granted and were preparing for the worst case scenario. Their only concern was that they did not have anyone else to could count on. It was just the two of them. They wanted to find other men to team up with if they needed to plan an escape. They both agreed to be on the lookout for fellow conspirators.

That's why Michael was pleased that Saturday afternoon when he ran into Jason. Michael was sitting outside in a commons area reading when he saw Jason walking by.

"Jason," Michael yelled out to get his attention.

Jason looked Michael's way and at first did not seem to recognize him.

"Jason, it's me Taylor," Michael said as he stood up so Jason could see him better.

"Michael Taylor, holy shit dude, you made it." Jason came running over and gave Michael a big hug. "I am so glad to see you made it Michael. I really am."

"Hi Jason, it's good to see you too. I'm glad to see you're still kicking."

The boys sat down on the grass and caught up.

"What trade are you working in?" Michael asked. He was hoping Jason's trade would be helpful to them.

"I work in the vehicle repair center. It's not too bad, I guess I could do that kind of work when I get out if I had to." Jason plucked a blade of grass and put it into his mouth.

"Do you ever get access to the key fobs?" Michael asked.

"Sometimes," Jason looked at Michael. "What do you have in mind Taylor?

"Do you have any idea what's going on in the community, the political battle over Modification?"

"Not really. Why?" Jason turned to face Michael.

"There is an election in a few weeks. If the pro-Modification candidates win they will pass a law that Modifies all criminals. That would make this place worthless. Everyone who is still here would be Modified."

Jason's jaw dropped open. "What the, I can't believe that."

"It's true. My girlfriend Liz is working for an anti-Modification group and shared information with me. Plus my friend

Victor's brother visits him every weekend and gives him updates. He said the same thing."

"We are trying to position ourselves to make a break for it if necessary. We are not going to let them Modify us if we can still fight." Michael punched into the ground. He was angry just from talking about it.

"Well count me in for sure. There is no way I intend to just roll over."

"That's great. Victor and I meet every morning at the dining hall to exchange information. We sit in the southwest corner. Why don't you meet with us in the morning?" Michael looked at Jason. "Are you sure you're up for this?"

"Hell yes."

"Do you have anyone here that you trust? We may need more manpower."

"I know a couple of guys that would jump in."

"Good. Don't say anything to them yet, and don't invite them to meet with us at breakfast yet. I want Victor to meet you first, understand?"

"Sure, I understand. Alright, I'm going to move on now. I don't want them to become suspicious and put a recording wand on us." Jason stood up to go.

Michael stood up and the guys hugged again. "See you in the morning," Michael said.

Michael sat down again and picked up his book. He watched Jason walk across the commons area. He thought it was ironic that Jason may be his ticket out of here after being the one who got him in here. He lay back onto the grass and basked in the sun.

80

The shoes fit well and the sports clothing was comfortable. Michael felt good as he headed to the athletic recreation area. He had been trying to take advantage of the gym since his arrival at the Rehabilitation Center. They had a wonderful gymnasium for basketball and a full weight room. They also had athletic fields and a track. The university that used to be there offered most sports to its students, and the government maintained the facilities for the inmates.

It was a nice fall day in Northern California, and Michael took in a deep breath as he crossed campus. In addition to the recreational aspects of working out or playing sports, he thought it was a good idea to stay in good physical condition.

He reached the gymnasium and had his data hand scanned by the supervising staff. Although things at the Center were much more relaxed than in Chino, they still kept tabs on who was where and when. There was a basketball game in progress. Michael walked over to the side where a few guys were hanging out waiting for the next game.

"You guys have a full team yet?" Michael asked.

"Sure Taylor, you can join us," one of the men said.

"Do I know you?" Michael asked.

"We crossed paths at Chino. I'm Ed Smith."

"Ed, of course, I remember you now." Michael went over to Ed and shook his hand. "I'm glad to see you made it out of that place."

"You too, how long have you been here?"

"About three weeks or so, how about you?" Michael asked.

"I just got here about five days ago." Ed had a basketball in his hands and he handed it to Michael. "Are you any good at this game?"

Michael laughed, "Not really, I just like to run around a little bit. It's good exercise." He bounced the ball a couple of times. "I came here to keep active. I never had time for sports in high school. I had to work, how about you?"

"I was enhanced for physical attributes. I was quite an athlete in high school. I won a lot of trophies and awards. I let myself get too big of a head though. That's how I ended up here. I got angry at a kid who worked in the locker room at the college I went to. I punched him out and broke his jaw. It was really stupid and a fucked up thing to do. I can see that now." Ed looked down at the ground while he spoke. Then he looked up at Michael and smiled. "Let's just try to have some fun, okay?"

"Sure, let's have some fun." Michael said.

"Have you been keeping up with the news about the upcoming elections?" Michael asked.

"Not too much. My head has been spinning what with my transfer and all." Ed had turned his attention to the game that was in progress. "They should be done in a minute," he said.

"Right, your transfer," Michael could see that Ed was getting ready to play the next game. His competiveness showed as he became mentally focused on the last few plays of the game on the floor. He decided to let it go for now. "Just play some ball for now," he said to himself, "Relax."

The game on the floor ended. Michael, Ed and the three other guys who had next game took the floor. They shot around and warmed up while the winners of the prior game got a water break. When the winners returned to play, they all shook hands and introduced themselves. Ed knew one of the guys on the winning team from high school.

"Taylor, this is Frank. We knew each other in high school." Ed said as he introduced the guys.

"Frank Headley, what did you say your name was?"

"Taylor, Michael Taylor, nice to meet you." Michael and Frank shook hands.

"Michael Taylor. Are you the guy that got Zack Cole's ass kicked when we were at Chino?" Frank laughed as he recalled the incident.

"That's him," Ed said as he nodded his head up and down.

Michael tried to ignore the question and not take it any further since Ed answered it.

"Did you guys hear that asshole got Modified?" Frank asked.

"Really?" Michael asked.

"Yeah, he got gaffoed up along with a couple of the Doctors. They were running a scam to send people to Modification for money," Ed said.

Michael became concerned for Dr. Carson all of a sudden. "It wasn't Dr. Carson was it?"

"No, not him, let's play." Frank said as he took the ball from Michael.

The game began and Michael became completely engrossed in the activity. He could sense the polished finish of the floor beneath his shoes as they squeaked with his cutting actions. He could also feel his body fall into a rhythm as he ran back and forth.

His team won, thanks to Ed, and they got to play another game, and then two more games. Michael was exhausted and actually thankful when they finally lost a game. It meant he could sit down and catch his breath.

The guys sat down to drink some water. "Maybe I'll see you here again," Michael said.

"Sure," Ed said.

"Nothing better to do," Frank said.

"Good. I'm done I'll catch you guys later."

The other guys nodded their heads, so Michael waved goodbye and headed back to his room. As he passed the weight room, he noticed his roommate stretching out. Stewart saw Michael and put his head down and turned away. Michael kept going.

81

Michael was feeling upbeat and had a smile on his face. He received an e-mail from Liz. She was going to visit on Saturday. It was a great way to start a new week.

"You're in a good mood for a Monday," Stewart said.

Michael immediately constrained himself. "Not really," he said. "Just another Monday."

He was determined not to give Stewart even a morsel of information about himself, and certainly nothing about Liz. He had learned the hard way to guard his personal life. Michael grabbed his book bag and headed out. He made it a point to try and leave before Stewart so he could meet up with Victor. He didn't need Stewart trying to tag along. He bolted down the stairs and emerged out into the common area.

It was a crisp, cool morning. Michael enjoyed all the colorful trees on campus. He headed toward the dining hall and thought of Billie. He wondered if Billie was able to enjoy a cool breeze.

When he reached the dining hall, he had his data hand scanned. Then he grabbed a tray and got into the food line. He saw a couple of guys from his tech program and exchanged greetings. Michael was settling into a routine now. At times he actually felt like a real college student.

He was glad they didn't have Mods serving food like at Chino. That was really depressing. He had not seen a Mod since his arrival in Redding. Someone told him they did not want to discourage the inmates who were being "rehabilitated." He wasn't sure if that was their reasoning, but he appreciated it just the same.

Michael took his tray and went to the rendezvous spot to meet Victor. Jason was supposed to meet them today. He kept a lookout for him. Michael saw Stewart enter the dining hall so he sat down and hid behind a pole. He did not want Stewart to see him. Victor walked up and set his tray on the table.

"What's up with you Taylor? Why you hiding behind pole?" Victor asked.

"I don't want someone to see me. Why else would I do it?" Michael said. "Why don't you sit down and quit drawing attention to me."

"Alright, alright," Victor took a seat.

"I asked someone to join us today. I knew him from my neighborhood. He may be able to help us if we need to do something drastic."

"You sure we can trust him?" Victor asked as he bit into a banana.

"Not totally. He's the reason I'm in here in the first place, but it was not completely his fault. I know he can take care of himself though. Besides, he works in the hover car shop. That could be a huge help to us." Michael began to eat his food when Jason walked up with a tray in his hand.

"Hey Michael," Jason said.

"Hey, have a seat," Michael said. He pointed to an empty chair next to Victor.

Jason sat down. Victor looked at Michael with a raised eyebrow.

"Jason this is Victor," Michael said.

The guys looked at each other.

"I was just telling Victor about your trade," Michael said.

"You have access to hover cars?" Victor asked.

"I can get one if I need to," Jason said.

"That is good."

"Did you get a visit this weekend?" Michael asked Victor.

"No, no news," Victor said.

"My girlfriend Liz is coming to visit Saturday. We can get an update on what's happening on the outside from her," Michael said.

"So what kind of a plan do you guys have worked out?" Jason asked.

"Not much really. I can maybe get some weapons from shop. Taylor may or may not be able to sabotage security system.

You may be able to get hover car. Pretty weak shit really, but we have to do something," Victor said.

"I guess we have to do something if they try to Modify all of us. I may be able to get a couple of guys to help us," Jason said.

"Let's wait on that until we have more of a plan. We need to think this through a little. I am also working on trying to line up more manpower," Michael said.

"I think if we have to do something, meal time is best," Victor said.

"Why's that?" Jason asked.

"Because everyone out in one place. Too many bodies to contain, easier to sneak out in chaos if place erupts," Victor said.

"That's good thinking," Michael said. "We could get some guys to set fires in different parts of the dining hall. That would create confusion to hide an escape attempt."

"I like this idea," Jason said. "My guys could take care of that easy."

"It's getting late, and we have to go to classes," Michael said. "Jason, can you make a map of the dining hall and look for good spots for the fires?"

"Sure, sounds good," Jason said.

"Victor, can you look for something we can set the fires with at your shop?"

Victor nodded his head acknowledging Michael.

"I am going to try to get as much information on the security system as I can," Michael said. "The thing we don't know is what their plan is for responding to an incident. We may have to set something off to see their response plan. Let's think about that, what could we do?"

Michael saw Stewart heading his way. "I have to go now," Michael said as he stood up. He grabbed his book bag and headed out.

Jason patted Victor on the back. "Nice to meet you Victor, see you tomorrow." Jason also made a quick departure.

Victor sat and finished the last few bites of his breakfast as Stewart walked by searching for someone.

82

Michael walked down the hallway of the counseling center. He needed to begin his preliminary psychological evaluation. He had to undergo an initial evaluation to establish a baseline of functioning early in the program. The actual counseling phase was in the last three months of his program. He was walking with his head down. He was looking at his data pad to see where to report.

"Hello Michael."

Michael looked up. He saw Dr. Carson standing in front of him, smiling.

"Dr. Carson, wow! What are you doing here? I mean, it's great to see you."

"Thank you Michael. It's great to see you too. You look very well."

"Thanks, I feel great. It's nice to be able to act like a normal person again. To get outside and exercise, and have some fun."

"I bet. To answer your question, I'm here for training. This facility has a staff training center. I'm up here for a month."

"Oh, that's cool."

"Yes, and in fact maybe you can help me out. I need to have someone enrolled here at the Rehabilitation Center participate in some of my training exercises. Would you be interested?"

"I guess so. What would I have to do?"

"Just take some tests, participate in therapy exercises, like we used to do back in Chino. I would get you excused from your regular classroom assignments during your participation."

"I would be happy to help out. I owe you a lot Dr. Carson. It would be nice to be able to pay you back a little."

"You really don't owe me Michael, but I would be pleased to be working with you again. I will make the necessary arrangements and notify you of the schedule by e-mail."

"Sure, okay. I will see you later."

"Thank you Michael," Dr. Carson said as he extended his hand to Michael.

Michael shook his hand. They paused, and smiled at each other. Then Michael moved off, and walked down the hallway to his appointment. He turned, and watched Dr. Carson walk in the other direction. "See you later Doc," Michael yelled after him.

Dr. Carson turned and waved to him.

83

The next morning the tech lab was not busy when Michael entered it and found a work station. He tried to find a spot with no one near him so he could go about his business. He was somewhat new to tech material, but was catching on quickly. He had some tech stuff in high school before he went to the continuation school. After that he just focused on graduating quickly. He always had a knack for it, however.

Today he was trying to navigate into the main frame of the Rehabilitation Center. He had not been able to penetrate it yet. The system was secure and he was not having much luck. He had been working at it for three days.

The lab was supervised by an inmate teaching assistant named Charles. He oversaw the other inmates work and assisted with glitches. Charles was a Normal who had intellectual enhancements. Charles came over and sat down next to Michael.

"Mr. Taylor," Charles said.

Michael looked up, and then sat back somewhat surprised.

"Mr. Taylor, here's the thing. I have been monitoring your work, and it appears as though you have been attempting to go places that you should not be going."

Michael just looked at Charles. He did not want to say anything that might incriminate himself.

"Okay, Mr. Taylor, let me do the talking," Charles said. "There are two possible scenarios that lead someone down the path you are on. One is to muck with the transcript records to ensure they graduate. The other is to be able to affect the center's systems, such as the security system. I have observed you in the short time you have been here and I am confident you don't need to worry about the first reason. So why don't you tell me why you think you need to do the second." Charles leaned forward so that he was very close to Michael.

Michael took a deep breath. He felt cornered. If Charles turned him in he would be screwed.

"Let me ask you a question Charles," Michael said. "How much time do you have left here?"

Charles looked Michael in the eyes. "Alright, I'll play along," he said. "I have three months left."

"One more question?" Michael asked. Charles nodded his head to Michael. "Do you have any idea what is going on outside of here, with the election in two weeks?"

"I do," Charles said.

"Then you know that if the election goes wrong for the Modification law, we will all be Modified well before your three months is up."

Charles sat back into his chair. He looked around the lab to see if anyone had moved to within earshot of them. Then he spoke, "I am aware of that Mr. Taylor. That fact has indeed been a source of great consternation for me lately."

"Yeah, well it's been freaking me out too. Only I intend to have a plan if things go south. I am not going to sit on my hands and be turned into a turnip." Michael was becoming more animated as he spoke. He checked himself however, so as not to draw attention to them.

"I understand Mr. Taylor. Perhaps we could come to some kind of an understanding with each other. For example if I do not report this incident. Perhaps we could work together, to help each other in time of need, if it comes to that of course."

"I think that is a good plan." Michael extended his hand to Charles. Charles shook his hand. Michael found it cold and clammy.

"Are you able to get into the security system Charles?" Michael asked.

"I am, but you can't do it through this lab. That is why I was on to you. It has to be done from one of the center's main terminals. There are only a few of them in public areas, but I know where they are and I can gain access." Charles anxiously looked around the lab again.

"Okay Charles, take a breath, relax man. We can talk about all of this later with fewer ears around, alright?"

"Okay Mr. Taylor. In the meantime you should stick to your lesson plans."

"Sounds good Charles, we can set up a meet before the end of lab. Think of a good time we can meet, and let me know when." Michael smiled at Charles. "And why don't you call me Michael?"

Charles stood up and took one more look around the lab. "Very good Mr. Taylor," he said. Then he walked away.

Michael sat back into his chair and took several deep breaths. "That was close," he said to himself.

Charles walked by his station later and passed Michael a note with a meeting place and a time on it.

84

Saturday finally arrived. Liz was coming to visit today. Michael had not seen her since Chino. That's when he found out Billie was working in her parent's home as a Mod.

He took a shower and dressed. It was great to have actual clothing to wear instead of the jumpsuits he wore at Chino. He also had shoes that fit. Stewart slept in or at least pretended to, so Michael went to breakfast early. He had some time to kill because visiting didn't start until eleven.

He saw Jason in the usual spot and went to sit with him.

"Don't we look all spiffed up?" Jason said when he saw Michael.

"Liz is coming to visit today," Michael said.

"Nice, good for you."

Victor sat down at the table. "Look at pretty boy today."

"His girlfriend is visiting," Jason offered.

"Good. Does she have friend for me?" Victor asked.

"I don't know but I'll ask," Michael said. "You do have a lot to offer a girl, after all."

"You have cruel heart Taylor," Victor said.

"Okay, listen," Michael said, lowering his voice. "I almost got my butt gaffoed up this week trying to hack the security system. The good news is the tech teaching assistant wants to throw in with us. I met with him last night and he is totally onboard. He is confident he can kill the alarm and any deterrent measures that are controlled electronically."

"That's great," Jason said. "I have two guys who are interested in helping. Between the three of us we can disable the security hover car and get key fobs for as many hover cars as we need." They had to talk louder now as the din of the busy dining hall rose.

Victor leaned forward so he could whisper and still be heard. "I have been giving thought to this. What we should do is set off disturbance, and then all go to garage to leave in hover cars. What we need is somewhere to go on outside. Somewhere to ditch hover cars from the Center so can't be tracked. We need exchange vehicles, money, and ID cards."

The guys listened to him intently. Jason looked discouraged. "You're right," he said. "If we just fly out of here with no transition plan, we are screwed. They will track those vehicles real fast."

"Can your brother help, could he get ID cards?" Michael asked.

Victor munched on his breakfast a little. He thought about it for a minute. "Maybe," he said. "I will ask him today."

"I can ask Liz for help from her political friends. They might be able to get some vehicles and money," Michael said. Someone walked behind his chair and bumped him. Michael spilled his juice and almost got some on his shirt. He quickly wiped it away.

"We'll know after the election next week if we need to do this. The new politicos take office three weeks later. If they put rush on it, we have new law in five or six weeks," Victor said.

The boys all sat in silence and looked at each other. The gravity of the situation was sinking in.

"I have some news about weapons," Victor finally broke the silence. "We have material to make small explosive. We can use to set fires."

"Excellent," Michael said. "Try to get some out for our trial run. If the election goes against us we will need to do that right away to figure out how to deal with their response."

Michael noticed Stewart sitting down at the table behind them. He was within earshot. Michael motioned to the guys to be quiet about their plans. They all concentrated on finishing their food.

Victor stood up to go first. "You enjoy your visit today Taylor," he said.

Michael and Jason also got up. "Thanks," Michael said.

The boys dispersed and Michael headed back to his room for a little rest before his visit.

85

It was finally time to go to the visiting yard. Michael checked himself once more in the mirror as he headed out to meet Liz. The visiting yard was next to the athletic fields so Michael had to walk across campus. It was cloudy and cool, but Michael was in an upbeat mood.

He checked in at the security gate to have his hand scanned, and body patted down. He received a table number and was pointed to the location. Procedures here were much more lax than in Chino where he had to be strip searched before and after his visit.

He saw Liz waiting for him and his heart leapt. She spotted him and stood up to greet him. He walked over to her and they embraced, at least as much of an embrace as was allowed. Which wasn't much, but he kissed and hugged her. She hugged him, and they finally let go of each other. They took a seat at a picnic table.

She looked tired and was staring down at the table. Michael reached out and held her hands. She looked up at him and smiled weakly.

"Are you alright Liz?" Michael asked.

Liz began to cry. Michael didn't know what to do. He was not allowed to go to her and comfort her. All he could do was sit there and hold her hands. After a few moments she gathered herself.

"I'm sorry," she said. "I'm sure this is not what you wanted to see from me." She took a Kleenex out of her purse and wiped her face.

"It's okay," Michael said. "What is going on? What's making you cry?"

"A lot has happened since I saw you the last time. I haven't told you in my e-mails because I wasn't sure who would see them."

"I kind of figured that out, that you were not telling me things. It's probably a good idea." Michael instinctively looked around as he spoke to see if anyone was trying to eavesdrop on them now. "Why don't you tell me now?"

Liz took a deep breath and then another. "Alright," she said. "First of all I joined an anti-Modification political group. That much you know. What you don't know is that I put a device on my father's data pad that allowed us, the group, to hack his data pad. We found some tapes of him and other people, like other businessmen, conspiring to undermine the election.

"Wow," Michael said.

"Yeah, wow," Liz said. "That's not the half of it. After the tapes were released to the media, my father freaked out and my parents moved out of the country."

"What?"

"He doesn't know it was me who betrayed him. They are still supporting me but I feel awful. For the last few weeks I have been holed up in my dorm room, just going to classes."

"I bet. Liz, I'm so sorry this happened." Michael shifted on his seat. He was unnerved by what she was saying but could only sit there.

"The election is next week. My group was hoping the tapes would turn the tide in our favor, but it doesn't look like it will. I did all of that for nothing, and now if they have their way you will be Modified anyway." Liz began to cry again.

Michael gave her a moment to cry herself out. Then he squeezed her hand tightly and waited while she took out another Kleenex. "There have been some things going on around here that are beginning to make more sense, now that you have told me this."

"What do you mean?" Liz asked.

"I think my roommate is a plant to watch over me."

"Really?" Liz sat up straight when she heard this.

"Yes really. Listen Liz, I'm going to share something with you. I want to ask for your help. I know it's probably not fair to ask you considering what you have done already, but it seems that you are invested in helping to stop this Modification thing." Michael leaned in as he spoke. He was not sure how she would react to what he was going to ask.

"What Michael?"

"We are aware of the election and what might happen. If the total Modification ticket wins, we are going to try to escape from here." He waited a moment to try and judge her reaction before going further. She dabbed her eyes again with her Kleenex. She was staring at him inquisitively, so he went on.

"If we do this we are going to need help from someone on the outside. We may have someone getting us fake ID's, but will need to go to a place nearby. Somewhere where we can ditch the hover cars from the center and get new ones. We will also need some money. Do you think the people in your group can help with that?" He watched her reaction. She sat back a little and thought about what he had said.

Finally she spoke. "I can ask them. Of course I will help you, Michael. You are all I have now. If not for you and my friend Alice, I am all alone."

Michael felt a great sense of relief wash over him. He reached out again for her hands. They sat there for a moment squeezing each other's hands. Finally Liz let out a little laugh. "We can be regular Bonnie and Clydes," she said. "Outlaws!"

Michael also let out a little laugh. "I guess we will be."

"If you are being watched, we will have to be extra careful," Liz said.

"You know, if I am being watched, then there is a good chance you are also."

"You're right." Liz suddenly slapped her hand on the table. Then she quickly laughed out loud to distract anyone who may have seen her do that.

"Okay, sweetie, just relax," Michael said. He became worried they were drawing too much attention to themselves. He didn't want staff to point a surveillance wand their way. He looked around again, and no seemed to be watching them.

"I'm sorry."

"Don't worry. Listen though. We need to make a plan to be able to communicate with each other. If we are being watched we have to be careful."

"What about our Lovers' Code?" Liz asked.

"Good thinking," Michael said. High school had been the last time they used it. They had devised it to be able to pass notes in class. They made up the code to prevent anyone else from being able to read their notes. It was a simple number/letter code.

"We can use the code to communicate in e-mail," Liz said. "I thought about using it before but I didn't want to get you in trouble. I wasn't sure."

"It's okay. We didn't really need it before. It's also probably best if you don't come here again until this is over. If we are both being watched they may figure out our plans. Just let me know if your group can help us. Tell me the location they pick with Lovers' Code. Tell them it will be very early in the morning." They both became silent again and looked into each other's eyes.

"How did this happen, Michael?" Liz asked. "How did things get to this point so quickly?"

"I don't know." Michael shook his head as he spoke.

The end of the visiting time was announced by the staff. Michael and Liz stood up and gave each other a hug goodbye. Michael watched her walk out the gate. He waited until he could no longer see her before he averted his eyes. He could not believe how much their lives had changed in such a short time.

86

Michael munched on a bran muffin and took a gulp of orange juice as Victor and Jason sat down. Michael took a quick look around to ensure his shadow Stewart was nowhere near. Then he began to update the guys on his visit with Liz.

"Liz thinks she can get her group to help with hover cars and money. She is going to ask them right away." Michael said as soon as they were seated.

"My brother will help with the ID cards," Victor said as he peeled a banana. "But I have question. Is test run really necessary?"

"Maybe, maybe not," Michael said. "It is a good way to really see their response to incidents. Remember when you first got to Chino? The first time an incident occurred? Did you have any idea what was going on? I know I didn't. If we know exactly what they do here, we can better plan for it."

"That makes sense," Jason said. "There hasn't been one incident since I got here. I have no idea what staff does."

"Okay, I guess it makes sense," Victor said. "I hope we not hanging ourselves though."

"Me too Victor, if you guys don't want a rehearsal let me know. This is not a dictatorship."

The guys all looked at each other for a moment. Jason spoke first, "I say we do the rehearsal."

Michael looked at Victor. Victor shrugged his shoulders. "Okay, let's do it then."

"It's settled then," Michael said. "What do you have Jason?"

"I have completed the map of the area and think I have a couple of good locations for preliminary fires," Jason said. "I was wondering what you guys think. Should we set fires in different locations for the test run than we will use for the real thing?" He dug into a bowl of oatmeal and scooped a spoonful into his mouth.

"Good question," Michael said. He wiped his mouth with a napkin and thought about it for a second. "I think we have a better surprise element if we use different locations."

"I agree," Victor said. "Let's use different locations."

"The election is in three days. If the pro-Modification people win, we will have to do our test run next week. Will you have enough explosives by then?" Michael looked at Victor as he spoke. Victor had a banana shoved half way down his throat. Michael began to laugh as he looked at him. "You can bite a piece off you know?"

"I did," Victor tried to say with a mouth full of banana. "Is just big bite."

All three of the guys had a good laugh at Victor. Then they got back down to business.

"The explosives?" Michael asked again.

"Yes, we have enough for test and real thing. Ready when you are." Victor then shoved the rest of the banana into his mouth.

The guys had finished their meals and went about making plans for their test run. Jason laid out the locations of the test fires.

"I want one of the incendiaries," Michael said.

"Really," Jason said. "What for?"

"I want to put it into my roommate's bag. I am pretty sure he was placed here to spy on me. We need to take him out of the picture before the real attempt. I don't want him sticking his nose into it and mucking things up. His bag is going to be the source of one of the test explosions. Plus it might help implicate him and take some heat off of us."

Jason and Victor looked at each other and shrugged. "Up to you Taylor, if you want I give to you tonight. Come to gym at seven tonight," Victor said.

"Perfect." Michael stood up and grabbed his bag. "See you guys later." He walked out of the dining hall.

87

Dr. Carson sent Michael a message to go to the Counseling Center the next morning. When he arrived at the Center, Dr. Carson was waiting for him.

"Good morning Michael," Dr. Carson said.

"Good morning Doctor."

"Let's go ahead inside." As they walked up stairs to the building Dr. Carson filled him in on the program. "We will be part of a group this morning. There will be other doctors and inmates like you. There will be an instructor teaching the doctors how to administer a new personality test. You will be there as my test subject. The results will not be included in your file."

"Okay, Dr. Carson." Michael said. "Can I ask you a question before we get in there?"

Dr. Carson stopped walking. "Sure Michael. What would you like to know?"

Michael moved closer to Dr. Carson and leaned over to whisper. "There are rumors that if certain people win the election next week they will modify everyone. That includes me, and the other guys in here. Do you think that will happen?"

Dr. Carson did not answer at first. For a moment he looked around them. Then he pulled Michael into a nearby empty classroom. When they were alone he answered Michael. "Yes. I do think that will happen."

The two men stood staring at each other, speechless for a moment. Finally Michael spoke, "What should I do?"

"I'm not really sure. It is almost certain the pro-Modification people are going to win the election. I will be out of a job myself. That's the real reason I'm up here. I'm looking for a job in Northern California. I want to be near my daughter at Stanford. But that is minor compared to your problem. I wish there was something I could do to help you." Dr. Carson sat into a nearby chair, and dropped his head into his hands.

Michael watched him. His heart was pumping so hard he thought his chest would explode. The doctor had just told him his worse fears would come true. Dr. Carson sat up and looked at Michael. He had tears in his eyes.

"Don't worry Doc," Michael said.

Dr. Carson stood up. "Michael, be assured, if there is anything I can do for you, to help you, I will."

"Thanks, Dr. Carson." Michael felt numb as Dr. Carson led him back into the hallway.

They headed into the training room and took a seat with the others. For the next few hours Michael's head was spinning because of the training. What he really wanted to do was work on ideas to make their escape successful.

88

The news stream stated that Mods were once again cleared to work in residences. It had been determined that prior attack was an aberration. No further problems were anticipated. Liz shook her head in disgust as she put down her data pad. She was going to have lunch with Alice.

She grabbed her sweater and headed out of the dorm. She walked across campus and was heading toward Alice's house. On the way she passed Ellie's house. She saw the small table and chairs in the front yard. The tea set was sitting on the table. But there was no sign of Ellie.

When she reached Alice's house she knocked and let herself in. She headed into the kitchen where she found Alice serving up bowls of salad.

"Hi Liz," Alice said. "How are you dear?" Alice walked over and gave Liz a hug.

"I'm alright," Liz said as she hugged Alice.

"Have a seat, lunch is served."

"I just heard on the news that they have approved Mods to work in residences again," Liz said as she took a seat.

Alice stopped serving for a second and looked at Liz. She put her hand to her mouth. "That's not good," she said.

"I know. It means the full Modification movement is gaining steam again."

Alice sat down and put salad dressing onto her lettuce. "Well, the election is tomorrow so we should know very soon how things will go."

Liz stuck her fork into her salad, but then set it down and sat back into her chair. "I need to ask you something very important."

"What's that?" Alice asked.

"I went to visit Michael at the Rehabilitation Center last weekend. He said that if the election is won by the pro-Modification, group they are going to attempt a breakout. He is afraid that they will be Modified if the law is changed."

Alice also put her fork down as Liz had her total attention. "Wow, that's big news."

"They want our help. They need hover cars and money. They also need a place to rendezvous with us to exchange the hover cars," Liz said. "I have some money but I was hoping our group could help with this."

Alice stood up and walked over to the sink. She leaned back to digest the information Liz just gave her.

"I know it's a lot to ask," Liz said.

"Have you thought about what you will do after the escape?"

"We haven't really talked about it, but we will have new ID cards. I guess we will move somewhere where no one knows us and try to start over. My family is gone so I don't have anyone here." Liz began to tear up as she spoke.

"Right," Alice said. She walked over and put her hand on Liz's back to console her. "Well, you know, after all you've done, we better help you and Michael. I'm going to call Frank and tell him we need to help you with this, Liz."

"Thank you Alice," Liz said.

"When would all of this take place?"

"Assuming the law will be changed, right after the election. They are afraid if they wait too long, security may be increased at the center."

"Sure, that makes sense," Alice said. "So we need to move on this right now." Alice walked over to the counter and picked up her phone. She dialed Frank's number. As she waited for Frank to answer, she looked at Liz and smiled. Liz attempted a smile, but she could not quite muster one.

89

Election activity had been streaming all day long. Liz had been checking the results off and on between classes. The east coast was three hours ahead, so they were already calling the initial results in some of the eastern states when she got home.

Modification had become the major issue of the election. It took center stage in all of the debates and all of the news reports. Each of the candidates had made their positions clear regarding Modification.

The country was split regarding the issue and most of the races were very close. Too close to call until the last votes were cast in every state. Liz checked the latest results as soon as she put her books down on the desk.

It was close, but the pro-Modification group was winning in the eastern states. The nation's final tallies would not be revealed until tomorrow morning. Liz found the process frustrating and exhausting.

Liz picked up an apple and lay back onto her bed to rest. As she bit into the apple her phone rang. It was the secure, non-vid phone Frank had given her.

"Hello," she said.

"Hi Liz, this is Frank."

She sat upright. "Yes Frank, how are you?"

"I'm fine. I wanted to call you because Alice told me about the trip you have planned."

"My trip? Oh yes, my trip. It's coming up very soon," she said. At first she did not realize he was talking about Michael and his escape attempt.

"Well I have some good news for you. We have decided to help you and we have made some travel arrangements."

"Wow, that's great Frank. That will help tremendously. I don't know how to thank you."

"Well you have put yourself on the line for us, so you deserve it."

"Thank you," she said.

"Alice is going to meet you on campus tomorrow at noon in front of the science building. She will have your travel packet. I want to wish you the best."

"Thank you Frank, so much," Liz said.

"You're welcome. Good luck Liz." Then he hung up.

It looked like she was about to embark on a strange new adventure. She would completely turn her life upside down if she went through with it. The worst part was she didn't really have anyone to talk to about it. She would e-mail Michael tomorrow with the details. She would also say goodbye to Alice, but other than that she had to keep to herself.

She lay back and took another bite of her apple.

90

The next morning Liz got out of bed and immediately reached for her data pad to get the final election results. The bad feeling she had the night before was validated. The pro-Modification ticket swept the country. Her heart sank.

She was supposed to meet Alice today if the escape was a go, so she checked her message center. There was a note from Alice. She would be in front of the Science building at noon. Liz sat for a moment considering the impact all of these recent events had on her.

She would most likely be on the run from the authorities in less than a week. She would leave behind all of her lifelong friends, and her family would be on the run in a foreign country. There were many arrangements to be made.

Liz pulled out her backpack to sort through her belongings. She knew she would have to travel light. She didn't care about that. Fancy clothes never meant much to her. She could not bring any data wear with her, because it may be traceable. She spent the whole morning packing her travel bag.

She didn't bother going to classes. There was no point. The more she thought about that, however, she decided she should go to classes tomorrow. If she was being watched, she didn't want to tip them off to her plan in any way.

At noon time she was standing in front of the science building. She saw Alice approaching her. She had a smile on her face. Liz would miss Alice, the sister she never had. Now she would have to say goodbye to her, forever.

"Hello," Liz said as she gave Alice a hug.

"Hi Liz." They hugged each other for the longest time. Each one was afraid to let go because they knew what that meant.

Finally they separated. "Why don't we have a seat on that bench?" Alice said.

They took a seat and Alice set a small envelope onto the bench. "This is for you Liz. Let's wait a second before you pick it up. If you are being watched, we don't want to be too obvious."

"Alright," Liz said.

She was filled with conflicting emotions and could not think straight, she was glad Alice was looking out for her.

"There is money and the address of a farmhouse that is owned by one of our group. You can meet Michael there to exchange hover cars. There will be two of them. They are standard family size cars that hold five people each. The owner of the house will dispose of the hover cars from the Rehabilitation Center. The contact's e-mail is also in the envelope in case there is a change of plan. Call him Uncle Bill.

Liz reached down and squeezed Alice's hand. "Thank you Alice."

Alice reached around and hugged Liz. "Take care of yourself Liz. You should wait a moment before you leave."

Alice stood up and smiled at Liz. Then she turned and walked away. Liz watched her go. Then she picked up the envelope and put it into her purse. She headed back to her dorm room where she opened the envelope. She examined what Alice had given her. Then she pulled out her data pad and sent Michael a message with the details of the plan.

When she finished, she packed her backpack with the contents of the envelope and her travel kit. She went down into the basement of the dorm. There was a storage area down there where each student was allowed to keep personal items.

She put her items into a space that was assigned to Jean Simmons. Jean was a student who left school last month because of drug abuse problems. Liz locked the storage space and looked around to be sure no one had seen what she did. If anyone searched her room or her storage space, they would not find the escape package.

She went back up to her room and sat down to work on a timetable and plan. She found that a shoot tube station was located less than a mile from the farmhouse. She could walk to the farmhouse from there. She felt oddly excited now. Maybe she was ready for this adventure.

91

Michael dressed quickly and bolted out of his room. He was supposed to meet Victor in the dining hall, but he needed to do something first. He needed one more piece of the puzzle before the escape plan would be complete.

He entered the residence hall next to his and went up to the second floor. He looked for a room. When he found it he knocked on the door. Ed Smith answered the door. He was still in his night clothes and looked surprised to see Michael.

"Taylor, what's up, what time is it?" Ed looked over his door to check the time.

"Can I come in Ed? I need to talk to you, it's important." He pushed himself past Ed and entered Ed's room. Ed shook his head and shut the door.

"I guess so," Ed said.

Michael took a seat at the desk. Ed did not have a roommate so they were alone.

"Have a seat Ed," Michael said.

Ed obediently sat on his bed. "What's this about Taylor?"

"Do you have any access to news outside the Center Ed?"

"Not really. I haven't had any visitors yet. You know they don't let us stream on the internet." Ed rubbed his eyes in an attempt to wake himself up.

"Well I do Ed. And yesterday there was an election. The pro-Modification candidates won by an overwhelming majority. Do you know what that means?" Michael leaned down to look Ed in the eyes. He wanted to be sure he had his attention.

Ed sat up. "Not really."

"It means that in about five or six weeks they will pass a law that will allow them to Modify us."

"What?" Ed suddenly stood up. "What the hell are you talking about Taylor?"

"That's right Ed. We are screwed." Michael also stood and was now face to face with him.

"What should we do?"

"We should get the fuck out of here, that's what we should do Ed."

Ed sat back down onto his bed. "This is crazy," he said.

"Yeah Ed, it is crazy. But we have a plan. A way out, and we could use your help. So I need to know if you are interested. Can we count on you to help us and then help yourself?"

Ed put his head down into his hands. He rocked back and forth for a moment while making a moaning sound. Then he stopped and stood up. He walked around the room for a second and then came back and stood in front of Michael.

"What do I need to do?" Ed asked.

Michael reached out and grabbed him by the shoulders. He shook him hard. "That's good Ed," Michael said.

Ed smiled and then began to laugh. "Tell me what to do Taylor. I do not want to be Modified."

"You work in the medical department, right?" Michael asked.

"Yes,"

"We need you to steal a data card removal tool. After we escape we will need to remove our data cards so they can't track us." Michael patted him on the shoulder again.

"Piece of cake," Ed said.

"Great," Michael said, "We will need it in the next two days. Can you manage that?"

"Sure." Ed nodded his head as he spoke as if to doubly verify his capabilities.

"Great," Michael said. "Be ready to go when I give you the word. Get the device as soon as you can. When I give you the word things will happen fast. Got it?"

"Got it."

"Don't say anything to anyone about this or you could screw it up for the rest of us. Not even to your buddy Frank. Can you handle that?"

"Not even Frank?"

"No!" Michael yelled. "I know he's your boy from way back, but we won't have room for him. You have to make a decision

Ed. Do you want to save your ass, or hang out with Frank as a Mod?"

Ed looked like he killed his best friend because in a way he was. "I get it," he said.

"Good, now steal the device and be ready to go. I will let you know what to do later."

Michael stuck his hand out to shake Ed's hand. Ed shook his hand and looked Michael in the eyes.

"Thanks Taylor. Thanks for including me. You won't regret it."

92

After Michael left Ed's room he hurried over to the dining hall. Victor and Jason had already finished breakfast.

"Nice of you to join us," Jason said.

Michael took a couple of deep breaths, and then spoke. "Listen up, I don't have much time. I have to get over to the counseling center to meet Dr. Carson. It looks like we are going to have to escape from here if we don't want to be turned into turnips. Liz e-mailed me and the election went against us. We have a location in place with transition hover cars and money. I lined up someone to get a data card removal device to take out our hand data cards. Victor you see your brother today right?"

The guys were staring at Michael wide eyed.

"Shit," Jason said. "I didn't really think we would have to go through with this."

"Yes, I see brother today," Victor said.

"Good," Michael said. "Let him know we will e-mail him the names of everyone who needs ID's. We will also send him the date, time, and location. Tell him it's within the next few days."

"Nice thinking Taylor, but our e-mails are reviewed. How I just tell him all that in e-mail?" Victor threw up his hands in frustration.

"I am going to teach you the code Liz and I use. You are going to teach it to him today during his visit. It's easy to learn, but it can appear complicated. I never met a teacher who could break it." Michael grabbed a napkin and pulled out a pen. "Look, here's how it works."

In a matter of a few minutes Victor sat back and smiled. "Very nice."

"You can send the list to him today. Also tell him to get our pictures off of our old social media accounts. I am sure they are still up. Here is the list of all the guys, and here is the address of where to meet us. Tell him to meet us there Wednesday morning at nine am. Got it?"

"Got it," Victor said as he took the information from Michael.

"We are going to do the trial run Monday morning during breakfast," Michael said. "Are you guys ready for this?"

"Totally," Jason said. "I will watch the garage, and my boys will set fires in the dining hall. Along the fence behind the old library to make it look like someone is trying to escape from there. We have a spot picked out by a gas line so once they figure that out, they will just think it was a leak explosion or a prank. We don't want to go on lockdown."

"Good," Michael said. "Charles will observe the reaction on the security feed. I will put a bomb in Stewart's bag. Victor you will be out on grounds to observe any hidden anti-aircraft guns they may have that we are not aware of. Any questions?"

No one said a word. They all stared at each other.

"Good," Michael finally said. "We should not meet again until Sunday night at dinner. Monday is the big event. Good luck guys."

93

The final meeting at Sunday night's dinner helped the guys finalize their plans. Modification fervor was sweeping the public. They knew they would have to go through with their escape if they were to avoid Modification. Michael had sent Liz the final details, and everything was in place for the trial run.

Stewart was in the shower so Michael took the opportunity to place the incendiary bomb into his backpack. He set the timer to go off in the middle of the breakfast hour. The guys had previously agreed on the detonation time. It should go off at the same time as the other charges.

Today the plan was for Michael to sit in a different location than he usually did to meet the guys. That was so Stewart would not find him. He did not want to be near Stewart when the bomb went off. The other guys had assignments to observe the proceedings at different locations around campus so they would not even be in the dining hall.

Michael left the room before Stewart returned and made his way to the dining hall. He passed Charles on the way. He was posted at one of the main data terminals. The guys shook hands as they greeted each other. Michael always found Charles' hands cold and clammy.

"Are you ready?" Michael asked.

"Yes Mr. Taylor," Charles said.

"You know what to do. This is just to see what their response will be. Don't risk getting caught." Charles looked nervous, and Michael wanted to be sure he was not going to freak out.

"Alright Mr. Taylor."

"We will talk about how it went tomorrow morning in the lab, alright?" Michael patted Charles on the shoulder and then continued on his way to the dining hall.

Michael entered the dining hall and got a tray of food. He went to a spot at the opposite end of the dining hall and found a seat.

He tried to keep a low profile so he avoided contact with anyone he knew. He wanted to be free to observe what would happen.

Stewart entered the dining hall, got a tray and went to the back corner where the guys usually sat. Michael could see him wandering around looking confused because they were not there. He finally gave up and took a seat.

Michael checked the time. Then he heard it, the explosion behind the old library went off. A moment later Stewart's backpack exploded into flames and another explosion rocked a vending machine. Stewart hit the floor to avoid the fallout. He suffered some minor burns to his face.

Alarms went off and a flurry of staff activity erupted. They instructed everyone to get down. That was the same protocol in Chino. The staff walked around with pulse batons and surveyed the dining hall as all the inmates lay on the floor. The fires were quickly extinguished. The staff evacuated the dining hall one section at a time. Everyone was searched as they left the dining hall.

All classes and programs were cancelled for the remainder of the day. All the inmates were directed to return to their rooms and await instructions. Stewart never returned to the room that night.

Near the end of the evening an announcement was made that regular programming would resume in the morning. Michael smiled to himself as he saw the notice. He would meet with the guys in the morning and find out how things went.

As he lay down to go to sleep for the night he thought of Liz. What would their new life be like? He wanted to move to the northwest. He had researched a nice little town in Oregon. That is where they would go.

94

The next morning the guys met in the dining hall for breakfast. Victor gave his report first. "Have three rooftop pulse rifles triangulate the yard. One top of residence hall three, one top of old library, and one roof of administration building. Manually operated so if guy can control security system, should not be a problem." He sat back and pulled apart a bran muffin as he looked toward Jason.

Jason took the cue. "They only have one response vehicle. It can easily be disabled before we start. I can also destroy all the key fobs for the hover cars we are not using. That way they can't follow us."

"Did your guys have any trouble planting the explosives?" Michael asked.

"Not really, we have a different location picked out for tomorrow. It will be on the opposite end of campus from the garage, and of course, the dining hall. That should draw them away from us." He smiled as he spoke.

"Nicely done," Michael said.

"They use the same protocols for group disturbances as Chino," Michael said. "We cannot be in here when it goes off. We have to be at the garage already, otherwise we will not be able to move around."

"Victor, is your brother set to deliver the ID's?" Jason asked.

"Yes, all is set. He will deliver tonight. He does not want to be there when we arrive. He is a little scared."

"That's smart of him," Michael said. "Please let him know how much we appreciate him."

"Sure," Victor said.

"Well guys it looks like we are ready for the real thing. Tomorrow morning head straight to the garage, and I will contact Charles and my guy for the data card removal device. I will tell them to meet us there. Today just do your normal routine." Michael looked across at Jason and Victor. "Do you know where you want to go?"

"I will move to mountains in Colorado," Victor said. "I know someone who will help me there."

"What about you Jason?" Michael asked.

"Texas, and then to Mexico, I always wanted to be a cowboy."

"That reminds me of Billie," Michael said. "He loved cowboy music."

Victor and Michael grew quiet for a moment thinking of Billie being Modified.

"Any news about Stewart?" Jason asked.

"They are looking at him as being involved because he had explosives in his bag," Michael said. "He never came back to the room last night. A staff came to talk to me about him, but I didn't know anything."

"He got what he deserve for being spy," Victor said.

"I'm not sure anyone deserves to be hurt, but we needed him out of the way." Michael said as he stood up. "Alright guys, hasta la vista!"

Jason also stood up. "Good luck everyone," Jason said.

"Will see you in morning at garage," Victor said as he grabbed his bag.

"Let's take separate exits," Michael said.

"Okay," Jason agreed. Then they all walked out of the dining hall.

95

Liz checked her data pad. There was an e-mail from Michael. It was partly written in Lover's Code. They were going through with the breakout today. She felt her heart skip a beat as she read it. A tear flowed from the corner of her eye. She wiped it away and went down to the basement to retrieve her travel pack.

She got her bag and went outside. It was very early and still dark. She had a bit of a journey ahead of her. As she walked toward the shoot tube station across campus, she looked around at the buildings of the University. She had marveled at them when she first arrived. They looked so majestic and made her feel safe and confident.

No one else was walking around the campus at this hour. It was a cool morning, and she wrapped her scarf tightly around her neck. Michael said he wanted to move to Oregon. She had never been there. It sounded alright, but she never lived in a small town before.

She wondered what her new identity would be. Michael said she would be getting a new ID. She felt the backpack to be sure the envelope of cash was still there as she walked. She knew they would need that to make a fresh start.

She reached the shoot tube and walked onto the platform. She entered the coordinates and took a seat on the facilitator. In a matter of moments she was deposited in the middle of the city of San Luis Obispo. Then she walked two blocks to another shoot tube. It took her to the beach area of the city. After two more trips when she felt confident she couldn't be tracked, Liz finally arrived at her final destination in the country.

She walked down from the platform and looked around. She was on the outskirts of a small town. No one was around. It was still dark. She opened her data pad and checked the map. After she got her bearings, she began the walk to the farmhouse.

She was on a small dirt road. Both sides of the road had agricultural fields lining them. They were devoid of crops now because it was so late in the year. Liz saw a murder of crows picking at the field, looking for something to eat. Perhaps something had escaped the harvest.

It took her about thirty minutes to reach the farmhouse. There was a light on in one of the windows. She walked up the pathway to the house and onto a porch. The old wood creaked with every step. Her heart was beating rapidly and her hands began to sweat.

She ignored her fears and knocked on the door. She could hear footsteps as someone approached the door. Finally the door opened. A man stood there looking at her. He did not speak. He looked as anxious as her.

Finally she broke the silence. "Uncle Bill. My name is Liz, Frank sent me here."

The man smiled and breathed what looked like a sigh of relief.

"Hi Liz, I'm Bill, come on in." the man said as he stepped aside and welcomed her into his home.

Liz walked in. The house was old with wooden floors and faded curtains. The smell of food caught her attention.

"Here Liz, let me take your stuff," Bill said. He helped her stow her bag and coat on a nearby chair. "Have you eaten breakfast?"

"No I haven't."

"Well then, come on in. Let's get something to eat before the fireworks start." He led her into the kitchen where a woman stood cooking next to the stove.

"This is Liz," Bill said to the woman. "Liz, this is my wife Sara."

"Hi Liz," Sara said as she came over and gave Liz a hug.

"Hello Sara," Liz said.

"Liz, you have a seat here," Bill said as he directed Liz to a chair.

Liz and Bill sat while Sara served them plates of eggs, potatoes, and bacon. There was a plate of toast on the table with a bowl of jam. Bill took a piece of the toast and spread some jam on it.

"Help yourself," Bill said as he pointed to the toast.

Liz focused on the potatoes and toast. She didn't want to insult them by claiming to be a vegetarian. Sara took a seat and Liz noticed a large picture of a boy in a football uniform in the middle of the table. She thought it was a rather odd spot for a photo.

Sara saw Liz staring at the photo. "That is our son Cameron," she said.

"He's very handsome," Liz said. "Is he still sleeping?"

Bill and Sara both remained quiet for a moment. Then Bill spoke, "Cameron was Modified last year."

Liz felt nauseous as she looked at their faces. She could see their grief. "I'm very sorry," she said.

"Thank you dear," Sara said.

Bill and Sara offered up no further information about Cameron and Liz did not ask any questions. They distracted themselves with small talk about the weather. They finally finished their meal and Bill stood up.

"Okay little lady," Bill said. "Let's get you outside to wait for the guys."

Bill gathered up Liz's bag and coat. He handed them to her and also gave her a small leather bag.

"A man came by to drop this off last night," Bill said.

Liz looked inside. The bag was filled with new ID cards. She reached into the bag and pulled one out. It was for her. "Christine Scott," she said as she read the name.

"That's a fine name," Bill said. Then he walked outside, Liz followed.

Michael woke up early and rolled out of his bed. The guys needed to be at the garage before most of the inmates arrived at the dining hall. In addition to the bombs, Victor had managed to get each of them a stun gun. He fashioned them with parts from old pulse batons that were recycled in his shop. Michael took his and put it into his backpack. With any luck he would not have to use it.

After he dressed he ate an apple he had saved from dinner last night. He wanted to have something in his stomach. He checked the time. He didn't want to draw attention to himself by being out too early. He lay back onto his bed to collect his thoughts.

His e-mail began to beep and he opened the message. It was from the administration. They wanted to interview him regarding the incident with Stewart. He was to report to the investigations office today at three.

Michael laughed to himself, "Don't think I'll be making that appointment."

He reread Liz's last e-mail. She sounded nervous, but she was going to be there today at the rendezvous point. He was nervous himself.

He checked the clock again and it was time to go. He grabbed his bag and headed out. Inmates were just beginning to leave their residences and head over to the dining hall. Michael kept his head low with a hat pulled down over his eyes. He just wanted to make a bee line to the garage.

There was one staff officer who worked in the garage. He had a coffee every morning and the plan was for Jason to spike it with a sleeping pill. Jason went to medical a week ago and complained of sleep problems. He was prescribed sleep medication that was administered by a nurse in his room every evening. He managed to cheek one for just this moment. The hope was the man would sleep through the entire event.

As Michael walked across campus he was stopped by a staff officer on a security sweep. "Can I scan your ID chip sir?" The staff officer asked.

"Yes sir," Michael responded, as he extended his arm. Michael's mind wandered to the pulse baton in his backpack.

"Can you explain why you are in this area of the campus at this time sir? According to my information, you have no reason to be here."

Michael broke out into a cold sweat. He tried to think of an excuse but his mind went blank from the stress.

"It's my fault Sir." Dr. Carson walked up.

"What do you mean Sir?" the staff officer asked.

"My name is Dr. Carson. I am here on a temporary training assignment, and this inmate is my subject. I asked him to meet with me early this morning. I wanted to review some of yesterday's material before class today. I guess I forgot to enter it into the master schedule. Sorry about that."

"May I scan your ID please?"

"Of course," Dr. Carson handed his ID to the staff officer.

After a moment he returned the ID. "Okay sir. Your story checks out. Please be sure to enter any unusual appointments in the master calendar in the future."

"Yes sir, I surely will," Dr. Carson said as he put his arm around Michael and led him away. "Which way are we heading Michael?"

As they walked away Dr. Carson looked Michael in the eyes. "Where are you going?"

"Out of here I hope." Michael said as he watched for a reaction.

"Good to hear. Let me escort you the rest of the way. Where to?" Dr. Carson smiled.

"The hover car garage." Michael hoped he wasn't making the biggest mistake of his life trusting him.

"Alright then," Dr. Carson said as they headed toward the garage. He reached into his pocket and pulled out a card. "Michael, this is the contact information for a friend of mine. He is sympathetic to your situation. If you ever need any help out there give him a call. Tell him you are a friend of mine."

Michael took the card and put it into his pants pocket. "Thanks Dr. Carson. It looks like you may have saved my life for a second time."

"My pleasure." When they reached the garage they shook hands again. "Good luck Michael."

"You too, Dr. Carson. You won't get into trouble for this will you?"

"No, I will just tell them you gave me the slip at the counseling center, or something. Don't you worry."

Michael turned and approached the garage. He slowly made his way through the main door and looked around. He didn't see anyone. Jason walked out from behind a wall.

"Hi Michael," he said.

Michael was startled and almost jumped out of his shoes. Jason laughed at him.

"What's the story?" Michael asked.

"The staff is out cold. I put a bomb in the rear engine compartment of the security response vehicle. It will go off at the same time as the other bombs. I have destroyed the key fobs of the hover cars we aren't using. My guys are waiting for us in the back garage. They planted the other bombs last night. We are good to go."

Michael put his arm around Jason, "Good job bro."

They walked together into the back garage, and Michael met Jason's two friends. Then they waited. The other guys streamed into the garage over the next five minutes. Charles, and then Ed arrived carrying their travel backpacks. Charles had his friend Frank with him. Michael saw Frank and immediately got upset.

Ed looked at Michael and shook his head. "Sorry Taylor, but I couldn't leave him behind."

"It's fine Ed. Don't worry about it. Let's just get the data cards out of us. "Welcome Frank," Michael said as extended his hand.

Frank shook his hand. "Thanks Taylor."

As Ed used the data card removal device to take the data cards out of their hands, Charles gave his report to Michael. "Mr. Taylor, I put a patch on the system. It will reroute the alarm protocol. The alarm will never alert anyone, so no pulse rifles, no security response, just confusion and noise."

"Great job Charles. Alright guys lets load up and wait for the explosions."

Just then a staff officer staggered into the back garage. He was rubbing his head. He looked up and saw them standing there. "What is going on here?" He asked.

Jason looked at Michael. "The sedative must have worn off," he said.

Michael was standing a little behind the staff and to his side. He reached into his bag and pulled out the stun gun.

"You people should not be in here. I need to report this immediately," the staff said. He reached up to his temple as if to activate his com system.

Michael moved lightning fast. He touched the stun gun to the staff's neck and released a charge into him. The man dropped to the floor and had a spasm. Michael reached down and checked him.

"He's breathing but unconscious," Michael said. "Grab something to tie him up and let's do this quickly."

Frank and Ed grabbed some electric cords and went to work on restraining the man.

"Okay everyone, let's get into the cars," Michael said. He returned the stun gun to his pocket.

They split up into two groups and loaded into the hover cars. Jason drove one with his two friends and Charles. Michael drove the other car with Victor, Ed and Frank. They piled the backpacks into the empty seat in Michael's car. Jason hit a button on his console and the back garage door opened.

A minute later the first explosion went off. Then the security hover car exploded.

"That's our cue," Jason said. He pushed the thrust lever forward and the car burst forward into the morning sun.

Michael saw him leave and pushed his lever forward. The car accelerated out of the garage. For a moment they were over the grounds of the Rehabilitation Center. They looked down and could see people running around in confusion.

Jason had preprogrammed the cars navigation systems, which suddenly took over. The cars turned sharply north and increased in speed. Michael looked over at Ed. He was staring at the countryside terrain.

The guys made the ten minute ride to the farmhouse in silence. The hover cars arrived at the programmed destination and landed. They were parked next to an old barn. They got out of the cars and looked around. Michael saw Liz walk out of the barn. She smiled at him and ran into his arms. He kissed her face and hugged her as hard as he could. Liz looked up into his eyes and they smiled at each other.

ABOUT THE AUTHOR

ROBERT S. CONBOY lives in Orange County California with his wife, and two Papillion dogs. He has a Ph.D. in psychology, and worked in the California Department of Corrections and Rehabilitation for more than 25 years.

CREDITS

Cover design by Ruth Conboy and Robert Conboy.

www.ingramcontent.com/pod-product-compliance
Lightning Source LLC
Chambersburg PA
CBHW060532180626
46817CB00002B/530